The ~~Watch~~

and

The Watchmaker

~

Tales from Cellanor

E J Shepherd

CONTENTS

~

ACKNOWLEDGMENTS

~

With thanks to those giants of imagination, Sir Terry Pratchett, and J R R Tolkien, who helped me through troubled times.

To my truly remarkable parents, who read my stories when I was a child, and who put up with my frequent bouts of insanity.

And to Bear: My life without you is like a broken pencil…pointless.

Pertaining to Cellanor

Imagine, if you will, a powerful goddess of creation. She can be beautiful, if you like, although it has never been mentioned in the tales, so she may well have looked like the wrong end of a dog for all we know. Anyway, the goddess Dantalis gave birth to twin boys, Cellanor and Prospanor. Although she loved both of her sons, Prospanor held a special place in her heart and she doted upon him without restraint. She created an entire world with people and animals, trees and rivers, for him to do with as he saw fit. Cellanor, although not forgotten, was left to his own devices, ever overshadowed by his sibling. Arcon, the father of the boys grew increasingly jealous of Prospanor. Overlooked and neglected by his lover Dantalis, Arcon slew Prospanor in a fit of envy.

Dantalis, heartbroken by this treachery, fled into the skies, never to return. Arcon, enraged but ashamed, hid himself away below the shadows of the world, his malice and shame twisting the lands and spirits around

him to reflect his own torment. Thus, he became the lord and master of his own world in the ethereal Vale

of Lament.

While Prospanor had enjoyed all the advantages and blessings bestowed upon him by his mother, Cellanor had not been idle. He had watched and learned that the world needed tending to. The crops his mother had created would wilt and die without care, the mortal inhabitants would starve, and the world would decay. Bereft of his twin and abandoned by his parents, Cellanor decided there was little choice

9

but to look after the world he had suddenly inherited.

Eventually, Cellanor fell in love with the mortal, Eloria. Dantalis, who could be seen as a distant light in the sky, began to take interest, and although she still refused to descend, she would gaze down upon the couple every night, to watch over them, lest Arcon took it upon himself to destroy them too.

Eloria gave birth to twins, a boy and a girl, who the couple named Brumail and Beltainia. Dantalis paid tribute to her half mortal grandchildren by bestowing upon them the power of full immortality. As the children grew, they discovered that they each had power over the cold and warm seasons. Brumail could usher in the rain to keep the lands lush, and the darkness for a time of rest and quiet contemplation. Beltainia found that she could banish the frost and make seeds grow in the light and warmth. The siblings realised that they were both as important as each other with regards to their father's world, and so they decided to take turns in presiding over the land.

As time passed, the children of Cellanor had children of their own. They were demi-gods charged with the task of overseeing a variety of aspects that affected life. There were the twins, Belenore and Aster, who were the guardians of day and night. Tegwen, the goddess of love. Talia, who presided over the trees and animals and all things which grew from the soil. Ethanial was the god of wealth and abundance. Valeria took care of health and good fortune. Delancey gave inspiration to artists and scholars. Galen was the god of rest and peace and he watched over the mortals as they slept and sent them pleasant dreams. Cambion, who shepherded the souls of the lost and hopeless, and finally the twins Yulia and Lamia. Yulia was the goddess of birth and fertility and Lamia acted as her counterpoint as the goddess of death.

With children and grandchildren all fully grown, Cellanor's beloved Eloria, grew old and died. Cellanor withdrew from the land and joined his mother in the skies, but always kept his eye upon the world he had saved.

Or so the legend has it.

Cellanor is a world much the same as any other. It has oceans and continents, mountains and deserts. There is war, famine, greed, kindness and freedom in varying degrees. As with most cultures, religion has its place and is even observed by some, the predominant belief system being that of Cellanorianism, the devotees giving praise to Cellanor the Saviour and fearing the vengeful Arcon and his demons. The lesser deities gained their own religious followers too. There was even a cult of Lamia, although it evolved over the ages to become a notorious guild of assassins, since killing other people seemed a lot more attractive than killing oneself.

In this tale, we are concerned with Eloria. Not the mortal lover of Cellanor, but the country, or rather its capitol, The Burning City of Bitterend.

'Burning' because the city is literally on fire, 'Bitterend' because its inhabitants seem determined to live there, regardless.

Morbus Brandish first established a small mining village at the feet of the Rothgar Mountain range in the Age of Aster 13:1. He named the hamlet Brandish Town because although he was hard working, he had little in the way of imagination.

Morbus and his sons stumbled upon a strange red rock within the Rothgar Mountains, which grew like a parasite from the rest of the grey stone. Upon seeing the discovery, Brandish's wife said the colour made her think back to the cautionary tales that she'd been told as a child, about the Fires of Remorse which apparently burned eternally in The Vale of Lament and she suggested that her husband name his discovery Arconian, after the disgraced god who resided there. This was probably well done, otherwise the stone would have ended up being known as Brandish Stone or something banal and descriptive such as Red Stone.

Arconian seemed to burn from within and had a tendency to explode if not handled with care, but regardless of its potentially hazardous nature, the rock was an excellent source of heat and lighting. It could also be used to generate steam to drive machinery and was soon regarded as a very valuable resource. People flocked to work in Brandish's mines and the village grew to accommodate its increase in population. Morbus Brandish was officially elected as mayor on 22nd of Thaw, Age of Aster 13:3.

As the demand for arconian grew, so did the mines. They began to creep further into the mountains and further beneath the village. It was recorded that three homes were lost due to land collapse within the first year alone after the extensive excavations began. There was also the strange phenomenon of the miners declining mental health. Long term exposure to the dust, which was produced when the arconian was chipped away from its growth point, seemed to make the miners act as though they'd had ten pints too many and then staggered from the tavern to the nearest opium den. The villagers called it Mine Madness.

Brandish himself was experiencing some peculiar side-effects due to spending too much time around the arconian, but the demand for the substance was such that he turned a blind eye.

It wasn't long until catastrophe struck.

Two miners, who had discovered a very lucrative side-line in the supplying of arconian dust to townspeople, developed an unfortunate predilection for sampling their wares before selling it on. The addlebrained pair were remiss about their safety precautions. The explosion had a domino effect. Half of the mining tunnels went up in flames that refused to be checked. Hundreds perished. The ground cracked open to reveal red pits of angry arconian. Half of the village disappeared into the burning chasm.

The result of this negligence was unremitting even two hundred years on.

People had survived, as people invariably do. They abandoned the ruined village and built a wall around it, in an attempt to hide it from view as much to prevent anyone from getting too close. New houses were built, new mines were dug. 'Dousers' were employed to continually monitor and control the underground inferno which simply refused to go out. More and more people descended upon the city, drawn by either morbid curiosity or by the fact that this was still the most affluent area in the whole of Eloria.

Mayor Brandish had perished in his attempt to help quell the fire and so his eldest surviving son had taken over the position. A Brandish had been in charge of the city ever since and after two centuries no one expected anything else.

Garrote Brandish renamed the rapidly growing city Bitterend and it thrived like a phoenix rising from its own ashes whilst choking on the smoke of an eighty-a-day cigarette habit.

26th Moribund, Age of Cambion 13:7

Hans Vogel was dying. He lay on his back and listened to the familiar ticking and tocking, which was punctuated by various chimes and bongs of different tones and pitch. He could literally count the remaining seconds of his life as they passed away.

Tick Tock Tick Tock Tick Tock

Hans Vogel was dying in a room above his beloved clockmaker's shop. It was an entirely anticipated event. Nevertheless, that did not detract from the fact that he found it terribly inconvenient and not at all good for business. He'd always been a practical man with a tidy mind and even tidier accounts. He had seen to it that his affairs were put in order quite some time ago, in the event of his death. About a decade ago, to be precise.

Vogel's Time Emporium, his reputable clockmaker's shop, would pass to his grandson Claus, although Hans did have some reservations about that. Claus was a good boy, but he was soft hearted and had a tendency to daydream. He was far too fond of experimenting and tinkering to be entirely business minded and wasted his time making small clockwork toys for no other purpose than his own amusement. Nevertheless, the clocks and the watches that the boy designed, when he actually applied himself, were little short of genius.

Tick Tock Tick Tock

Eva, Hans's daughter had become pregnant with Claus out of wedlock and the scandal had forced the family to leave their ancestral home in the frozen hilltop country of Skorda. They boarded an Air Coach and voyaged south to Eloria. They established their business in Bitterend, the prosperous and chaotic capitol, which was known by the local populace as The Burning City. Things went well for the family, until Eva met an untimely death.

Hans had raised the boy from a young age and taught his grandson everything he knew about the business of watchmaking. He comforted himself with the thought that Claus was still very young and that he would no doubt grow out of his fanciful inclinations. Responsibility tended to have that effect on young men.

Claus was sitting at the end of his grandfather's bed, reading a newspaper, although the term 'reading' can be loosely applied here. He'd been staring blindly at the same advertisement for a good ten minutes now.

*'Cordage's Patented Tea Re-flavourment Longevity Strainer. Cut household expenditure and needless waste! Makes tea leaves last up to five times longer. *warning- may cause adverse perspiration, heart palpitations and shortness of breath.'*

Claus disturbed himself from his reverie with a shiver and moved quietly across the floorboards to the open sash window. The physician had indicated that Hans should get plenty of fresh air, a commodity that was hard to come by in Bitterend. Claus thought that a trip to the seaside would have been more beneficial than an open window, but the mines of Rothgar would have to freeze over before his grandfather would ever consent to abandon his beloved shop. It seemed likely that the bedroom would freeze over, as the late Moribund air filled the room. Claus could see his own breath when he exhaled.

He gazed down at the wide thoroughfare of Sovereign Street. It was situated in Heartfelt, a region in the southwest of the city, which was proclaimed to be 'the right side of the river'. The river in question was called The Dolorous, and its source was Gal Rimnol Falls, which cascaded from the Rothgar Mountains, fed by the snow and ice which capped those lofty giants. The river bisected the city and flowed all the way to The Tiahn Ocean.

The location of Sovereign Street had a direct effect upon the price of the goods sold in the shops there. Nevertheless, it was busy with late afternoon shoppers, who hurried about their business, either to catch the shops before closing time, or to stave off the biting chill.

A diluted sun was setting in a bleak sky and frost was already beginning to form patterns upon the glass of the windowpane, entombing the ever-present smuts of ash. Claus tried to slide it closed but the cold had made the mechanism as stiff as an old man's back, so he had to put some force into the action. The thud of the window frame meeting the casement was all but unnoticeable amid the ambient sound of the many clocks. The noises from outside, the clatter of horse's hooves, the rumble of carriage wheels on cobble stone and the voices of the shoppers, became distant.

Tick Tock Tick

"Are you quite comfortable, Grandfather?" asked Claus. He drew the curtains and moved around the room, lighting candles as he went.

"Tolerably," Hans wheezed. "Although I would have been happier if you hadn't closed the shop early. Matis Day is fast approaching. Think of all the customers we might have lost."

Claus chose to ignore this complaint. He knew it would be a waste of breath to argue.

"Is there anything I can do for you?"

"You can stop burning all those bloody candles. It's a waste of wax. And don't even think about lighting a fire!"

"Grandfather, this is no time to be...' Claus sought hastily for a polite

16

version of the word that was on the tip of his tongue. 'Thrifty," he sighed. "You must keep warm."

"I must do nothing but die." The old man spoke irritably, but he meant no unkindness. It was just his way. Claus was about to protest but Hans held up a gnarled hand to forestall him. It was amazingly steady.

"Light a fire if you must. I know how you hate the cold. It's just as well that you were not brought up in Skorda. Then you would really have something to complain about."

Claus turned his back to conceal his look of exasperation and got to work on the fire. There was no housekeeper employed at The Time Emporium, nor any other staff come to that. Consequently, with an aged grandfather whose health was failing, the responsibility of all the chores, cooking and cleaning, fell to Claus. Suffice it to say, Claus was under the impression that the feather duster was some sort of strange, exotic ornament and the pair would surely have starved had it not been for the many eating establishments which were located in close proximity.

The carriage clock on the mantelpiece chimed Five, somewhat redundantly since (according to Claus's last stock take) forty-seven other timepieces went off simultaneously.

"Claus…"

Claus looked over his shoulder. Hans was frowning at him. Not his usual type of frown either. He looked troubled and indecisive.

"What is it?"

Hans drew his tongue along his dry lips. He had never intimated to his grandson the presence of a most curious artefact that had lain undisturbed in the attic for many years.

"There is…an item of peculiarity," he hesitated. This discomforted Claus. His grandfather was not and never had been, a hesitant person.

17

"Do you remember the broken grandfather clock with the ebony face? The one that would always run fast or slow, no matter what I did to it?"

"In the attic?" Claus glanced upwards, as if he could see through the ceilings and floors and into the rooms above him.

The building was five stories tall and part of a grand and sprawling terrace of grey Rothgar Stone. There was a large basement that served as a workshop, while the ground floor was devoted to the business of selling the timepieces, with a showroom filled with examples of their craft, from the largest and most grandiloquent grandfather clocks, to the smallest, utilitarian pocket watch. There was also an overcrowded office which was squeezed into one corner, as if it had been added as an afterthought.

The first floor was their primary living quarters. It was more like living in an apartment than a house, with everything on one level. The upper three floors had been abandoned after Claus's mother and grandmother had died. Hans had insisted that it would be a frightful waste of money to heat and maintain the other rooms when there was merely two of them living there. Claus could see the logic in this now that he was older, but when he had been a child, the silent rooms above, still filled with old furniture and memories, had taken on the stagnant ambience of a mausoleum and had filled him with a sense of dread.

He and his friends had made a game of sneaking up there to tell ghost stories to one another and Claus would hide his fear with fierce bravado, until he was alone in his bed at night and the hairs on the back of his neck would prickle as he listened to the sounds that houses only ever seem to make during the hours of darkness.

The attic had been like a playroom filled with wonders, which could only be reached via running the gauntlet of the abandoned floors.

Tick Tock

"There is a reason that clock never told the correct time," continued Hans. "Something is hidden in it. Something very important, perhaps

18

dangerous even."

"Alright…" Claus was perplexed. Perhaps the medications prescribed by the physician were clouding his grandfather's mind. He perched on the chair by the bed and took the old man's hand in his. "Is there something you want me to do?"

"You must promise me that you will locate the item and destroy it. Although, that might be easier said than done."

"What is it? Why must I destroy it?"

"I just told you! It could be dangerous!" Hans propped himself up on his elbows in agitation. "I've been protecting it for years and I wasn't going to tell you about it," he wheezed urgently, "but now that I'm going to die the burden falls to you. If you cannot destroy it then you must give it to-"

"You're not going to die!" interrupted Claus.

Tock

Hans fell back into his pillows, dead.

"Oh," said Claus.

~

Miss Henrietta Temperance Tempest had, on occasion, lamented whatever reason, or rather lack of it, which had compelled her parents to choose that name in particular for her. She didn't feel that it was a very glamorous name. It conjured images of little old ladies wearing grey and knitting unsavoury scarves for their unfortunate relatives, for their own twisted amusement. She had briefly dabbled with the idea of going by her middle name, but that was scarcely any better. The name Temperance seemed to convey moralistic inclinations and yet, apart from her grandfather, who had been born in Denali and raised as a devout Cellanorian, her family had shown not the slightest interest in any religion. She thought that perhaps it might be a personality trait that her parents, apparently lacking it themselves, had admired and wished to be bestowed upon their only daughter. As luck would have it, either by natural attribute or by the years of practice she had endured living with an irate father, a silly mother and an irritating brother, Henrietta Temperance Tempest was indeed, temperate for the most part. Until it came to the subject of food at least.

To watch Miss Tempest eat, fellow diners could be forgiven for forming the opinion that she must wear a corset of herculean strength to give the impression of such a narrow waist. It must be noted that she did not *overeat* as such, but the rate at which she devoured her meals was quite startling. Perhaps she had endured a long, self-imposed starvation, which she was only now breaking, because she was at a dinner party? (Apparently this was quite the rage for fashionable young ladies, so that they could socialise regularly without the risk of losing their figures).

No.

Miss Tempest had always been very enthusiastic about food. The only person she knew with a healthier appetite than her own, was her twin brother, Henry. As small children, Henry could eat twice the amount of anyone else, at twice the speed and then still look for seconds or thirds, which if not rapidly forthcoming, he would steal from his sister's plate as soon as their nanny had turned her back. In order to protect her share of the food, Henrietta had developed a habit of eating at an astonishing rate, lest it be taken away from her. Unfortunately, she had never grown out of this practice and in truth, nor had her twin brother.

Currently, Henrietta was sitting at a busy dining table, listening to the pleasant tinkling sound of cutlery upon crockery, her own plate empty before her, waiting patiently for her companions to finish their puddings. She let her eyes wander around her surroundings and gazed at the faces of the other diners who sat around the table.

The room was finely furnished and of good proportions, befitting the gathering of females present, some of which were the daughters of lords and of peers of the realm. Henrietta was certainly not either of these. Everyone knew that her father was in trade but for some reason that didn't appear to matter. Henrietta had a suspicion that her father might have merely bullied his way to the top of the social ladder.

No one present was over the age of one-and-twenty (apart from the staff who attended them) indeed, a number of the all-female guests were barely sixteen and in consequence the conversations were mostly shallow and punctuated by much giggling. Henrietta sighed. She wasn't much of a giggler. She harboured a love of fashion, which helped under these circumstances, at least she could discuss this with her fellow guests, but she couldn't abide boring gossip. If one was going to gossip, it should at least be diverting, if not scandalous.

Besides fashion, she was also interested in the occult, medicine and modern scientific discovery, subjects which, on the whole, were neither desirable nor suitable topics for young ladies of quality. Her host, Miss Mary Honeydew, who was an altogether more sensible creature than most of her guests, caught Henrietta's eye and smiled.

"Ladies." Mary delicately tapped the edge of her silver knife against her crystal glass to get everyone's attention. "Now that we have all finished eating, I propose that we retire to the parlour for the evening's entertainment."

The young ladies looked around at one another and there were excited murmurings at the mention of 'entertainment'.

"Are we to have dancing?" asked one.

"In the parlour? I shouldn't think so!" scoffed another. "We're not in Furthermoor!"

"Anyway, there aren't any gentlemen present!" a young lady with a rather nasal voice observed. Henrietta noted that the butler didn't even blink.

"Ooh! Are there gentlemen to be found in the parlour? *Eligible* gentlemen?"

"You mean rich gentlemen!" laughed a pretty blonde girl. There were several delighted gasps following this lewd comment.

"All will be revealed," said Mary enigmatically, as she stood up to lead the way.

The parlour was much changed from the last time that Henrietta had seen it. The drapes were all pulled closed against the cold moribund gloom, but this afforded little cosiness, as the fire which danced in the hearth burned with a disconcerting greenish-blue hue. This phenomenon intrigued Henrietta until she remembered reading somewhere that burning driftwood produced this very same effect. It was an impressive spectacle none the less and gave the parlour, normally so warm and inviting, an occult and vaguely uncomfortable ambience. Upon noticing that some of the other young ladies looked rather scared, Henrietta perceived that this was the desired response. She glanced sidelong at Mary and smirked.

The atmosphere was heavy with the smoke of burning incense, a musky, exotic scent, which pervaded the air in a rather more aromatic mimicry of the smog in the streets. All of the fine and elegant lamps had been covered with shawls and handkerchiefs to diffuse the light and, in addition to the spectral fire, add further tones of muted alien colour to the room.

Most of the usual furniture that occupied the space had either been pushed to the very extremities of the room, or removed entirely, making way for lots of small, circular tables, chairs, footstools and pouffes. A teapot and two cups had been placed upon each table. The most intriguing feature of the room was not the outlandish lighting effects, nor the peculiar furniture arrangement, but the woman who sat upon a high-backed chair in front of an ornamental Katamese screen. She looked elderly in years but perversely she seemed to have more energy about her than many of the young guests. Henrietta wasn't sure how she had come to this conclusion, as the woman wasn't moving about. She was as still as a statue, as if in some form of trance or meditative state, but nevertheless, that was the impression she got.

The woman had a great profusion of pure white hair which roamed freely over her dress, which was black and unornamented, apart from a black lace shawl that fell around her angular shoulders. The simplicity of the dress was more than compensated by the vast array of rings, bracelets and necklaces which adorned her person and glittered in the spectral light.

As Henrietta made her appraisal, the old woman opened her eyes and stared back at her with obvious disregard for politeness. Henrietta almost flinched beneath the unyielding gaze of those milky white eyes, until she realised that the woman was almost certainly blind.

The young ladies had ceased their chattering and giggling the moment they had entered the parlour and in the absence of their ambient noise was a somewhat pregnant silence.

"Allow me to introduce Madam Nimueh," announced Mary Honeydew, in the most whimsical and mystical voice she could muster. "The Blind Seeress of Katamatown."

There was a collective sigh of comprehension from the gathered young ladies.

"Are we to commune with the spirits?" asked one.

"Madam Nimueh is going to instruct us in the ancient art of Tasseography," declared Mary. Her statement was met with silence and blank stares.

"Tea leaf reading," said Henrietta, which garnered lots of 'Oohs' and 'Aahs' and much nodding from the other young ladies.

~

Claus stood at the parlour window and sipped a medicinal brandy. It was not a particularly good brandy, which was why he considered it medicinal rather than enjoyable. It burned as he swallowed and he shuddered at the taste, but he had heard somewhere that it was good for those who had suffered a shock. Not that the death of his grandfather had come as a shock as such, the old man had extrapolated about his imminent demise for the past ten years or so. The physician had visited to confirm the obvious and the undertaker had removed the late Hans Vogel, leaving Claus alone.

Claus had, on occasion, felt loneliness. He'd spent the majority of his life in a basement workshop after all. He'd never met his father and his mother and grandmother had departed the world when he was just a small boy, but Hans Vogel had remained. Constant. Consistent. Constipated.

Now he was gone, and Claus was beginning to understand the difference between feeling lonely and feeling alone.

He gazed out at the dark horizon, the Rothgar mountain range was a deeper black against the night sky. It didn't matter where you went in the city, the mountains would always be looming in the background, illuminated by the ethereal glow of the subterranean arconian fire. The arconian mines had been ablaze for over two hundred and sixty years now. People had tried to extinguish the inferno, of course, but apparently arconian didn't care about that. It grew from the stone within the Rothgar Mountains in great, red stalagmite and stalactite formations. It could be turned into expensive jewellery if polished. It could be used to heat homes and generate steam to power machinery. Scientists were even talking about harnessing the energy that was contained within the arconian itself. And of course, arconian dust was big business. It was highly illegal and consequently highly lucrative. The powder could be sniffed like snuff, or smoked in a pipe, or mixed into a tincture. Either way, ingesting the red powder gave one an altered sense of reality, feelings of euphoria and a complete disregard for health and safety. Allegedly, this effect was discovered by accident when there was a cave-in and the miners inadvertently breathed in the dust.

Claus heard movement from behind and turned around. He wasn't utterly alone. He had Agatha. Agatha was his cat, and she was a consummate rat killer and so the house, although dusty, was blessedly devoid of vermin. Claus had designed and constructed a pair of brass clockwork mice for her to chase. Sometimes she managed to bat one with her paw, but the brass skins were impenetrable, and the metal rodent would speed away upon tiny wheels, unharmed, until its clockwork wound down.

He watched her skittering around the floor after them, feeling strangely numb and unsure of his next course of action. He looked around the parlour. It felt empty. He shuffled over to the fireplace and made a fire in the grate, half expecting to hear his grandfather bellow at him about wasting arconian.

One of the advantages (or disadvantages) of residing in a clock makers shop, was that one invariably knew what time it was. Several clocks of various size and design began to chime Nine o'clock. The cacophony awoke within Claus a single-minded desire to remove all but the quietest of the time pieces to either the showroom, or the workshop. He removed his jacket, waistcoat and cravat, rolled back his shirt sleeves and got to work. It was a laborious task and he soon began to sweat with exertion, but at least it kept him occupied.

He struggled with the heaviest- a handsome grandfather clock- and became trapped on the staircase which led down to the shop, when one of the ornately carved feet became lodged on a loose nail, protruding from one of the rough wooden steps. He was squashed against the wall, unable to move up or down the steps, but he couldn't relinquish his hold on the clock for fear that it would topple and crash to the floor below. Much sweating and breathless profanity ensued before he finally managed to pivot the body of the clock enough to free its foot, the only injury sustained was a torn shirt sleeve. When he eventually attained safe footing at the bottom of the stairs, he suddenly realised that if he had fallen, there would have been no one there to assist him. He might have been trapped beneath the grandfather clock and not discovered until Henry or a customer came to call. He might have fallen awkwardly, and broken his neck, just as his mother had years ago. He frowned at the staircase with a sudden and bitter loathing. There was nothing amusing about his thoughts, but for some reason he uttered a slightly hysterical giggle, which sounded peculiar to his own ears. He shook his head as if to clear his mind. Perhaps he was suffering from shock after all. Maybe he ought to go to bed. He glanced at one of the time pieces and learned that it was almost Half past Eleven. He realised that he had lost all track of time in his pursuit to eradicate it from his living quarters.

The clock he had glanced at had an ebony face with bronze numerals and encased in a grand oak body. It was the same design as the broken clock in the attic. Hans Vogel's dying wish was that his grandson locate and destroy whatever was hidden within that clock. Claus shrugged. Even if the old man had taken leave of his senses in his final moments, there was no harm in taking a look.

He slowly made his way back up the stairs. Out of habit, his feet wanted to take him towards his bedroom, and he faltered slightly on the landing. He peered at the stairs which led up. He knew that he was being childish but the dark void at the top made him nervous. He turned his feet towards the parlour to retrieve a candle and to put his coat on. No doubt the abandoned floors above would be freezing.

As Claus mounted the dreaded stairs, they obliged him with an ominous creaking sound, which was popular amongst unused staircases at the time. He tried not to think of the many ghost stories he had long since dismissed as childhood nonsense. When he reached the landing, he glanced down the corridor towards rooms he could barely remember. It was as cold as he'd anticipated, and the air smelt musty and damp. There were no curtains at any of the windows to block out the draughts, nor the light from the crescent moon, which illuminated the dust swirling sedately in the air, spurred into half-hearted action by his

26

trespassing presence. He noticed that there was ash upon the floor, even up here. The damn stuff got everywhere. Claus shivered as the sweat on his back cooled and prickled his skin and he pulled his coat tightly around himself.

He carried on up the stairs to the next level. He didn't bother to stop to look around. He moved quickly through the dark, surprised at how sure footed he was, despite the amount of time that had elapsed since he had last been up there.

He reached the fifth-floor landing and came to a halt. The staircase which led to the attic was at the other end of the passage. He'd have to pass by three open doorways to reach it. He swallowed noisily and decided that he wouldn't even glance into the rooms beyond those doors. He knew that he was being ridiculous, but some primitive part of his brain recoiled at the thought of looking into those cold, abandoned rooms. He tried to imagine what his friend Henry would say if he were with him. He'd probably laugh and give him a good ribbing. Claus smiled and felt a little bolstered at the thought and marched along the corridor with a little more confidence.

The staircase at the other end was more like a glorified stepladder. It was bare wood and had gaps between the steps and slanted at a steep seventy-degree angle. There were no handrails. Claus fought against a plethora of boyhood memories as he put one foot on the first step. Perhaps he should have waited until daylight to do this? He felt a feathery light touch upon this shin.

"Gah!" Claus stumbled backwards and almost dropped the candle. "Agatha!"

"Meooow," replied Agatha.

"You nearly frightened me to death!"

The cat looked up at him with an expression of benign disinterest. He bent down and scratched her ear.

"I'll tell you what, if you come with me, I'll buy you some salmon tomorrow."

Agatha meowed and Claus chose to interpret this as a sign of acquiescence.

"Good," he said. He didn't know why, but he felt less nervous having someone to talk to, even if that someone had four legs and fur and couldn't talk back. He tried not to look down the desolate hallway as he scooped Agatha up with his free arm. He turned back to face the steps.

"Come along then," he said in an overly cheerful manner as he began to climb.

There was a tiny landing at the top of the ladder, barely three-foot square. The door was small and plain. Claus pushed at it and was surprised at how readily the hinges obeyed, almost as if the attic was eager to welcome him back after their long years of separation. He had to stoop a little as he crossed the threshold. He had grown much taller since he'd last entered the attic. He held his candle aloft before him like a talisman, but the little flame seemed to make the space all the more eerie, its insufficient light casting sinister looking shadows all around. His mother's old dress making mannequin gave him quite a start and he had to wait for his heart to return to its normal rhythm before he could continue. He tried to remember the layout of the attic, as he had known it when he was a small boy. He knew that it must be exactly the same, as no one had been up here for years.

The broken grandfather clock held a particular horrific fascination for Claus, not because it was sinister in any way, but because it had earned him quite a few lashes from his grandfather's belt. As a young boy, he had used it to check the time when he was up here, not realising that it was faulty. He had once arrived an hour late for supper because of that clock

He moved carefully towards the corner in which he thought it stood and stubbed his toe on an old tea chest. He swore under his breath and decided that careful shuffling steps would be prudent. He made his way towards the light of the nearest window without further injury and wished that the moon was full. In what little moonlight there was, he recognised the sight of a battered chest of drawers. It was nursery furniture and had once upon a time been painted blue and adorned with crudely painted cat faces and paw prints, which had now mostly chipped off. Atop it sat a moth-eaten, wind-up monkey, wearing a red fez hat and a military coat. It held a pair of symbols in its hands. A dog-eared book with a crippled spine lay next to the toy. Claus didn't need to look at the cover to remember that it contained a collection of the works of Rattlepole, the famous poet and playwright. When they weren't telling ghost stories, or getting into trouble, Henry's twin sister, Henrietta, used to insist that they enact the plays. Henry used to get bored and complain, or deliberately say the wrong lines, just to vex his sister, but Claus had rather enjoyed it. There had been a multitude of 'props' to be found around the attic -if you applied a liberal dose of imagination- and plenty of musty old fabric which Henrietta somehow managed to turn into rather impressive costumes. The monkey had been a favourite toy of all three of them.

Claus smiled in the darkness and found that he could remember where most things were now that he'd stopped panicking. It was only a dusty old room after all.

He set Agatha down on the floor. She had been squirming to be released, no doubt eager to explore this unknown territory. Claus moved forward, carefully, so as not to stub any more toes. He approached the broken grandfather clock with purpose and held the candle up to its ebony face. Claus stared in confusion as the hands moved stoically, albeit backwards, regardless of the clock not being wound for who knew how long. He frowned in puzzlement and reached out for the little brass door handle. From inside his head, he heard the voice of his grandfather, like a message from beyond the grave...It could be dangerous. He stopped and looked around the attic and selected a heavy bronze statuette of a ballerina from a nearby sideboard. Well, better safe than sorry. He stuck the candle in a tarnished old candelabra and set it on the floor beside him. He held the ballerina figure by its head, the heavy, rectangular base raised high like an oddly shaped mattock. He reached out to the clock, his face slightly averted, his eyes screwed up, the ballerina held out before him and... swung open the little door with a flinch.

Nothing happened.

Claus stopped squinting, dropped his arm and peered inside the cavity. Beneath the pendulum, which apparently swung of its own volition, there was a small canvas bag and a rolled-up piece of paper. That was all. Claus let out his breath. Nothing dangerous about paper, unless you had a morbid fear of paper cuts. He retrieved the items and looked around for a relatively clean space in which to examine them. He realised that he should probably just retreat downstairs with his treasure, but he was so curious that he just couldn't wait. He found a dented table and pushed the debris of unwanted objects aside with his forearm. He unrolled the paper and put various weighty items at each corner to hold it flat, then retrieved his candle and held it aloft, careful to prevent any wax dripping onto the paper.

"Schematics for a watch?" Claus frowned and then chuckled to himself. "Is that all?"

He scrutinized the paper just in case he had missed something. It did seem to be a very elaborate design, but he felt certain that he was up to the task. His grandfather had been a celebrated master Timesmith and he had taught Claus well. He picked up the bag and gently tipped its contents out onto the table with a metallic tinkle. He scrambled to keep the tiny parts from rolling off the tabletop and gathered them into a neat pile. They shimmered in the candlelight and seemed to emit a faint, phosphorescent, red glow. Claus pulled a small pair of tweezers from his pocket- he had a habit of storing tools about his person, sometimes to the extent that he emitted faint clattering noises when he walked-carefully picked up a cog from the top of the glittering mound and inspected it. He smiled and carefully replaced all of the components into the canvas bag, which he put in his pocket, and rolled the paper up and tucked it under his arm. He made his way purposefully across the attic floorboards with an urgent desire to visit the workshop. As Hans had always liked to say, there was no time like the present. He called to Agatha and picked up the stuffed monkey toy as he departed.

27th Moribund

It seemed to Henry Tempest that anywhere he stood, regardless of how many times he moved, he was still in the way. He would receive a filthy look and hastily shuffle to the left, where upon he would hear a very pointed sigh, too loud to be mistaken for a natural exhalation, at which point he would move backwards and upset a skillet pan on the stove top or a rolling pin on the table. Most people would decide to depart at this point, but Henry Tempest was not most people.

"Master Henry!" exclaimed Cook in exasperation. "Must you stand there?"

"Where would you have me stand?" Henry asked amiably.

"Anywhere but in the kitchen! Go back upstairs, to the breakfast room, with the rest of them!"

'The rest of them' were Henry's family. Henry sighed and looked at his pocket notebook. The page was entirely blank, and Cook was growing evermore surly with every question that he asked her. Indeed, there was something decidedly threatening about the way in which she wielded the kitchen knife.

The previous evening, Henry had hit upon the ingenious idea of interviewing his family's staff. He had already interviewed two of the maids. Unfortunately, the scullery maid, who was named Sally, had come to entirely the wrong conclusion when the young master of the house had begun to ask her probing questions about her life, and she had fled from the room in tears. The maid of all works, Hattie, a sturdy, reliable sort of woman, turned out to be a much more willing subject. As it happened, she had led quite an interesting life and revealed that she had once been in the service of a great family in Furthermoor, whose daughter had turned out to be a vampire or some such creature. Henry had enjoyed her candid narrative and felt sure that his father would be impressed by the evident improvement of his son's journalistic skills.

Henry Tempest Senior, owner and chief editor of *The Tempest's Eye*, was unrelenting in his decree that his son would not be permitted to write for his newspaper until he had gained experience and the necessary skills of diplomacy with which to deal with people. Henry Junior found this rather irksome, not to mention unfair. He would often ask in a petulant tone how he was supposed to gain experience if his father wouldn't let him write anything for the paper?

"Use your brain," his father would reply. "That's what it's there for."

So, Henry had used his brain. As it turned out, it wasn't as bad as he thought it would be and he decided that he might be inclined to do it a little more often from now on.

"But what inspired you to become a cook?" Henry pressed. He had to raise his voice above the din produced by so much activity. It put him in mind of a beehive. Pots clattered, pans were scrubbed, and flatware was polished. The kitchen seemed too small to contain all these busy souls, trying to complete their individual tasks, which amounted to one conjoined effort: mealtimes for them upstairs. Cook wiped her arm across her sweaty forehead and raised her eyes skywards, as if offering up a silent prayer to the gods.

"If I feed you, will you go away?" she asked.

Henry raised an eyebrow and looked at the buns which she had just taken out of the oven. The kitchen was like a patchwork blanket of smells, stitched together by deliciousness. Freshly baked bread, sizzling sausages and more bacon grease than you could shake a pig at. He

33

deliberated for a very brief moment and then nodded. He opened his mouth to thank her but cook stuffed one of the buns in before he had a chance to speak, for fear that he was about to ask her another question.

~

Henry arrived at the breakfast table still chewing.

"I think that the preferred method is that you wait until breakfast is served *before* you start eating it dear," cooed Missus Tempest indulgently.

"This is why I shall never attend any social events in the company of my dear brother. Honestly, I've seen creatures at the zoo with better table manners than Henry," smirked Henrietta.

"You were late home last night," replied Henry, slumping down into a chair. "Out with some new beau, were you?" He looked towards his mother as he said this so that he could watch her reaction.

"I don't have a beau, new or old, as well you know," said Henrietta smoothly. "If you must know, I was with Mary Honeydew."

"Such a lovely young lady," mused Missus Tempest as she buttered a slice of toast.

"She hired a mystic for after dinner entertainment. It was thoroughly gripping."

Henry snorted.

"Your sister can read the future in tea leaves now, can't you darling?" smiled Missus Tempest.

Henry rolled his eyes and turned to watch impatiently as a servant brought a dish of scrambled eggs towards the table.

"Well, not entirely. It is quite involved actually," demurred Henrietta. "Though the mystic was a real proficient. They call her 'The Blind Seeress of Katamatown'."

34

"How can she read tea leaves if she's blind?" frowned Henry as he helped himself to six rashers of bacon.

"Oh, brother. You have such a lack of imagination."

"Don't worry. You seem to have enough for the both of us," Henry reached towards the sausages, but Henrietta was quicker. She tipped the last remaining three onto her plate and began devouring them without pause.

"So, what did the witch 'see' in your teacup?" asked Henry rather sulkily, as he watched the sausages disappear one after another.

Henrietta paused very briefly between bites and a dark look overshadowed her countenance.

"Ah, don't tell me," smiled Henry. "Death by sausage?"

"It was difficult to interpret," Henrietta resumed chewing, "Apparently," she added.

"Well, I wouldn't worry too much if I were you. It's all hogwash anyway. Where is Father? I have something to show him."

"Brisk Street. Something went wrong with a printing press," replied Missus Tempest.

"Then I shall go there directly," he gazed longingly at the kippers which had just been placed on the table. "Well, almost directly."

~

"Wha…?" groaned Claus. He lifted his head from the work bench which had served as his pillow and wiped the spittle from the side of his face. He was still wearing his goggles and the world looked blurred and oddly magnified. He was stiff and cold, and the candles had burned down to waxy coagulations. The rapping on the tiny basement window was most insistent.

"Claus!"

Claus tried to marshal his thoughts as he got up from the stool and stumbled over to the thin strip of glass high up in the workshop wall. The window was on a level with the pavement above and served no other purpose than to let in daylight, unless one had a mind to study other people's footwear. All Claus could see was a pair of freshly polished brogues. The figure crouched down on the cobbles and waved frantically through the glass.

"Henry?" Claus's voice was hoarse with sleep as he raised it. "Why don't you try using the front door?"

"I did! It's locked and no one answered when I knocked!"

"That's because I was asleep," Claus shook his head and thumbed in the direction of the shop. Henry nodded, stood up and disappeared from view.

Claus didn't worry too much about his appearance as he unlocked the shop door and ushered his friend inside. They had both seen each other the worse for wear over the years. Henry was far too excited to notice Claus's disheveled state in any case.

"What is it?" Claus removed his goggles and rubbed his eyes.

"Sorry to wake you, old chap, but it's the most diverting thing ever!" Henry Tempest looked like he was about to burst. He was dressed smartly in a woollen tweed suit, which now unfortunately had dirty marks on the knees. "Where's Hans? He'll think this a hoot!"

"He's dead."

Henry stared at his friend, as if waiting for the punch line of an unamusing joke. Upon realisation that the punch line had already been delivered, he blinked and removed his hat.

"When?"

"Last night."

"I can't believe it. Are you alright?"

36

"It's not like I didn't know it was coming," Claus shrugged miserably. "I hardly know what to feel. I'm going to miss him."

Henry clasped his friend's shoulder and shook his head dejectedly. "My news doesn't seem very amusing now."

"Have on, Henry," Claus tried to smile, although the movement seemed to defy the wishes of his facial muscles. "I could really use the distraction."

"Well, you won't give credence to it..." Henry ran a hand through his curly dark hair, which stuck up in all directions now that he had removed his top hat. He leaned against one of the glass fronted cabinets which held many examples of Vogel pocket watches. "I was on my way to the office when I heard a dreadful kerfuffle coming from Beverstone's tea shop. Seeing as how it's one of our favourite haunts, I decided to take a closer look."

"Curiosity killed the cat you know."

"I'm heir to a newspaper firm. It's not curiosity, it is *investigative journalism*. And as far as I know, there was no cat involved. But there *were* monkeys. A lot of monkeys," Henry grinned. He paused for dramatic effect and waited for Claus's inevitable question.

"Monkeys?"

"Monkeys. In suits. Running amok with Missus Beverstone's best porcelain."

"What happened?" Claus couldn't help but grin.

"Pandemonium. By the time I left to fetch you, a couple of Bobbies were at the scene. Could be that it's still going on."

"What are we waiting for?" Claus snatched up a jacket and his top hat and headed for the door. He turned around when he realised that Henry hadn't followed.

"Are you sure you're... well enough to go out?" he asked hesitantly.

37

Claus nodded. "I could really do with getting some fresh air."

Henry looked concerned but nodded and put his hat back on.

"Very well. But if it's fresh air you're after, I think you're in the wrong place."

~

It was a short sprint from Vogel's Time Emporium in Sovereign Street to Beverstone's Tea shop. Claus frequented the establishment with regularity. It was the ideal place for a spot of breakfast. No one fried an egg quite like Missus Beverstone. It was all in the bacon grease apparently.

The pair came to a standstill outside the tea shop. Claus knew that it was considered ungentlemanly to stare, but he just couldn't help himself. He stood with his mouth open and positively goggled. No longer a sanguine retreat for the noble past time of tea drinking, the place looked more like a zoo. There was a troupe of primates that reminded Claus of the small, skittish creatures he'd seen at fairs or involved in street theatre. They were normally accompanied by a man playing an accordion or a grind organ. They were all wearing red tailcoats and were leaping around, upending furniture, screaming furiously and throwing crockery, scones and chocolate éclairs with wild abandon.

The rotund figure of Missus Beverstone was like a beleaguered island in the midst of a ferocious sea. The poor woman seemed to be trapped within her teashop. She was screaming just as much as the monkeys were and was apparently attempting to hide behind her own apron. Claus ducked as a crumpet soared out of the open door and narrowly missed his head. More police officers had arrived in an attempt to quell the situation, but the fracas had already begun to spill out onto the street.

"Come on!" Henry tugged upon Claus's arm. "I need to get details!"

38

Claus rolled his eyes but let himself be drawn closer to the melee. The pair came to an abrupt halt as a table smashed through the front bay window, sending a shower of glittering shards of glass onto the cobbles.

"I say!" exclaimed Henry.

"Step back, Sir's, step back, please," ordered one of the police constables.

"What's going on?" asked Claus.

"Monkey business," responded the constable, without a hint of amusement.

"Yes, we can see that. To whom do the monkeys belong?" asked Henry.

"Don't know, Sir. According to Missus Beverstone they just started piling in through the front door and began drinking all the tea. When there wasn't any tea left, they went berserk."

Claus bit the insides of his cheeks to prevent himself laughing.

"What do you intend to do?" asked Henry. He was scribbling frantically in his pocket notebook.

"I intend to stay away from the hairy little blighters. We've got chaps from the zoological society on their way, with nets and tranquilizer darts. I'd wager the Natural History Museum wouldn't mind a new specimen or two to stuff and put behind glass neither."

One of the monkeys stopped in mid-action of eviscerating a current bun and stared over at the policeman, as if it had somehow overheard this threat. Claus stared back and noticed that there was something peculiar about the primate. Its features seemed slightly blurred, or not quite fully formed, as though Claus had forgotten to remove his goggles and was viewing the creature through the magnifying lenses. It opened its mouth to reveal rows of disconcertingly long, sharp teeth and let out a scream which made the hairs on the back of Claus's neck rise. He observed that upon hearing the cry, the rest of the rioting monkeys began to scramble out of the door and broken window, before bounding off down Sovereign Street, amidst a plethora of shouts and screams from the human pedestrians.

Small children laughed. Smaller children burst into tears. A horse took off in the wrong direction, heedless to the remonstrations of the man who'd been unloading sacks of flour from the wagon it was tethered to. A small dog that was being carried by a lady, urinated without restraint. (Although, it must be noted that this might not have occurred as a direct result of being afraid of the monkey horde. The dog may just have had a weak bladder.)

"Well. That's not something you see every day," commented the policeman.

~

Claus and Henry spent the best part of the morning tracking the primate's progress across the south-western regions of Bitterend, although 'progress' tends to indicate a positive action. The term 'rampage' might have been more of an accurate description. They ransacked a further seven tea shops in the area, before going into hiding, and the police would have been inclined to call it a crime spree, had they not feared that the public would laugh at them. Claus felt a little concerned that they seemed to be targeting his favourite places to eat. Henry was enthralled by the whole affair and fidgeted as they sat down to lunch in an (as yet) unmolested restaurant.

"I thought you were meant to be going to the office this morning. You realise that we are heading in entirely the wrong direction for Brisk Street. Not to mention you're…" Claus took out his watch. "Four hours late."

Henry shrugged. "That's your fault. You coerced me into having lunch with you."

"You never need any encouragement to eat," protested Claus. "And I didn't even have any breakfast this morning. I was starving!"

"Well, no matter," Henry waved a forkful of beef dismissively. "There has to be some perks to being related to your boss."

"I thought you said that your father wanted you to be more responsible?"

"This is responsible. This monkey business will make a great article. It's not as if I'm doing this for my own amusement!"

Claus raised his eyebrows.

"Well, you'll have to be quick to write up your report. I'm sure that escaped monkeys terrorising respectable tea shops is front page news."

"I know. I just wish I could interview some of the proprietors," Henry frowned.

Claus shook his head and sighed.

"You'd have to wait until Missus Beverstone stopped screaming."

"Well, it would benefit her as much as me. The best way to get over trauma is to talk about it, after all."

"Really?"

"Yes," Henry seemed to miss the sarcasm in Claus's tone. "If only my sister were here. She has a way with people."

"Yes. You'd never believe the two of you are twins."

"Indeed. What's that supposed to mean?"

Claus laughed. He felt better for spending the morning chasing escaped monkeys with Henry. It seemed bizarrely normal. Besides, anything was better than moping around the depressingly quiet Time Emporium. He would have consented to chase dragons if it meant he had company.

"Do you think they've taken roost in Eldarn Forest then?" Henry asked.

"Do monkeys roost?" Claus frowned.

Henry shrugged. "Maybe we should go and talk to a zoologist?"

"Or try to find out where the monkeys have escaped from," Claus cut and speared a forkful of his pork chop.

"Agreed. I think we should do some research. How are you fixed for tomorrow? Or have you got..." Henry faltered, "You know, funeral business to attend to?"

The pork Claus had just swallowed seemed to turn to lead in his stomach.

"It's all in hand. I must see the solicitor later on today, but everything else is arranged. You know how well-organized Hans was, he'd arranged his own funeral by the time he was our age."

Claus and Henry stared at each other in silence for a moment, in mutual sorrow, before Henry turned his attention back to his meal. Claus watched in awe as his friend shoveled beef loin and roast potatoes into his mouth at breakneck speed and wondered how he managed to breathe. It was one of life's great mysteries that Henry had never choked to death.

"Food!" Claus suddenly exclaimed, the spectacle of Henry at lunch had jogged his memory. "I need to arrange food for the wake."

"Hans didn't? How remiss of him," Henry smirked. Hans had acquired a reputation for being a little tight fisted. Claus often disputed this misunderstanding. Hans had been positively miserly in some respects.

"I would have asked Missus Beverstone to provide the catering, if she hadn't just suffered at the hands of those hairy little blighters."

"Well, at least in that respect I can be of some assistance. The

42

Tempest's will see to it. I'm sure Father will want to help in any way he can, although I'm not looking forward to breaking the news to the rest of the Tempest clan. We were all rather fond of Hans," Henry sighed. "Cantankerous old git," he added sadly.

Claus nodded.

~

Upon his return to the Time Emporium, Claus noticed a man loitering outside the shop. He was peering in through the large front window, his hands cupped around his eyes so that he could see better through the glass. Claus sighed. It was late afternoon and customers would expect the shop to be open for business. The cab ground to a halt and Claus disembarked.

"Can I help you?" he called, after paying the driver.

The man turned around. He was immaculately dressed, with perfectly coiffed hair and a very impressive walrus moustache. His physique was also reminiscent of that creature.

"Mister Claus Vogel?" he asked in a pleasant and friendly manner.

"Yes?"

"My, how you've changed!" The man darted forward on unexpectedly nimble feet and wrung Claus's hand.

"Um, have we met?" asked Claus, hoping that he didn't sound rude.

"Oh, forgive me dear boy! You were very young when last I saw you. My name is Ambrose Alltard. I have the honor of being your family's solicitor." The man spoke as if he was on a stage, addressing a great audience.

"Of course," Claus nodded. "Am I late?"

"No, no. Not at all! I'm early. My wife has been badgering me to lose some weight," he patted his ample stomach with a rueful smile. "So, I promised her that I would walk everywhere from now on!" He suddenly dropped his voice dramatically to a conspiratorial whisper. "A lie of course, but in order to keep up the pretense, I must leave the house early, walk to the end of the road and hail a cab once I'm safely out of sight. A ruse which unfortunately means that I arrive *unfashionably* early for all of my appointments."

Claus nodded in polite bewilderment. He found his key, unlocked the door and ushered the solicitor inside The Emporium.

The low brumail sun managed to infiltrate the smog briefly, and shone in through the bay window, which took up most of the front wall of the showroom. The light glittered upon the many watches which were displayed in glass cabinets around the walls. Claus moved towards the right of the shop where a long, L shaped counter stood, which supported an appointment ledger and various catalogues of designs for watches. He slipped behind it to the door of the office which stood beyond.

"Right this way, Mister Alltard," Claus was privately dubious that his guest would fit behind the counter. Alltard seemed to be thinking the same thing, but he managed to follow Claus into the small room beyond, by breathing in and shuffling sideways like a crab.

The office was cluttered but well organised. Another large window faced out onto the street so that the room felt light and airy, despite how much was packed into it. There were two armchairs positioned in the window, with a small tea table between them, a fireplace with tea making facilities and five filing cabinets lined up against the wall. In the space below the staircase, which led to the upstairs living quarters, were rows upon rows of shelves, straining beneath the weight of hundreds of ledgers, containing information about every time piece and every sale that Hans Vogel had ever made.

There were no stairs leading down into the workshop, instead a large brass cage was suspended over a hole in the floor. It was transporting contrivance that worked by a system of levers and pulleys and cogs. It was an exact replica of those used in the mines of Rothgar, to raise the notoriously temperamental arconian, or 'red gold' as it was sometime called, from the deeps. It made bringing heavy clocks up from the basement a lot easier, safer and faster. Hans had disliked it on the principle of it being 'new-fangled' and unnecessary. It had been Claus's mother who had insisted that it be installed. Although Claus had barely had enough time with his mother to discern her character, by all accounts she had been very interested in new inventions and was a bit of a dabbler herself. Hans had always complained that this was probably where Claus got his 'frivolous inclinations' from, which Claus chose to take as a compliment.

Ambrose Alltard was staring at the transporter, a look of admiration upon his face.

"Marvellous invention. Hans hated it I know, but I'm all for labour saving devices."

"I'm surprised my grandfather ever agreed to it."

Alltard laughed. "Your mother was a formidable woman."

"You knew her?" Claus raised his eyebrows in surprise.

"Indeed." A shadow crossed the solicitor's amiable face. "I sorted things out when dear Eva passed away too."

"Please, take a seat, Sir," Claus indicated one of the armchairs.

"If you insist. You might need to use that contraption to get me up again though."

Claus laughed before he could stop himself, but Alltard was smiling.

"Tea?"

"Yes, please."

A dreadful yowling screech filled the air. Alltard shot up out of his seat without the aid of the transporter and Agatha streaked across the office floor, nothing more than a black and white blur.

"Oh! I'm so sorry. I seem to have sat on your cat!"

"Er. That's alright," Claus peered anxiously into the shop to make sure that Agatha had not been flattened. Alltard sat back down and pulled some papers out of a leather file. Claus stoked the fire, waited for the kettle to boil, filled the teapot and then set the tea tray down in the middle of the table, before taking the chair opposite the solicitor. Alltard seemed to fill up a lot of space.

"I need some signatures from you, Claus. Do you mind me calling you Claus?"

"Not at all," Claus answered honestly.

"Your grandfather left you his entire estate. You are his sole beneficiary. I'm not sure if he discussed this with you?"

Claus shook his head and poured the tea. "Not at any great length. He told me that he wanted me to take over the family business, but that was always the plan. He didn't spend all those years teaching me for nothing."

"There's more than the business and the property. When Eva died, she left you an inheritance to be paid to you upon your Twenty First birthday *or* in the event of your Grandfather's death. Your mother took my advice and invested the money well. This is the final amount that you will receive." Alltard scribbled the figure onto a blank page in his pocketbook. A true gentleman would never utter a sum like that aloud. He passed it to Claus, who stared at the number. He turned pale, stood up abruptly and then fell back down again into his chair.

"Might I discuss some investment plans with you?" asked Alltard pleasantly.

Claus opened and closed his mouth several times, but no sound was forthcoming.

Alltard nodded sympathetically.

"Perhaps at a later date then," he sipped his tea, made a face and added five sugar lumps to his cup.

"And to think," Claus frowned, suddenly feeling quite agitated. His hands clenched on the arm rests of the chair. "Hans wouldn't let me light the fire because he said the price of arconian was extortionate these days!"

Alltard reached over the table and patted Claus paternally on the hand.

"Well, now you can buy all the arconian you want. You could buy shares in the mine if you had the fancy. Not a bad investment actually," he mused. "You should probably put some sugar in your tea, Claus. It's supposed to help with shock."

Claus wrinkled his nose. He liked sweet tea even less than the kind of brandy his Grandfather insisted on buying. It dawned on him that he could afford very good brandy now, in the event of future shocks. Alltard pushed the paperwork towards him.

"I can see that you need some time for all of this to sink in, so I'll leave these papers with you to read through and sign at your leisure. I'll pop by in a few days to collect them."

"I'll just sign them now," Claus reached out for the pen, the thought of good brandy still predominant in his mind.

"Some free advice," smiled the solicitor, he held the pen out of reach. "*Never* sign *anything* unless you have read the small print."

"Even if it's from you?"

"Especially if it's from me!" Alltard laughed. Claus raised an eyebrow but nodded. Alltard looked as if he were about to stand up to leave, but then changed his mind at the last moment. The chair groaned as he redistributed his weight.

"Speaking of the small print…There is something that I feel I ought to mention, in fact I believe that I would be doing you a grave disservice if

47

I did not bring it up. In addition to your inheritance, Eva left behind a pocket watch. Not remarkable in the least given your family profession, but apparently this watch is a family heirloom of sorts, which Eva stipulated upon her death, must pass into the possession of the most senior member of the family."

Claus nodded uncertainly.

"Which, at the time of course, was her father, Hans," continued Alltard. "Now that your Grandfather is deceased, the watch must pass on to the next most senior member of the family."

"Well, I *am* the most senior member of the family. I am the *only* member of the family."

"You have the watch in question then?"

"I have never even heard of a family heirloom until now. What does it look like?"

"I am afraid that I do not have the faintest idea."

"But did Hans not elaborate as to its whereabouts in his will? It seems strangely remiss of him if he neglected to divulge the location of something valuable."

"Perhaps he was under the impression that you already knew of it?" suggested the solicitor.

Claus shook his head.

The many clocks in the showroom began to chime Three o'clock, in various tones and volume.

"No? Well, I'll let you get on." Alltard stood up. "I'll show myself out. Don't forget to read the paperwork."

Claus stood and shook the solicitor's hand. He listened to the man's surprisingly light step as he made his way to the front door.

Claus sat back down in his seat and poured himself another cup of tea.

He couldn't bring himself to put sugar in it. Agatha leapt silently into his lap and began to purr. He buried his face in her warm fur and his voice sounded muffled as he spoke.

"Don't be angry with me, Aggie, I'm afraid that I forgot to get your salmon. I'll get it tomorrow. And a big tin of tuna."

~

Claus chewed disconsolately on his hastily prepared supper of slightly stale bread, cheese and cold ham. With all the excitement of chasing errant monkeys, meeting with Ambrose Alltard and finding out that he was now very wealthy indeed, Claus had quite forgotten the existence of the mysterious watch which had been dismantled and stuffed unceremoniously into the clock in the attic. Forgotten, that is, until the solicitor had mentioned the family heirloom. Could it be the very same watch that Alltard had been referring to? If so, why would his grandfather not have mentioned it until he was on his deathbed? If it had belonged to Claus's mother, why had it been dismantled and hidden in the attic all these years? Moreover, why would Hans insist that Claus destroy it? It didn't make sense. Hans must have been very confused in the final moments of his life.

Claus abandoned his paltry supper and went down to the workshop. The pocket watch sat amongst the detritus on the cluttered workbench where he'd left it, quiet, benign and not at all dangerous looking. He picked it up and admired his handiwork. It was a beautiful watch. The thought that it might have once belonged to his mother made it all the more precious.

The outer casing, which had been inside the pouch along with the complications, was made of a metal that Claus couldn't identify. It was a peculiar colour. Too dark to be silver, too light to be described as black and certainly too lustrous to be termed grey. It seemed to absorb all colours and both light and shadow and project them in a manner wholly confusing and utterly beguiling to the human eye. Claus could

49

only assume it had been subjected to some chemical process which he was not familiar with. It was covered in an intricate filigree engraving and had small windows cut out in the Half Hunter style, so that one could read the time without opening the case. The numerals were silver inlaid in a black face with another circular widow cut out at its centre, exposing the intricate cogs and complications of its inner workings, which were silver, bronze and red. Claus had a deep suspicion that the red components might be arconian, although he had never heard of anyone using the substance for such a purpose.

Not only did the watch tell the time, it also displayed a tiny calendar. It was nothing short of beautiful. Claus couldn't imagine why his grandfather would have wanted it destroyed. It had been surprisingly easy to put together, almost as if the watch had wanted to be brought to life. The hands moved gracefully as they quietly ticked the seconds by. It was five minutes to midnight. The calendar showed Twenty Seventh of Moribund Age of Cambion 13:7. He felt inexplicably excited at the prospect of seeing that date change.

There came a rapping at the basement window.

Claus raised his eyes but could see no one at street level. It was too dark outside. Probably someone playing silly beggars, or Henry come round to check up on him. His gaze returned to the watch. Four minutes to go.

Scratch, scratch, scratch.

"Henry!" Claus yelled, not bothering to look up. "Why can't you just come to the front door, like everyone else?"

Scratch, scratch, clonk.

"What in the world are you doing?" he demanded. He laid the pocket watch down on the workbench to glare up at the window.

Clonk, clonk, crash!

Claus watched in bewilderment as a large and heavy stone smashed

50

through the glass and came hurtling through the air towards him. Instinctually, he ducked his head down and heard the stone crash against the wall behind him. Claus sprang to his feet and gathered his wits in time to see a monkey, wearing a red coat and a fez, flying towards him like some hairy projectile from the now broken window. It landed beside him on top of the workbench, upsetting all manner of tools and equipment. The creature snatched up Claus's empty tea cup from the previous evening. It looked downcast for a moment at the lack of contents, before it tossed the cup aside and started to screech. Claus had a brief window of opportunity to examine the creature. It didn't look like the other monkeys who had laid siege to the local teashops. Although dressed in the same outfit, its face was different, and it seemed more scared and panicked than enraged and violent. It began to hurtle around the workshop, either in search of tea or an alternate means of egress. Either way, it was making quite a mess and so Claus laid hold of the little creature, in a bid to stop it from damaging anything of real value. The monkey struggled vehemently, apparently under the impression it was in danger. It writhed in Claus's grasp, climbed up onto his shoulders, grabbed little fistfuls of his hair and yanked, seemingly intent upon trying to twist his head off, as if it was a stubborn lid on a jam jar.

"Tea!" shrieked Claus in desperation. "You want tea? Is that it? I'll go and brew some!"

He staggered in the general direction of the transporter and tripped over his stool. He raised his arms to break his fall and knocked the pocket watch form the workbench.

Claus felt a very odd sensation that had nothing to do with having a monkey on his head. It felt as though someone was trying to pull his navel out through the back of his spine. He felt dizzy and nauseous. The world seemed to grind to a halt momentarily before the monkey suddenly released him and sprang back upon the bench. The teacup mended itself and flew through the air, back into the monkey's hand, apparently undamaged and complete with dried up tea leaves. Then the monkey flew backwards through the air and out of the window, as if it were being tugged by an invisible rope that was tied around its middle. The stone promptly followed the monkey's lead and the shattered glass gathered itself up from the floor, only to replace itself in the window frame, seemingly as good as new.

Claus sat down heavily upon the sawdust covered floor and let out his breath. His heart seemed to want to break through his ribcage. He uttered a profanity and scrabbled beneath the bench for the pocket watch. Once he had located it, he examined it for any signs of damage. There was not one single scratch upon it, but the time was wrong. The hands pointed at twenty-seven minutes to midnight. Claus swore again. He frowned up at the window and knew that what he was thinking was impossible.

"An item of peculiarity," he breathed.

Without further ado, he ran to boil some water and used the biggest tea pot he could find, in which to brew some very strong tea. He went outside and set the pot on the ground by the basement window. Anyone watching him might have thought he had gone funny in the head, but luckily it was late, and no one was around to observe his actions. He went back inside and gathered some lengths of wood, some nails, a hammer and a ladder and proceeded to board up the basement window from the inside. When he had hammered in the final nails, he returned to his seat and stared at the pocket watch.

At five minutes to twelve there came a rapping at the window. Clause counted silently as he watched the seconds tick past. Four minutes to twelve.

Scratch, scratch, scratch.

Then silence for a moment, followed by a gentle clatter of ceramic on cobblestone, then silence again.

Claus held his breath. The minutes ticked by without incident. He

52

breathed again and watched as the date changed to the Twenty Eighth of Moribund.

~

Brenna McGrath wrapped a shawl around her angular shoulders before pouring the tea into a cup. She took a sip. It was stewed, just the way she liked it. She stooped to scratch Bodkin beneath his chin. He was a huge, greyish black cat, of about the same proportions as a medium sized dog. He was missing the tip of one of his ears and had fierce orange eyes. Brenna made cooing noises at him and he purred.

Her home consisted of two rather barren rooms above an apothecary, which sold various remedies and potions to cure a wide range of ailments, which Brenna concocted herself. She was considered a witch by some people, a quack by others and a reputable healer and midwife by those destitute enough to require her services. The shop, which also sold second hand (and in some cases, third hand) books of an occult nature, alongside other mystical curios, was currently swathed in darkness. Brenna couldn't see the point of lighting candles, other than for the purpose of witchcraft, because she was quite blind.

The worn floorboards creaked as she made her way towards the staircase. She used the sound much as a bat would use echo to navigate its surroundings. An unwary observer might have felt concern to see an aging blind woman attempting to descend such a steep staircase. Perhaps they would offer assistance, under the misapprehension that she was a doddering old lady who required aid, but only if they were quite unacquainted with the lady in question. Brenna descended the steps without hesitation and with the vigor of a woman twenty years her junior. She pulled aside the curtain at the foot of the stairs and entered the shop. No one had knocked upon the door yet, but she anticipated that her guest would be arriving soon, so she unlocked the door and sat in an old, winged chair in the corner of the room. Bodkin, who followed his mistress everywhere, sat at her feet and purred happily.

53

~

Ambrose Alltard pulled the collar of his coat up to his ears. He moved in his oddly prancing manner into the shadows of the alleyway beside the apothecary. There was no illumination to been seen from within the premises, not even from upstairs and Alltard supposed that the old woman might have fallen asleep due to the lateness of the hour. He had intended to make his visit earlier. A hastily concluded visit, that would leave him free to go back to the well-lit, evenly cobbled, better smelling and frankly altogether more wholesome streets of Heartfelt. Unfortunately (or fortunately, depending on how one viewed the situation) he had bumped into an old friend who had invited him to a dinner party. It would have been rude for Alltard to refuse and he could not have left before pudding, even if he had wanted to. Eyebrows would have been raised.

Still, eyebrows would certainly be raised if anyone were to see him now. Solicitors of good reputation should not be seen to be skulking in dark alleyways, in very questionable areas, paying late night visits to very peculiar women. What if one of his clients were to see him? Mind you, he couldn't imagine why any of his clients would want to come near Blacktemple. For that matter, he couldn't imagine the inhabitants of Blacktemple wanting to come near Blacktemple.

He observed an aging Katamesian man as he walked past the mouth of the alleyway. He was whistling a cheerful music hall tune and seemed quite at his leisure. Ambrose Alltard was so busy marvelling at this man, who seemed to be entirely composed and at his ease in these dubious surroundings, he did not notice the pair of Mahjians who were approaching, until they came to a halt directly in front of him. They appraised his attire and then turned to each other and conversed in their foreign tongue. Alltard shifted uneasily. It was quite a task for a man of his proportions, but he attempted to make himself appear small and inconsequential. He pressed his back against the filthy wall and sidestepped his way around the corner. The men seemed to be addressing him, so Alltard tipped his hat towards them, so as not to appear discourteous and the pair laughed. He fumbled with the door handle of the shop and almost fell inside in his haste to get off the street. He slammed the door behind himself and fumbled with the latch. After a few minutes, he got his breath back and marveled at the fact that the old woman had left the front door unlocked. He was relieved that she had, but he thought that she must either be very brave, very stupid, or gone a bit senile.

He looked around the musty interior, but he could only make out vague shapes in the darkness. The smell of cats, herbs and decaying paper were prevalent in his nostrils. He stepped carefully towards the shelves and scrutinised the items upon them. There were not only books, but other objects too, some recognisable, others less so. There were miscellaneous bottles and jars lined up in neat rows, but he couldn't see any labels to disclose their contents or purpose.

He reached out towards something which looked very much like a crystal ball. Whether it reflected light from a source which Alltard could not detect, or it glowed from within with its own strange luminescence, the solicitor couldn't decide. He removed one of his gloves and tapped its cold, smooth surface with a fingernail. Nothing happened and he set it down. Next, he came to a small, angular object which, in the darkness, he could not hazard a guess as to what it was, nor its use. He carefully picked it up to examine it and found it to be very light.

There was a sharp scratching noise from behind him and a sudden blinding flash of light. Startled, he spun around to face Brenna McGrath. The scratching sound had been the old woman striking a match to light a candle. Alltard let his breath out. He looked down at the object in his palm which he had almost forgotten about.

"Blessed raven skull," said Brenna.

Alltard flinched and wrinkled his nose in disgust. The old woman's hand shot out to intercept the falling skull. It landed without harm in the palm of her hand.

"Well?" she asked. "Does the boy have it?"

Alltard wiped his hand on the front of his coat.

"He says no. He didn't seem to know what I was talking about."

"And you believe him?"

"Yes," said the solicitor a little defensively. "He's a very nice young man."

"And not at all capable of deception, I'm sure," sneered the old woman.

"You still believe it to be hidden in the Emporium somewhere?"

Brenna shrugged.

"Well, I've done what you asked of me." Alltard turned as if to make his way out of the shop.

"I asked that you get proof, one way or the other. This is important. Forgive me if I don't take the boy at his word," Brenna did not sound as if she required forgiveness, in this matter or any other, come to that.

Bodkin hissed as if to agree with his mistress's words. Alltard stared uneasily at the feral looking monster which had slunk silently through the shadows towards him. Alltard didn't know if it were preferable to be inside the apothecary, with this deranged woman and her demonic familiar, or outside with the Mahjians, finger-smiths and cutthroats. Brenna seemed to sense Alltard's nervous glances out of the window.

"You're a jittery one, aren't you?" she said with unconcern.

The solicitor didn't seem to know how to respond. He pulled out his pocket watch.

"It's almost midnight. I really ought to be on my way."

"I think I shall pay a visit to the boy myself. There's no one to stop me now that the old man is dead," said Brenna, more to herself than to Alltard. She fished around in her purse and produced some coins and a crisp bank note. "Your remittance, Solicitor. I no longer require your services. It seems you have outlived your usefulness."

Alltard accepted the payment with a slightly indignant word of thanks. Some of the shillings slipped through his fingers as he fumbled for his purse. He might have left them where they lay on the floor to save himself the indignity of groping around like a beggar, but the thought of leaving the money behind seemed churlish. He collected the coins as swiftly as he could, bid the old woman good evening and made his way out of the door and disappeared into the night.

Brenna was overcome by a sudden light-headedness. She stumbled slightly and fell back into the chair. She gagged as a dreadful sense of nausea clutched at her insides. The room and space around her felt vacuous and intangible, yet somehow claustrophobic and crushing, simultaneously pulling and pushing at her from every angle. The little flame of the candle she held flickered but strived to stay alight. Bodkin growled.

The old woman took a few minutes to regain her composure before expelling a vociferous array of language, not commonly heard in even the least polite society. She remained seated and waited for the inevitable.

The bell above the shop door tinkled and Alltard practically fell into the apothecary. He slammed the door closed behind himself and Brenna heard him fumble with the latch.

"Oh!" he exclaimed as he turned and, by the light of the candle, caught sight of the old woman in the chair. He cast the creature who sat at her feet a dubious glance. "Forgive the lateness of my visit, Madam. I have performed the task you set me. I don't think Claus has the item. He didn't seem to know what I was talking about."

57

Brenna sighed and resigned herself to asking the question: "And you believe him?"

"Yes," said the solicitor a little defensively. "He's a very nice young man."

Brenna made a disgruntled sound.

"You still believe it to be hidden in the Emporium somewhere?" asked Alltard.

"Aye! I bloody well know it is!" Brenna yelled. She groaned and put her head in her hands.

Alltard stepped back in alarm and knocked into the shelves behind him. Something fell and he caught it automatically. He peered at the item resting on his palm. Brenna sighed and made her way over to the solicitor.

"Blessed raven skull," she said.

Alltard flinched and wrinkled his nose in disgust. The old woman's hand shot out to intercept the falling skull. It landed without harm in the palm of her hand. She clutched her head again and took a deep breath.

"I say, are you alright?" Alltard asked.

Brenna didn't respond and there followed an awkward silence as Alltard stood in indecision as to whether he should offer aid to the surly old lady.

"What just happened?" demanded Brenna.

"Um. I came to tell you that Claus doesn't have the item." Alltard decided that the old woman was definitely a bit senile after all.

"He lied," said Brenna. She squared her shoulders and moved with surprisingly determined steps towards a curtained doorway at the rear of the shop. Alltard watched her move and, not knowing what else to do, followed her.

"How can you know that?" he asked.

Brenna ripped open the curtain to reveal a small back room that resembled a fortune teller's tent, which Alltard had once seen when he was a boy visiting the circus. There were swathes of gauzy, mismatched fabric strewn across every available surface, candles and crystals, small figurines of various deities, and many talismans were strung from the low ceiling. There was a small round table in the centre of the space, covered with a cloth. Two chairs were positioned facing one another. Alltard sat on one so as not to get in the way.

Brenna had retrieved a pack of cards and was now shuffling them furiously.

"He has the watch and what's more, he just used it."

"But how do you *know*?" Alltard persisted, intrigued in spite of himself.

"I felt it. And if *I* felt it, there is a very good chance that others did too."

She began to pick cards, seemingly at random, laying them face down upon the table in such a violent manner that Alltard leaned back in his seat, which creaked ominously.

"If you break the chair, you have to pay for it," she snapped. "I can't afford new furniture, I'm just an old woman."

Alltard almost laughed. He was beginning to perceive that she was anything but 'just an old woman'.

Brenna finished laying the cards out and turned the first one over, so that the picture faced upwards. Alltard leaned over to look. Although the image was well drawn, it meant nothing to him. He frowned at Brenna and waited for an explanation.

"The fool," she obliged. "The boy, obviously. Ignorant of this world and its machinations."

She turned over the next card.

"The Ace of Swords. A new beginning of some sort, possibly on several fronts. Sometimes preceded by a separation of some kind. Hans's death, I would assume."

Bodkin suddenly jumped up onto the table next to the cards. Alltard knew he was being ridiculous, but he had an overwhelming belief that the cat was as interested in the proceedings as he was.

Brenna turned over another card.

"Temperance. Hm. Balance and relationships. Friendships, family, romantic partnerships. Alchemy."

"Alchemy? He's a clock maker, not an alchemist," said Alltard before he could stop himself.

"Don't be so literal," said Brenna. "It could signify experimentation. He may have to try several approaches to something, before he finds his right path."

"His right path?" The solicitor frowned. "What is his right path?"

"How should I know?" Brenna snorted.

Alltard looked back down at the cards, inexplicably eager to know what was next. Brenna indulged his curiosity.

"Seven of Cups. A card of hard choices. It often indicates confusion and can also point to disorganization and too much going on. He will experience the sensation of being overwhelmed. Idiot."
"Can we not help him?" Alltard asked, a tone of pleading coloured his question.

Brenna responded with a grunt and flipped over another card.

"Justice. Karma-"

"Karma?" Alltard said the word slowly. "What is that?"

Brenna huffed in exasperation. "I suppose *you* might know it as something a little like the law of cause and effect, only on more of a cosmic level. All events, and all people, are connected. His actions could have far reaching consequences that he didn't foresee."

"Forgive me, Madam, but how can you interpret these cards? You can't see them."

"They talk to me."

"I see." Alltard nodded. He didn't see. "But could they be misinterpreted? Might you be wrong?"

"I'm not in the habit of being wrong, Mister Alltard," Brenna growled as she reached out and turned over the final card in the spread. Bodkin hissed.

"But I surely hope that I am."

Alltard stared at the card which needed no introduction.

Death.

Somewhere upstairs a clock struck midnight.

28th Moribund

Claus was lying beneath his blankets, staring up at the ceiling. He hadn't slept well. The peculiar pocket watch ticked innocently on his bedside table. He turned over onto his side, reached out and picked it up carefully. Surely what he had witnessed last night had been some sort of hallucination, probably brought on by the distress of losing his grandfather. Whatever the cause of the strange events, he realised that he wasn't going to get any more sleep. He needed to ascertain whether or not he was losing his mind. He swung his legs out of bed, shivered, and wrapped himself in a dressing gown, then carefully dropped the watch onto the bed. Nothing happened.

The 'peculiarity' had occurred when the watch had fallen to the floor. Maybe it needed a heavier impact than what a duck feather mattress could offer. He dropped it as gently as he could onto the floor. Again, nothing of note occurred. He decided to try winding it backwards just a little and experienced the same uncomfortable feeling in his stomach as he had when the monkey had attacked him. He looked around his bedroom, but nothing had changed.

"Of course!" he said to himself.

He picked up the jug of water from the sideboard and tipped the contents onto the floor. He stepped back and wound the watch again. He held his breath in anticipation of seeing the water flow backwards into the jug. He felt nauseous but that was all. The water remained upon the floorboards. Slightly crestfallen and a bit annoyed that now he had to clean up an entire jug full of spilt water, Claus was becoming more than a little convinced that the events of the previous night had occurred only in his imagination.

He fetched a cloth to clean up the water, then got dressed in a desultory manner. He decided to visit Beverstone's for some breakfast, before he remembered that it probably wouldn't be open, and he'd have to find somewhere else to have his morning repast. Unless the monkeys had also been part of his delusions. He sighed heartily.

The sight of Henry and his twin sister Henrietta, loitering by the front door of the Time Emporium was a welcome one. Claus felt a sense of normality as he stepped outside to greet them.

"We want to go and have a gander at Beverstone's," said Henry without preamble. "Assess the damage, so to speak."

Claus smiled. He hadn't imagined the monkeys. That was a good sign. Sort of.

Henrietta reached out a gloved hand and squeezed Claus's arm.

"How are you? I was so sad when Henry told me about Hans."

"I'm…trying to adjust."

"Did everything go well with the solicitor?" asked Henry. "You look done in old chap," he added with a frown.

"Er…yes," Claus shrugged "I had a disturbing…disturbed night," he faltered. He was reluctant to mention his unexpected windfall, as for some reason it made him feel embarrassed. He certainly didn't want to talk about the monkey attack and the strange occurrence with the watch. He'd probably sound as if he was raving. He needed time to marshal his thoughts before he shared them with anyone else. He felt as if his entire life had taken an unexpected turn of strangeness.

"Come on," he said.

Henrietta linked arms with the boys and the trio made off along Sovereign Street to assess the damage done to their favourite eatery.

63

~

The broken window had been boarded up and a 'closed until further notice' sign hung resolutely upon the door.

"Do you think Missus Beverstone would let us in for a look?" wondered Henry.

"I say, Henry! There's no need to be insensitive," scolded his sister. "This was Missus Beverstone's livelihood."

"No, I didn't mean that I wanted to pry," Henry looked unusually smug. "It's just that Father was so impressed by the report that I wrote about the marauding monkeys, he wants me to do a feature. Me! He says if it's good enough, he might even publish it!"

"Gosh, well done, Henry," smiled Claus. "But perhaps you should wait a little while to question Missus Beverstone. The poor woman's probably still a bit traumatised."

"Perhaps you're right," Henry admitted.

"Anyway, where are we going to go for breakfast?" urged Claus, as his stomach rumbled.

"I know a nice place," smiled Henrietta, ignoring the undignified sound and leading the way.

They ended up sipping tea in an attractive shop on Eldarn Avenue. It was rather crowded, probably due to the fact that many of the local establishments had been forced to close temporarily after the monkey attacks. The view of the street outside was obscured, not only by the demure white lace curtains, but also by a dense fog of condensation on the inside of the windows, due to the large amount of customers sipping from steaming cups. Claus chewed a mouthful of black pudding and had to admit to himself that the breakfast he had been served was every bit as good as the one at Beverstone's, not that he would ever say it aloud, due to a sense of loyalty. Plus, Missus Beverstone always gave him extra bacon rashers because he was a regular customer. Henrietta picked up the teapot to pour them each another cup of tea, but as she reached across the table to fill up Claus's cup, the sleeve of her dress caught the small flower vase. It tipped over, spilling its single pink rose bud and the water within, all over the pristine white tablecloth.

"Have a care, sister. We wanted tea, not a bath," teased Henry, as he moved his hat out of the reach of the spreading puddle.

"I'm awfully sorry. It's these sleeves! Big cuffs are all the rage in Denali at the moment, but I must admit, they're not entirely practical. Mother would have a fit if she saw me making a hash of pouring tea," Henrietta blushed. Claus stared at her with his mouth open.

"I say, it's only a bit of spilt water, Claus," Henry raised an eyebrow at his friend's stricken expression and began to dab at the spillage with his napkin.

"Yes…yes, it is," Claus reached inside his waistcoat and pulled out the peculiar watch. He slowly wound it back a little and held his breath. The water that was soaking into the table linen flowed backwards into the vase, which righted itself, complete with rose bud, in the centre of the table. Henrietta moved the teapot around the table, which sucked the amber liquid out of the cups. She set it down and leaned back in her seat.

"My word!" exclaimed Claus. Several of the nearby diners turned to look at him.

"Whatever is the matter, Claus? You look as if you have seen a ghost," Henrietta said with evident concern. She and Henry seemed completely oblivious to the fact that time had just run backwards for a brief moment.

"Er…"

"Would you like some more tea?"

"Yes, please," Claus mumbled through lips which felt numb. He

65

wanted to shout out 'I'm not mad! Hurrah!'" Instead, he reached out and swiftly moved the flower vase to the other side of the table. Henrietta poured them all another cup of tea with her usual grace and dexterity, regardless of the size of her cuffs. Claus began to laugh, and the Tempest siblings exchanged a worried glance.

"Anyway…" Henry said awkwardly, trying not to notice his friend's odd behaviour as he turned towards his sister. "Yesterday, Claus suggested that it would be a good start to find out where these monkeys came from, didn't you, Claus? After all, they must belong to someone."

Claus looked vague.

"For my article!" snapped Henry.

"Oh. Oh, yes. Good idea," nodded Claus.

"It was *your* idea!"

"Yes," agreed Claus dispassionately.

Henry carried on talking but Claus couldn't focus on what his friend was saying and so had to resort to nodding at what he hoped was appropriate moments. Why had the watch worked this time? Why had it not worked on the water he had spilt in his bedroom? It had worked during the incident with the monkey and the teacup and again with Henrietta and the tea pot. He needed to consider the variables. The only thing these two episodes had in common was the presence of tea. Claus was the first to admit that he was exceptionally fond of tea and believed that the beverage had many agreeable effects, but he seriously doubted that it was a conduit for time travel.

"Maybe the people at the zoological society could help?" came Henrietta's voice. Claus tried hard to concentrate upon the conversation. "If someone had come home from travelling abroad, with an exotic pet, or in this case, a whole menagerie of them, they might have gone there for information about how to look after the creatures. The staff there would surely remember someone who came to inquire about the best way to look after thirty or so primates."

"I don't know," frowned Henry. "If the owner is careless enough to lose a small army of monkeys, I doubt he's that bothered about their welfare. Maybe he grew tired of their antics and turned them loose on purpose."

"I seriously doubt it," Henrietta raised an eyebrow. "They were all wearing little coats and hats. Someone must care about them if they went to the trouble of dressing them all."

"Shipping records," said Claus, believing that he had caught up enough with the conversation to be able to participate. "There would be records of someone bringing exotic animals into the country, not to mention quarantine restrictions."

"Good thinking!" grinned Henry.

"It would have to be someone very rich, surely?" suggested Henrietta.

"And very eccentric," nodded Claus.

Henry went to take a piece of toast and looked disappointed to find that there was none left.

"You get more for your money at Beverstone's. I'm still hungry," he whispered.

Claus nodded and then grinned as an idea struck him. He concealed the pocket watch beneath the table and wound it back twenty minutes.

It turned out that observing his friends eating in reverse was not a pleasant sight. When the time shift stopped, Henry and Henrietta were repeating a conversation which they had already had, and a waiter was walking towards them with their breakfast.

"That looks good, Claus," said Henry, for the second time, with an appraising look at the plate.

"You should have ordered one," said Claus

"No, no. Poached eggs, sausage and toast will fill me up. I want to save room for lunch. Cook promised to bake me an entire trout."

Henrietta sniggered.

"What's so funny?"

"I heard that Cook means to keep you as full as she can, so that you'll stay out of the kitchen from now on."

"Henry could eat *two* baked trout and still have room for pudding," commented Claus, not unjustly. "Anyway, I'm not quite as hungry as I thought I was. Share half of this with me. I insist."

"Well, if you *insist*," Henry held his plate out and received half of Claus's breakfast on top of his own.

"Why are you grinning like a Cheshire cat?" enquired Henrietta. "I've never seen anyone so keen to give away half their meal."

Claus shrugged.

So, it seemed that Claus was the only person to notice that time had run backwards. Was it because he was the one who *wound* the pocket watch, or because he was the one who had made it? Why could he affect no change when he was alone? Was he somehow immune to the watches power? He needed to conduct further experiments, although he had a feeling his grandfather would be furious with him. Henrietta poured yet more tea and Claus noticed that his bladder was becoming uncomfortably full.

He sat through the ensuing conversations with as much patience as he could muster, though he had to try very hard not to finish the twins' sentences for them.

"Yesterday, Claus suggested that it would be a good start to find out where these monkeys came from, didn't you Claus? After all, they must belong to someone" said Henry.

Claus smiled and nodded.

"Maybe the people at the zoological society could help?" said Henrietta. "If someone had come home from travelling abroad, with an exotic pet, or in this case, a whole menagerie of them, they might have gone there for information about how to look after the creatures. The staff there would surely remember someone who came to inquire about the best way to look after thirty or so primates."

"I don't know," frowned Henry. "If the owner is careless enough to lose a small army of monkeys, I doubt he's that bothered about their welfare. Maybe he grew tired of their antics and turned them loose on purpose."

"I seriously doubt it," Henrietta raised an eyebrow. "They were all wearing little coats and hats. Someone must care about them if they went to the trouble of dressing them all," she suddenly screwed up her eyes and put a hand to her head.

"Sister? Are you quite well?" Henry put his hand on her shoulder.

"I have the most terrible sense of Deja vu!"

Claus bit his lip, concerned.

"Ah, well," said Henry autocratically. "That's what you get if you spend too much time around witches."

"What? Déjà vu?" asked Henrietta incredulously.

"No! Peculiar happenings, unusual occurrences..." Henry gestured at his twin as though she were exhibit 'A' in a body of evidence. "Strangeness!"

"I thought you didn't believe in witchcraft?" Henrietta snapped.

"I don't! She probably laced your tea with some sort of mind-altering substance to make you *think* you were witnessing occult phenomena."

"You've been spending time with witches?" Claus interrupted in confusion.

"No. Henry is being silly," huffed Henrietta. "I visited Mary

69

Honeydew a couple of nights ago. She had a prognosticator."

"Oh dear," Claus frowned. "I'm very sorry to hear that. Is it contagious?"

Henrietta snorted a laugh.

"A prognosticator is a clairvoyant," she grinned. "You know, a fortune teller, like at the circus."

"Oh, I see. Wait, that's an idea," Claus mused. "There's some sort of travelling circus or carnival camped out in Katamatown at the moment. They're just passing through, but we should check to see if they have any performing monkeys. And we should check the shipping records," said Claus, keeping an eye on Henrietta. He was worried she might suffer another attack of Déjà vu at his repeated words. "There would be records of someone bringing exotic animals into the country, not to mention quarantine restrictions."

"Brilliant!" exclaimed Henry. "So, we have a list of potential leads at least. Shipping records, the carnival and eccentric aristocrats. Hm, I might do a bit of snooping around the archives at the office. Could be someone did a piece for the social column. *Wealthy weirdo turns mansion into primate playground.'* you know, that sort of thing. Where should we start?"

"Wherever you want. This is your bailiwick after all," shrugged Claus, giving Henrietta a covert glance. She looked a little less pale now.

"Might as well get Katamatown out of the way," Henry sighed, as he glanced at his pocket watch. "It's still early, hopefully the pickpockets aren't up and about yet."

"No time like the present," said Claus before he could stop himself.

"Are you sure you are well, Henrietta?" Henry asked solicitously. "You do look a bit off colour. We could hail a carriage and drop you off at home first, if you'd prefer?"

"Don't fuss, brother dear. I'm quite well. I just had an overwhelming feeling that we had had that conversation before."

Claus felt horribly guilty as they made ready to leave. He hoped that he had not caused Henrietta any lasting ill effect. His grandfather had warned him that the item of peculiarity might be dangerous. Claus would endeavour to be more cautious with his experiments in the future.

~

Claus had always felt a strange affection for Blacktemple, or rather Katamatown, which was situated to the north of the region. Bitterend was a city which assaulted the senses. It was a chaos of varying degrees of order, which included no order at all. The myriad sights and sounds could lead the unwary astray, even unto death. Claus had spent most of his life, thus far, learning the art of watch making. It was complicated and filled with tiny, seemingly inconsequential parts which worked together to make the whole, not unlike the city in which he dwelt. His occupation had taught him to pay attention to the little details, which were so easily overlooked. Sometimes Claus wished that he *could* overlook certain details, as Bitterend was also a city which was filled with smells and some, admittedly, were not exactly pleasant. Katamatown had a scent all of its own. It smelt *exciting*. It smelt like foreign foods and exotic spices and travellers from far off places. It was the sort of place where anything could happen and most probably *would* if you lingered long enough.

As it was early morning, the carnival folk were inactive, and most were asleep. That is not to say that Katamatown was quiet. It was never quiet.

"There doesn't seem to be anyone around that we could ask about livestock," said Henrietta. Claus looked around and realised that she was correct in her deduction. There were plenty of people milling about, but they all seemed otherwise engaged, entirely unapproachable or unable to speak Elorian.

71

"There's an old lady over there," Claus inclined his head towards a woman, who was sitting outside a dilapidated looking shop. "Maybe we should ask her?"

The woman was perched atop an upturned bucket, by the doorway of the shop, smoking a pipe, seemingly at her leisure.

"She looks like a nomad," commented Henry, with an expression of deep mistrust. She was wearing a dress sewn together out of various patches of mismatched fabric and a rough woollen garment, which looked to be a khaki-coloured fisherman's jumper. A vast array of shawls and scarves were wrapped around her shoulders. Multiple strands of beads and talismans were strung around her neck and large rings of dubious quality glittered on her fingers, which lay exposed to the elements below the remnants of her tatty fingerless gloves. A wide brimmed, brown leather hat crowned her mane of exceedingly long, pure white hair.

"You can't trust nomads." added Henry urgently, in case his friends had failed to notice his concern.

Claus shrugged, undeterred and ushered his companions forward. The shop was as run-down as the rest of Blacktemple. The wooden door and the window frame were splintered and rotting. Behind the smog smeared glass of the bay window and its diaphanous yet moth eaten purple drapes, was a display of faded and discoloured books of magic and the arcane. Palmistry, tarot, spiritualism and tasseography manuals, all propped up neatly, despite their broken spines, to tempt the window shopper's eye. Claus mused that their battered and dog-eared appearance only lent credence to their supernatural auras.

"It's her!" hissed Henrietta as they approached. "She's the mystic, the one I told you about. I believe she goes by the name of Madam Nimueh, if memory serves."

"Gad! You would think that the Honeydew's of all people could afford someone a little less…moth eaten."

"Henry! Really! She was most convincing."

"I am sure she was. I have no doubt that she has had plenty of practice at swindling fools out of their money over the years."

Henrietta looked just about ready to stamp her foot.

"I am not a fool. And she didn't swindle me or anyone else. We had a ripping time."

"Then *you* go and talk to her, sister," Henry pushed Henrietta towards the old woman.

"Why me?"

"You're less threatening."

"Compared to what?"

"Claus and I."

Henrietta looked incredulous. "Yes. You're positively terrifying," she said sardonically.

"Let's all go," said Claus decisively, tired of the twins bickering.

As they drew closer to the old woman, she stood up, mounted the step at the shop doorway and gestured at them to enter.

"Good morning," chirped Henrietta. "Madam Nimueh? Sorry to disturb you. We just wanted to know-"

"Not out here," the women cut sharply across Henrietta's words. The trio looked at one another.

The mystic turned her back on them and entered the shop.

"An Irkish nomad!" hissed Henry. "That's the very worst kind!"

"She can't be a nomad! She has a shop!" snapped Henrietta, as she tugged on her brother's arm.

"Very well," shrugged Henry. "But we are *not* buying anything. Not even a clothes peg!"

73

Claus was the last to enter. He looked around the shop, which reminded him of the interior of a Nafreskan tent, or at least what he had read of them and seen in drawings. He didn't mention this to Henry, although he'd never heard his friend say a bad word about the desert dwelling tribes, he didn't want to risk another panic about Nomads. At the centre of the ceiling, a great number of brightly patterned lengths of fabric hung in swathes and were gathered together like curtains and nailed to the walls, giving the room the bevelled appearance of a circus tent. Between the fabrics were rows upon rows of shelves, bowing under the great weight of musty smelling books, dark glass bottles, jars and curiosities. There were threadbare carpets of various design upon the floor and large furs draped around haphazardly. There was one chair in the corner by the counter and a number of large cushions scattered about, presumably to languish upon should the need arise. There were several low tables upon which was set tea making apparatus and various small items of an occult persuasion. At the back of the shop was a room not much larger than a cupboard. The curtain which hung across the entrance was pulled back and Claus discerned something which looked very much like a crystal ball sat in the middle of a table. He heard Henry fail in his attempt to suppress a groan.

"Cross my palm with silver," said the old woman.

"We do not want our fortunes told, thank you," said Henry resolutely and he folded his arms across his chest.

"Who said anything about telling your fortune?" snapped the mystic. "If you want my time, you'll have to pay for it. I was busy."

"You didn't look busy," Henry scoffed.

Henrietta hastily fumbled for some coins, which she pressed into the old woman's hand.

"So, what *do* you want?" asked Madam Nimueh. "Man trouble is it?"

"Oh! No. Nothing like that," Henrietta blushed.

Madam Nimueh nodded and moved on towards Henry.

"Boils need lancing?" she suggested with an accusatory tone to her voice. "Bad breath? Hair loss? Something funny going on with your-"

"No!" Henry interrupted. "None of those things. Especially not the last one," he added defensively.

Madam Nimueh's mouth twitched at one corner in an almost-smile and she stepped towards Claus.

Close up, Claus realised that the old woman was blind. He felt sorry for that and decided to give her a little extra money before they left.

"We just wanted some information," he said.

"What do you want to know?" asked Madam Nimueh.

"You sell books?" frowned Henry. "A blind bookseller. That must be difficult. How do you find the titles when customers request them?"

Henrietta elbowed her brother sharply in the ribs.

"Is that your question?" asked the old woman.

"No," Henry wheezed and rubbed his side. "We want to find out about the carnival that recently arrived. Do you know anything of it?"

"We really just wanted to know if they keep any animals," said Henrietta placidly. "Monkeys, to be precise."

Madam Nimueh turned her head in Henrietta's direction.

"I met a Katamesian woman that's got a couple. Nice lass, she gave me some of that green tea. If anyone offers you a cup, decline it. It tastes like piss."

Henrietta giggled.

Henry took his notebook out of his inside pocket.

"Have you seen, er-" he faltered. "Are you aware of them being let out? For exercise maybe?"

The old woman laughed and sucked on her pipe. The fumes she exhaled made Claus feel a little lightheaded, but not in an unpleasant way.

"They wouldn't thank you for exercise. They're too old. Like me."

"How many of them are there?"

"Just the two. Like I said."

Henry looked disappointed.

Claus froze as something warm and hairy brushed against his leg. He looked down to see a large, grey shaggy rug on legs. It had a pair of bright orange eyes and it was staring up at him. It made a deep, gravelly noise, which sounded a bit like someone scraping rocks together.

"Bodkin," said Madam Nimueh. "He must like you, which is unusual. Bodkin doesn't normally like anyone he doesn't know, or anything he can't eat or hump."

"Er, he can probably smell Agatha. My cat," Claus leaned down and scratched Bodkin behind his stub of ear. The huge cat made more grinding rock noises. Claus interpreted this sound as Bodkin's version of purring.

"Hm. Well I shouldn't stand too long in one place if I were you. Just to be on the safe side. He's a bugger to get off once he's got his claws in."

Claus stood upright, rather abruptly.

Henry cleared his throat. "Erm. Well, thank you. Good day, Madam…"

"Madam Nimueh," supplied Henrietta.

Without further ado, Henry ushered his sister out of the shop. Claus rummaged for some money.

"For your time, Madam Nimueh," he reached out and placed the coins

76

in her palm and turned to leave, but her fingers closed about his hand, surprisingly strong for a woman of her advanced years.

"My name is actually Brenna McGrath," she paused expectantly, as if she were waiting for a specific response of some kind. When Claus remained silent, she continued. "Madam Nimueh is a nom de theatre. It sounds more mystical."

"Oh. Yes, I suppose it does," Claus felt a little awkward and turned towards the door.

"Take care," she hissed.

Claus nodded and then remembered that she was blind.

"Yes," he said. "Thank you."

Assuming that she had spoken out of gratitude for the money, he tried to make for the door again, but she still held fast to his hand.

"You should destroy it, before it is too late."

"Pardon?"

"There is trouble heading your way. I've cast your tarot over and over, but your course has become unclear. There are too many futures now possible."

Claus felt the hairs on the back of his neck prickle. For some years now, he had openly denied his belief in the occult abilities of clairvoyants and the like, for the sake of his grandfather, in an attempt to dispel his belief that his grandson was too prone to whimsical notions.

"Er...yes. Thank you," Claus forcibly pulled away and almost ran to the door, but Madam Nimueh wasn't quite finished.

"One more thing…"

~

"What were you doing in there? You didn't buy anything did you?" Henry grimaced as Claus emerged from the apothecary. "Don't tell me you let her look into your future?"

"She couldn't see it. Apparently, I have too many," Claus tried to sound blithely unconcerned.

"Too many futures?" Henrietta frowned. "How is that even possible?"

Claus shrugged.

"It seemed as if she knew me. Or at least, she thought that she did."

"Perhaps she mistook you for someone else?" suggested Henrietta.

"I suppose she might have mistaken the sound of my voice."

"Utter waste of time," Henry interrupted, as he crossed out the word 'Carnival' from the list in his notebook.

"She had a message for you, Henry," said Claus.

"Oh no. Unless it's about marauding monkeys, I'm not interested."

"She said, fortunately for you, some people are a lot more than what they appear to be."

"More? More what?"

"I don't know. Just *more*," Claus shrugged. "And she told me to give you this."

Henry huffed as Claus passed him the item.

"What is it?" asked Henrietta.

Henry stared at the object in his palm for a moment with a look of disbelief.

"It's a wooden clothes peg."

His sister grinned.

~

The stench of Bitterend hit Niall's olfactory glands like a pugilist's fist to the face. It had been many years since he'd spent any time here and if circumstances had not forced him to flee the place, then the smell surely would have.

His legs felt stiff from the long and tedious journey from Bightport Bay and as he stepped down from the train carriage, he stumbled into a passing gentleman.

"Forgive me, Sir!" said Niall, all a fluster. "I must have lost my footing."

"No harm done," said the gentleman, as he steadied his assailant.

Niall smiled, tipped his hat and turned back to the carriage to help his stepdaughter down onto the busy platform.

The pair weaved their way through the crowd of harassed looking travellers and exited the station to join the masses on the street outside.

"It's snowing," said Arabella. She poked at one of the flakes which had landed on her sleeve and frowned as it left a powdery grey smudge.

Niall laughed at her look of indignation.

"It isn't snow. It's ash."

The girl looked up into the sky with wide eyes.

"It's everywhere!"

"Aye. Put your parasol up," instructed Niall. "Hurry up. We need to find some digs. Perhaps somewhere near the river. To remind you of home."

Arabella nodded and smiled as she took her stepfather's arm, but as they ventured further down the street, her smile dissolved into a grimace.

"So many people," she commented and chewed nervously at her

bottom lip.

She had thought that Bightport Bay was overpopulated, compared to the rural village in which she had spent most of her childhood, but Bitterend was entirely overwhelming. She stared at the Rothgar Mountains which looked like gigantic broken teeth tearing into the sky.

"Aye. All the better for us, in our line of trade," Niall patted her hand and lead her on towards the northeast of the city.

"Did you take something from that gentleman?" Arabella whispered.

"Oh. Aye, I'll show you later," Niall patted his pocket in which the silver watch was hidden, that had, until very lately, belonged to the well-meaning stranger, who had steadied a fellow passenger.

A crease of concern appeared on Arabella's brow and she looked around as if expecting to see the owner of the watch coming after them.

"Don't fret so," grinned Niall. "He was hurrying to board the train."

"You didn't need to rob the man. We have our savings after all."

"Our savings aren't going to go far in this town, my dear. I'll do whatever I can to provide for you."

"I still don't understand why we had to come here. Business you say. What business? And why did we have to leave so hastily? Like a pair of felons fleeing the gallows!"

Niall declined to answer but hastened his stepdaughter onwards.

"There's an inn near the river. The Pretty Penny. I think you might even be able to hear a gull or two from there. Might remind you of home."

Arabella looked sceptical.

"There'll be plenty of gin," he commented with a wry smile. This seemed to raise the girl's spirits somewhat. She'd developed quite a taste for it over the past year.

~

Claus and the twins had met with another dead end when they paid a visit to the dockyard. It turned out that there were no records in the recent past of anyone importing a large number of monkeys, by boat or air ship, nor any other exotic creature come to that. Henry deployed Henrietta to charm the man in charge of the shipping records into giving up any information he might have. The man obliged by foraging through his filing cabinets, searching for quarantine records, unfortunately to no avail. A few aristocrats had brought back an unusual pet or two from abroad, but nothing on the scale of the monkey horde.

"Tea," said Claus.

"Good idea," smiled Henry. "I could do with a restorative. This futile search is exhausting."

"No, I mean the monkeys. They were specifically after the tea. Why?"

"Perhaps *they* needed a restorative?" suggested Henrietta.

Claus smiled. "It just seems a bit peculiar that they would hunt *specifically* for tea. Animals aren't usually so fussy about their sustenance, are they?"

"The entire affair is peculiar, but it does seem unusual, now that you mention it."

"Maybe it's an acquired taste," said Henry.

"You mean that someone has trained them to drink tea?" Claus looked out of the carriage window as the trio travelled back towards Sovereign Street. He had a mind to open the shop the following day and planned on spending the remainder of the afternoon getting it ready.

"Wealthy, eccentric tea fanatic. In Bitterend. Doesn't really narrow our search down much," Henrietta smiled.

"Let's examine what we have deduced so far," said Henry with absolute seriousness, pulling forth his notebook like some hackneyed detective from a penny crime novel. Claus and Henrietta exchanged a smirk. "Whoever we are looking for, must have travelled to exotic locations to procure the beasts at some point, that or he hired someone to breed them, either way, he must have plenty of money."

"*He?* We are assuming this person is male then?" Henrietta said archly.

"Oh, well…I just thought…" Henry floundered and looked at Claus for aid.

"A highly plausible assumption. No woman would dress those poor creatures so tastelessly," Henrietta grinned.

Claus laughed.

Henry cleared his throat and continued to divulge his suppositions.

"He would probably have fed the monkeys tea on a regular basis in order for them to have developed such an overwhelming desire for it," he paused for a moment and looked thoughtful. "Who are the main tea barons around here? Come on! Name some tea companies!"

"I say Henry, that's an idea," nodded Claus.

"Should we make a list of potential suspects?" teased Henrietta.

Henry didn't take the bait. It was notoriously difficult to tease Henry Tempest. Not because he had any particular ability to rise above it, he just tended not to notice.

"I'm afraid I won't be able to join you in your investigations tomorrow," said Claus. "I really must open the Emporium."

"Yes, of course, Claus. We shall visit you in the evening to present our findings," smiled Henry.

Before Claus retired for the evening, he brewed a large pot of tea and set it down outside the basement window. Perhaps tea was the only way to pacify these pillaging primates? He felt rather sorry for them in a way. It was clearly the fault of the owner that these monkeys were running amok.

29th Moribund

Brenna McGrath was a bold woman, but she was not so foolhardy as to go traipsing the dark streets alone, from Blacktemple to Northwall. She took Bodkin along with her, as well as a long and heavy staff. It helped her to negotiate unfamiliar terrain and it had a knobbly bit on the end, which was useful for hitting people with. Bodkin prowled just ahead of her, he was wearing a collar and a lead, much like a dog, but if it displeased him, he showed no sign of it.

It was early morning. The sun had yet to rise and the air was bitter cold. Elsewhere in the city, a frost would be on the ground, but not here. The ground under Northwall was always warm to the touch. When it rained, the entire area turned into a free steam bath. Puddles evaporated. Even snow could not endure the heat for long.

Brenna made her way along Courtesan Road and past The King's Ransom ale house, which was still serving customers. Unless you happened to be a copper, the gin palaces, beer houses and dram shops were all open for business. If you happened to be an off-duty copper, your coin was as good as anyone else's. The brothels and arconian dust dens also operated on an 'open all hours' basis, although the general hush indicated otherwise. By now, most of the patrons were subdued or insensible, having had their fill of whatever particular vice they were martyr to.

The silent, ragged vagrants, who had nowhere else to go, milled around in the street, searching for anything they could put to use, eat or sell. Their souls were like dim flickers of candlelight in Brenna's mind's

84

eye. One stiff breeze and they would be snuffed out of existence. They smelled of hopelessness and death.

Northwall was the region in the city that was closest to the mountains. Or the closest that was habitable at least, although the term 'habitable' could be applied loosely. No body actually wanted to live there. To say it was 'the wrong side of the river' was a gross understatement. An artificial tributary of The Dolorous had been directed to snake through the region. There were great waterwheels erected at strategic points, which forced the water below ground, therefore flooding some of the subterranean tunnels, in a desperate attempt to prevent the fire from spreading any further beneath the city. A great wall had been erected around the perimeter, to close off what had once been the mining town of Arcon. The fire, like some terrible infection, had spread beneath the ground and the area was prone to sink holes and explosions. The sparse remnants of the long-abandoned dwellings stood like broken gravestones.

The only people permitted entrance beyond the wall were the arconian miners, the Dampeners and those who had earned special dispensation from the mayor. This was a rare privilege only extended to murderers and the most persistent of wrongdoers. Civilians were strictly prohibited beyond the wall. No one disputed this, because no one in their right mind would *want* to go beyond the wall. Not only was there a persistent risk of agonising, burning death, but there was also talk of hauntings and curses.

The miners were viewed as heroes by most people. They risked life and limb on a daily basis for the prosperity of the city. On the whole, they seemed curiously relaxed about the potentially terminal nature of their work, although this could be attributed to the fact that they were regularly exposed to high levels of arconian dust.

The Dampeners, on the other hand, were generally viewed as insane and/or suicidal. Their job was to control the subterranean fires. Unfortunately, the protective clothing and breathing apparatus they wore stopped any arconian dust from entering their bodies, which meant that they saw all of the danger and horror and none of the dancing unicorns and spiraling rainbows.

Brenna could feel the increase in temperature through the soles of her boots as she made her way closer to The Wall. She could tell when she'd arrived in Clinker Street. You could bake a potato in the ground if you buried it for a couple of hours. Brenna had no intention of spending that long in this part of the city though. People that lived this close to the mountain tended to have some funny ways. Breathe in too much of those ashes and you'd be mad as a miner in no time.

She turned down a side street which was too insignificant to merit a name. In truth it was little more than a gap between the buildings and led to nowhere of consequence. Nowhere of Consequence was a ramshackle, wooden construction, which may have at some point been worthy of the term 'building'. Many of the roof tiles were missing and the holes had been patched with apparently whatever could be scavenged from the surrounding area. Brenna used her staff to negotiate the rotting steps which led to the door. Instead of knocking and waiting for an answer, she pushed open the door and stepped inside, where she promptly stumbled over a pair of legs. She felt around and discovered a torso attached to the limbs. It was warm and she could hear breathing. Just as well, she thought. It was never a good omen to go tripping over a corpse this early in the day. She soon deduced, with the aid of her staff, that there were many slumbering bodies strewn across the floor, some of which got a rude awakening as the heavy stick came into contact with a ribcage or worse. She could smell the grease and oil of the perpetually silent cotton looms. The machinery didn't work after all. The looms were merely a decoy.

"Click Clack!" she bellowed. She reached out and found a banister, which belonged to the staircase leading to the floor above. She called out again but there was no response, so she began to mount the steps. The timber groaned. The perpetually warm, damp climate had taken its toll and the entire edifice was succumbing to rot. There was always a risk of falling through the floorboards, even when one had the ability to see. She used her staff to prod at each step before she would trust it to support her weight and was not surprised when the stout wooden stick sank through one of the spongy steps. There was no sound of cracking or splintering, as the wood was as soft and moist as a good fruit cake. Eventually she made it to the top of the stairs in this irksome fashion and called out again. The unmistakable sound which announced the approach of the proprietor met her ears.

Click Clack. Click Clack. Click Clack.

The staccato sound of wood striking on wood.

"Madam Nimueh. To what do I owe this pleasure, at such an unsociable hour?" asked Click Clack the Locust.

"Good morning."

"It's the middle of the night. I suppose you'll be wanting tea," he offered in a tone full of feigned inconvenience.

Brenna's lips twitched minutely in her own version of a smile.

It was common knowledge, not to mention *obvious*, that Click Clack had earned his name from the sound that his wooden legs made when he walked. '*The Locust*' was a little more obscure, but many believed that it referred to his plague of 'boys' who followed him around like a faithful entourage to a king. He had come to Eloria from Katama, many years ago, as a young man, wishing to seek his fortune. Regrettably it had been his fate to lose both of his lower legs in an industrial accident, which left him fit for no legitimate purpose. Fortunately for Click Clack, he seemed to excel at non legitimate purposes. He had very long, black hair which he wore in a braid down his back and he sported a well fitted suit of good cloth, which spoke plainly, given his surroundings, of ill-gotten gain. He spoke with a broad Northwall accent and proclaimed himself an entrepreneur. Indeed, owning a 'fabric manufactory' was one of his lesser concerns and in truth it was merely a smoke screen for his more lucrative business ventures. Click Clack had his fingers in more pies than Jack Horner. Whether you wanted to hire protection or obtain valuable information, if you needed a spy or an item procured, contraband of any variety, someone found or someone permanently lost, you visited The Locust.

"You should pull down this rat-hole before it falls into the ground," said Brenna, as Click Clack turned to fetch some tea. "It's a health hazard."

"I would, if I had anywhere else to live," he called from the next room. "Perhaps I could come and live with you. I could be your eyes and you could be my legs."

Brenna grunted in what might have been amusement.

"Or your conscience?" she suggested. "Anyway, don't you give me that old blarney, my lad, I know full well that you have a nice house off Threefold Square."

Click Clack moved smoothly on his wooden legs. The tea tray didn't even wobble.

"But this place *does* have a certain charm."

"Aye. It's positively palatial," Brenna reached her hand out to receive a teacup and sniffed at its contents before sipping it. "It's green," she stated.

"So?"

"Tea should be brown."

Click Clack huffed and tried to remove the offending beverage, but Brenna held fast to the cup and began to drink it regardless of its colour.

"So, what brings you to my *rat-hole*? I assume you didn't come here just to insult my tea?"

Brenna took a deep breath.

"No. I need to find a man."

"But you have me!"

Brenna scowled.

"This is serious, Yusheng."

Click Clack raised his eyebrows at the sound of his real name and lost all trace of joviality.

"Go on."

"He poses a great threat to someone… whom I would rather not have come to harm. I need to know if he's in Bitterend. Or if he arrives in Bitterend and what he does when he's here. I'm not entirely sure if he's still alive. In some ways I hope he isn't."

"You want him offed?"

Brenna seemed to consider this briefly for a moment before she shook her head.

"No. Just watched."

"Does he have a name?"

"Niall McGrath."

~

After a makeshift breakfast of cold muffins and cheese and several cups of tea, Claus made ready to open the shop. He felt a dreadful sense of loss as he turned the sign upon the door to display the word 'open'. The emporium didn't feel as though it belonged to him. It was still his grandfather's. Claus missed the old man terribly. He even missed his perpetual complaints. For as long as Claus could remember, he had done his best *not* to hear his grandfather's litany of grievances about the weather, or his 'blasted leg' or that the tea was stewed, or that Claus had left the workshop in a 'bloody shambles again.' Now Claus felt that he would give just about anything to hear himself moaned at again.

"This watch has stopped working. *Again.*" A voice from behind Claus startled him. He spun around to face a disgruntled looking old gentleman.

That's not what I meant thought Claus. He took a deep breath.

"Let me see," Claus held out his hand and the customer thrust the pocket watch into his palm.

"I saw old Vogel's obituary in the newspaper," the old man stated in a creaky voice. "I always read the obituary," he added, somewhat morosely.

Claus carried on inspecting the watch.

"Pity," said the old man, when Claus failed to respond.

"There," said Claus. He passed the timepiece back. "You have to *wind* it, Mister Higgins. *Every day.*"

"Well, why didn't you tell me that?" huffed Mister Higgins.

"I do. Every day," Claus smiled as he turned away and Mister Higgins shuffled towards the shop door, muttering to himself about smart-mouthed whippersnappers, only to very nearly collide with someone coming in the other direction. The person entering pushed on with very little regard for the old gentleman who was in his way.

"No respect," grumbled Mister Higgins, who seemed to change his mind about leaving in preference of glaring at the newcomer, with the kind of expression one can only master after a lifetime training in the art of eating lemons.

Claus was surprised when he turned back to see *two* customers in his shop. Business was never what one could call 'booming' at the Time Emporium. People just didn't want to buy clocks or watches on a regular basis as they would do with food or clothing for instance, but the Vogel's had built up a good reputation over the years and attracted customers who wanted the prestige of owning a Vogel timepiece, even if that meant they could only afford the premade designs that were displayed in the showroom. The *real* money came from designing bespoke timepieces for special occasions, on behalf of the very wealthy patrons.

"Good morning, Sir," said Claus with automatic politeness.

"Aye. That it is." agreed the customer.

As the newcomer walked forward, Claus had a brief moment to appraise him. In years, he looked to be around his mid-thirties. He was fairly tall and lean but well-muscled, as though he were no stranger to manual work. He had a curiously sinuous way of moving, not unlike a cat stalking its prey. He spoke with an Irkish accent, although it was somewhat diluted, perhaps from spending prolonged periods of time away from his native home. His hair was almost as black as that of the Tempest twins and his eyes were of an uncommonly bright blue. His suit was of good quality, but his face was unshaven. His boots had been polished and the leather was excellent, but they had been re-soled several times.

"I'd like to speak with the proprietor," said the stranger.

"I am he," smiled Claus amiably.

"You are Vogel?"

"Indeed. Claus Vogel, to be precise."

The customer frowned.

"So, the old man really is dead."

Mister Higgins could be heard huffing in the background, muttering words like 'rude' and 'insensitive'.

"My Grandfather passed away recently, yes," Claus replied. "Did you know him?"

"Aye, I knew him alright," smiled the man with bright blue eyes.

"Seen you before too. Doubt you remember me. You were about this high," he held his hand out at just below waist height.

"No, I'm afraid I don't recall you."

"Aye, well perhaps that's all to the good. I was a bit of rascal back then." The man grinned and revealed what looked like a gold tooth.

"Hans's funeral is being held at eleven o'clock, on the third of Brevis, at the Chapel of Galen in Five Martyr's. The wake is being held here in the shop. You are welcome to come, if you have a mind to."

"That's very gracious of you," said the man with bright blue eyes. He touched the brim of his hat and without another word, turned on his heel and left as abruptly as he had entered.

"Strange sort of fellow," frowned Claus, more to himself than to Mister Higgins, as Claus had quite forgotten that the old man was present.

"Disagreeable I'd say," commented the old man.

After Mister Higgins had departed, Claus kept himself busy in the shop by doing some cleaning and rearranging. This was unchartered territory for Claus, but after a little hunting, he found some vinegar and old newspapers and buffed the glass cabinets until they gleamed, just as Hans used to. When he had exhausted that particular exercise in killing time, he thought briefly about doing a stock take, but there really wasn't any need. Nobody had bought anything since Hans had died and he had kept the books in ferociously good order. Claus retrieved the ledger from beneath the counter and flipped through it idly, not really paying attention to what was written on the pages. The bell tinkled above the door, announcing another customer. Three in five hours. A veritable stampede.

"Can I help you?" smiled Claus.

A woman, who looked very well-to-do, approached the counter. The coat she was wearing looked like it cost more than most people's yearly income.

"I require a watch for my son. Not just any watch. The best you have. He is soon to turn one and twenty."

"I see. Did you want to look at what I have in stock? Or perhaps you'd like something specially crafted for the occasion..." Claus trailed off as it became apparent that the woman wasn't listening to him but frowning around the shop with an air of impatient expectation.

"Where is the proprietor?" she demanded.

"That would be me, ma'am."

The woman looked down her nose at him.

"*You*? You're a *master watchmaker*, are you?"

"Indeed," Claus didn't bother with the 'Ma'am' this time.

The woman peered at him in a disconcerting manner.

"You're terribly young."

"I've been younger," replied Claus, without a hint of sarcasm. He could imagine Hans giving him a clip around the ear and tried not to grin. "Would you like to see my credentials? I have a recent letter of thanks from Lord Windersale, Earl of Wherewithal. He was very pleased with my work."

The woman raised her eyebrows.

"The Earl of Wherewithal? Well...in that case. I think I should like something custom made."

"Very good," Claus inclined his head graciously. "With an engraving perhaps? Something personal?"

"Yes, that would be nice."

Claus tried not to sigh as he pulled out a ledger full of designs and a pocketbook and pen.

"If you would like to sit down and look through these? Let me know if there's anything you like, and I can sketch some designs based on whatever you think would be fitting."

The woman smiled, safe in the knowledge that her son would receive a watch fit for an Earl.

After what felt like an eternity, the woman, who had turned out to be one Lady Drummond, pointed out some watches which she liked, paid a heavy deposit and left. Claus retired to the office for a restorative cup of tea and left the door open so that he could hear the shop bell, although the thought of more than three customers in one day was unconscionable. Although, Claus couldn't count the Irkish man as a customer and, in truth, Mister Higgins only ever came in because he wanted someone to talk to.

Claus held his cup and saucer to his chest and gazed out of the window at nothing in particular. Sovereign Street was as busy as ever, but then a solitary figure in the crowd caught his eye. It was the old mystic woman from Katamatown. She looked so out of place that Claus was surprised she wasn't garnering more attention from the other pedestrians. Strangely, other than himself, no one seemed to notice her at all, and even the people who moved out of her way did so without glancing at her. It was as if she were invisible and merely repelled people with some occult force of will. Claus shook his head and dismissed this idea as nonsense. He wasn't sure why, but he found the sight of her unsettling somehow. It was similar to the feeling of forgetting to do something important, but not being able to remember what that something was. She was stood as still as a statue, with what looked like a wizard's staff in her hand and the huge grey cat at her side. As Claus watched, she turned very deliberately and met his gaze. He gasped and stepped behind the curtain before laughing and mentally admonishing himself. What was he thinking? She couldn't see him, she was blind. Anyway, what did he have to fear from some old woman?

The bell over the shop door gave a shrill tinkle. Claus felt his heart begin to race and he peered cautiously around the office doorframe.

"Henry! You're early!" Claus darted forward and practically dragged his friend into the shop.

"My sister got bored and kept complaining, then ended up going home, so I've come in search of a more stalwart companion."

"Good grief! No one has ever accused me of being stalwart!" Claus reached towards the shop door and turned the sign over, so that it displayed the word 'closed'. He surreptitiously glanced across the street for the mystic, but she was nowhere to be seen. He shut the door and drew the latch.

"See," grinned Henry. "You've closed the shop early on my account. *Stalwart.*"

"I've had to deal with *three* customers today Henry!"

"Dreadful! How on Cellanor have you coped?"

Claus laughed and beckoned Henry to follow him into the office for refreshment.

"So, am I right to deduce that the investigations went ill?"

Henry looked sour and nodded.

"I don't blame Henrietta for giving up. Our search has been entirely fruitless."

"Well, we have the afternoon to carry on, if you have the heart?"

"If you are sure that you don't mind closing the shop early?"

"Entirely sure. I have made enough money this morning to live comfortably for the next month," said Claus.

Not to mention I have my inheritance money, he added to himself, feeling rather guilty that he still hadn't mentioned this to his friends.

Henry raised his eyebrows.

"Lady Drummond," Claus rolled his eyes. "Special custom order for her son, no doubt some intolerable fop. Anyway, with a little expert assistance from yours truly, she chose the most expensive casing and components. Even the complications are gold plated. It will be a hideous piece no doubt. Plus, she incurred a ten percent surcharge."

"On account of what?"

"On account of being generally disagreeable."

"I say, Claus! I think your grandfather was wrong about you not having any business sense."

"I wouldn't go that far. I just didn't like her."

Henry laughed.

"So, who are we going to investigate?" asked Claus.

Henry retrieved and consulted the list he had made in his pocket notebook. "I still have Whitmore, Jacksons and Cordage to interview."

"Let's do Cordage. I like Cordage."

"You realise that we will have to pretend to be proper reporters."

"Is that illegal?"

"Not *terribly*, I think."

Claus smiled and shook his head. "In any case, surely these companies would welcome publicity?"

"Not if it's the sort of publicity which includes maniac monkeys destroying other people's property, premises and livelihoods. There could even be legal action taken against the negligent owner, once he is identified."

"That's a fair point, I hadn't thought of that," Claus nodded. "So, what is our cover story?"

"That our readers are interested to know the bloke behind the brew.

The captain behind the cuppa. The chap behind the char. The…the…"

"Yes, Henry. I get the point."

"That way I can ask probing personal questions."

"Not too personal. You'll get us thrown out."

~

The pair left the shop and hailed a carriage, which came to a halt some thirty minutes later. Heartfelt – which was a prestigious region in its own right- was merely a prelude to Ardent, which was a leafy suburb, where birds chirped in the trees that lined the road. This was the southern outskirts, on the very edge of Bitterend, where the smoke and squalor had yet to spread. Ardent seemed to blend seamlessly with the edge of the Eldarn Forest, a wild and dense expanse of trees, which separated Bitterend from its neighbouring county of Wherewithal.

Claus got out and looked around.

"It's so very quiet," he observed. "And there's no ash!"

Henry brushed his suit down self-consciously.

"Let's hope that they allow us in," he said and gestured at the impeccable white manor house that loomed before them.

They marched up a gravel carriageway, which was lined with small topiary evergreen trees and tugged on the bell pull. After a brief wait, the door was opened slowly and somewhat regally.

"Tradesmen are supposed to use the side door," said the butler by way of greeting, as he glared imperiously at the visitors.

"Oh, we are not tradesmen, we are reporters," Henry smiled.

The butler raised an eyebrow.

Henry reached inside his lapel and produced his father's business card, which he'd filched earlier that day.

"The Tempest's Eye," stated the butler after he glanced at the card. He didn't seem impressed. "And what exactly do you want?"

"We want to interview Lord Cordage, if he is agreeable. I'm sure his vast knowledge of the tea industry would make for some compelling reading. But what we'd really like, is to get some background information from him. His life, his hobbies and interests. Let our readers get to know the bloke behind the brew. The chap behind the char. The-"

Claus stood firmly on Henry's foot before he could get too carried away.

"Ow! Oh yes! Could be quite good for publicity."

"Hm. Follow me. I'll see if his lordship is disposed to arrange an interview with you, although I doubt that he will have the time to speak with you personally. His Lordship is *very* busy," said the butler, as he ushered them inside without a smile.

Claus gazed around at the opulent entrance hall and decided that he was in the wrong trade. They followed the butler, as he led them imperiously down a lavish corridor and stopped before the farthest door. He reached out and tapped elegantly with a pristine white gloved hand.

"His lordship doesn't like to be disturbed. He's been working on a new blend. I haven't seen him since the day before yesterday. Sometimes he shuts himself up for days, so I wouldn't get your hopes up," he said, before knocking again, a little louder. There was no answer from within. They stood in silence for a moment. The butler opened the door a fraction and peeped inside.

"Good gracious me!" he exclaimed and flung the door open and hurried inside. After a brief moment of indecision, Claus and Henry followed.

Lord Cordage was sprawled upon the floor, one of his arms resting at a very peculiar angle. There was a pool of congealed blood around his head and a broken teapot lay nearby. There was a lot of smashed porcelain and tea leaves strewn about. The room was in utter disarray, with broken furniture, upturned tables and shattered windows, as if some terrible fight had occurred. Worst of all, (with the exception of the corpse) there seemed to be a substance which looked an awful lot like excrement smeared across the wallpaper.

The butler crouched down beside his fallen master and peered at him.

"He's dead!" he gasped, his snobbish facade fell away as he stared up, wide eyed and ashen faced at the visitors. "I must fetch help!"

He sprang up and raced from the room, leaving Claus and Henry with little else to do than to stare at the man on the floor.

"What in the world?" Henry breathed. "Dead? Is he really? Does he look dead to you, Claus?"

"He doesn't look very lively."

Claus decided that he'd had enough of staring at the corpse and turned his attention to the room in which they stood. The furniture was all made from light wicker and the floor was covered by a large Katamesian style carpet. The low brumail sun streamed in through south facing Bonancian doors, which opened out onto a landscaped garden. No doubt the view was probably rather splendid in the warm beltainian months. Claus thought that the room would be very nice without the addition of the dead body and faeces.

He stepped carefully around the late Lord Cordage and made his way towards the Bonancian doors, the glass of which seemed to be intact. The glazed panels on either side however, had not been so fortunate, and were smashed to smithereens. Claus frowned.

"Henry, the glass is all over the lawn."

"There's shit up the walls, but you're concerned about the state of the turf?"

"The glass is *outside*. Whoever did this was breaking out, not in."

As Claus turned back to look at Henry, a strange looking cabinet caught his eye. He glanced towards the door to make sure that they were still unsupervised and went to have a better look at the curiously incongruous item of furniture. It was similar to a large sideboard in proportion and design. A wooden, rectangular shape with two doors which opened up to reveal two separate compartments within, one of which had been partially ripped from its hinges and hung like a broken limb. The internal space, which was surprisingly capacious, had deep gauges scored into the wood and, disturbingly, what appeared to be bite marks.

What had initially attracted Claus's attention, was an abundance of tubing and copper wires, mounted upon the top and disappearing into a sealed compartment. There was also a pyramid shaped lump of arconian, about the same size as Claus's fist, which had been polished and glittered like a crystal, set into a metal prong. There was a dial which had been set to 'maximum' and a handle on the side of the cabinet, which Claus reached out for and turned before he could stop himself. There followed a series of sharp popping noises, a whirring sound and a light show of disconcerting magnitude. Claus leapt backwards into a small wicker table. A meagre amount of crockery, that had managed to survive the previous disaster, shattered onto the floor. Claus looked around guiltily at Henry, whose mouth hung slightly agape.

"What is that?" he whispered, staring at the cabinet.

"I've never seen anything like it."

Henry grimaced as he stepped gingerly over the corpse. He stooped to pick up the table which Claus had knocked over.

"Hallo. No one will miss these."

"Henry! What are you doing?" hissed Claus. Henry had picked up a pile of letters that had fallen on to the floor along with the crockery and stuffed them inside his waistcoat.

"They could be clues!" Henry hissed back.

"Better the police have them then!"

"Not a chance. This isn't the story I came here for, but it's a whopper of a story! This could mean a big promotion for me!"

"And big trouble," Claus shook his head. "And what do you mean *promotion*? Technically you haven't even been hired yet!"

At which point a maid entered the room. Claus was somewhat relieved. At least it meant that Henry couldn't steal anything else. The maid stared at the corpse of her fallen master and turned pale.

"I ain't never seen a dead person before," she spoke as if to herself.

"Um…" said Claus, not sure how to respond.

"He was alright y'know," she continued. "To work for, I mean."

"Yes…I'm sure," Claus said. "Do we need to remain here? Until the police arrive, I mean?"

"Oh no. Mister Hogarth told me to get rid of you. Said he didn't want no reporters sticking their noses in what didn't concern them."

"Mister Hogarth?" frowned Henry.

"The butler," said the maid and rolled her eyes. "Anyway, I have to find Dahljeeling."

"Um, it's in Mahjia isn't it?" asked Henry.

"No, no," said the maid. "Not the place. Dahljeeling's the other butler. The monkey."

"A monkey butler!" Henry almost shouted.

The girl raised her eyebrows at the outburst but nodded.

"He's…he *was* the master's chief tea taster. His Lordship said Dahljeeling was a…*Conner-sewer*."

"A what?" Henry frowned.

101

"An expert," explained the maid.

"How does a monkey indicate whether or not the tea is up to scratch?" Henry asked with a look of incredulity.

"Well, if he thought the blend was a good'un, he'd get really excited and jump up and down."

"And if he didn't like it?"

The girl shuddered and her eyes darted towards the soiled wallpaper, before answering quietly "He'd throw a handful of his own doings at you."

Henry's mouth fell open. "I'm never drinking Cordage's again," he muttered.

Claus cleared his throat. "Does Dahljeeling happen to wear a red tailcoat and a fez?"

"Yes! That's him! Have you seen him then?"

"No," said Claus and Henry in unison.

"But I'm sure he'll turn up." added Claus.

"He can't have gone far," Henry tried to sound reassuring. There was no point in worrying the poor girl.

"No. He can't have. Dahljeeling has Angoraphobia."

Claus and Henry glanced at each other in confusion.

"Fear of rabbits?" ventured Claus.

"No. He hates big crowds and wide-open spaces, that sort of thing. If he gets upset, he usually hides in a cupboard or somewhere small, which means I'm going to have to hunt all over the house for him."

"Ah. Well, we'll let you get on with it then," Henry tipped his hat and made for the door.

"Good day, Miss," said Claus.

~

"Dahljeeling has to be our man. I mean our monkey," said Henry. He was pacing in agitated excitement up and down the length of Claus's workshop, or at least as much as anyone *could* pace in an overcrowded basement. Nevertheless, it seemed like a good location for a clandestine discussion.

"But he's just *one* monkey," protested Claus.

"How many do you need?"

"Well, I'd have said between twenty and thirty!"

"Yes. I suppose you're right," Henry looked momentarily crestfallen, before brightening once more. "But it all seems too much of a *coincidence*. The butler said that he hadn't seen Lord Cordage for a couple of days. That's when the monkey attacks began. And Dahljeeling is missing."

"And Lord Cordage is dead," said Claus. He got up to light a few more candles. The basement was gloomy, the sun had long since set. Claus bit his lip. He hoped that Henry would depart or fall asleep before he had to offer his tea tribute. He didn't want to divulge this nightly ritual, as he was painfully aware that it would seem very peculiar, not to mention that in light of recent discoveries, Claus might well be aiding- or at least supplying tea to- Lord Cordage's killer.

"I think we should open the letters," stated Henry.

"It's an arrestable offence you know? Opening another person's mail," said Claus without any real conviction.

"It's *already* been opened. I'm just reading it," insisted Henry.

"Do you want a drink?"

Henry nodded. "And I could use a bit more light!" he called, as Claus stepped into the Transporter and began to wind the lever.

Claus returned quickly, with a plate of biscuits, which he had found hidden in a jar, lurking at the back of a cupboard, and a bottle of brandy. Not the medicinal kind.

"I thought this might perk us up."

"Jolly good show. Shall we?" Henry picked up the first letter.

Claus nodded, resigned.

Henry shook open the sheet of paper and began to read aloud.

Medius 8th. Age of Cambion 13:7

Lord Cordage,

I was quite overcome by your interest in my work. I had no idea that my little toys could rise to the attention of such esteemed gentry. It would, of course, be my privilege to visit you at your convenience and I will bring some items which I believe may amuse you.

Sincerely

N Todorovich

~

"Toys?" frowned Claus.

Henry shrugged, discarded the letter and picked up the next.

Lamtis 1st. Age of Cambion 13:7

Dear Lord Cordage.

I was so pleased to learn that you liked my little gift. You must visit me in my workshop, where I can show you some of my larger experiments, I think you'll be quite impressed, if that is not too bold of me to say. With regards to your invitation of tea, just let me know when.

Yours sincerely

N Todorovich

~

Ochre 12th. Age of Cambion 13:7

Dear Lord Cordage,

I have finished the plans for our little endeavour and enclosed them with this letter. Look them over and let me know if you want any modifications made. If not, I will proceed without delay.

Your friend,

N Todorovich

~

Henry glanced at the back of the letter and then scanned the rest of the missives with a frown.

"There's no plans here. Bother. They must still be at Cordage's house."

"Well, go on with the next letter," shrugged Claus. "Perhaps this Todorovich chap will elaborate."

Moribund 17th. Age of Cambion 13:7.

Dear William,

The device should be delivered to your home by the 20th. You might even have it with you before you receive this letter. Who can tell given the lamentable state of the Elorian postal system? A note of caution, please do not attempt to operate the device without me. It is, after all, rather experimental and I wish to oversee your first attempt, in order to avoid any disappointment or injury. I will call round on the morning of the 22nd unless this is inconvenient.

Fond wishes,

Your friend,

N Todorovich

Moribund 22nd· Age of Cambion 13:7.

My Dear William,

I am disappointed to inform you that our experiment must wait a further week. It is an errand of mercy which drags me away. I must attend a relative who is unwell. Hopefully, it is not a serious affliction. I must stress once again that you should NOT operate the device without me, I know how impatient you get! I must dash now if I am to make the train.

N

~

"What in the world is all that about?" said Henry with disgust. He tossed the letter down and sipped his brandy with a frown. Henry hated mysteries as much as he loved to solve them. He had been that way for as long as Claus could remember. When they were boys it had always been Henry's curiosity which had got them into trouble and earned Claus a few lashings into the bargain.

"The cabinet?" suggested Claus. It was the first thing that sprang to his mind. It had certainly looked experimental.

Henry nodded. "Perhaps. It was strange indeed. All those wires. What do you suppose is its purpose?"

Claus shrugged. "Not just to make peculiar noises and flashing lights, I'm sure."

"I think we should try to find out about this Todorovich character."

"Agreed. I wonder who will inform him that Lord Cordage is dead. I hope he doesn't read about it in the paper. It seems that they were close."

"I expect the police will want to talk to all of Lord Cordage's friends and acquaintances. There's no way that he wasn't murdered. Unless he decided to commit suicide by beating himself to death with his best porcelain."

~

"I'm out," said the portly man, whose name Niall had learnt and then quickly forgotten, discarding the information as useless. Ted, on the other hand, was worth watching. Niall had marked him from the beginning of the game as the most accomplished player out of the five men, who were gathered around the table, in a secluded corner of the inn. Niall had never been remarkably good at card games, but that hardly mattered and he always kept in mind the old adage 'Unlucky at cards, lucky in love'. He smiled bitterly as he thought of Arabella's mother.

"Fancy your chances, do you?" asked Ted, misconstruing his opponent's smile.

Niall bared his teeth in a roguish grin as he turned his gaze upon Ted, his gold tooth flashing in the dim light of the candle. They were now the only two players left.

"All in."

Ted smirked and laid his cards down.

"Royal Flush," he said with an air of smugness.

"Bah! Got me again! You must have a guardian angel watching over you tonight my friend," Niall tossed his own cards down on the table in disgust.

"Two pairs?" exclaimed one of the other men in horror. "You went all in on *two pairs*? Were you banking on the luck of the Irkish?"

Niall shrugged good-naturedly, stood up and made his way to the bar.

"Another round, if you'd be so good Landlord," he said jovially.

The landlord of The Pretty Penny gave Niall a significant look before leaning over the bar towards him.

"I hope you can afford to pay for your lodgings after that?" he asked in a low tone.

"Give me an hour. I'll have it all back in my pocket and then some."

The landlord shook his head in a despairing way, which plainly conveyed the thought "*on your own head be it.*"

"And pour me a very large brandy," Niall grinned.

He stumbled back to his new friends with the tray of drinks and pushed the glass of brandy towards Ted.

"To the victor the spoils!"

Ted laughed and reached for the glass.

"You're a good sport, Nomad. We'll have to do this again!"

"We bloody won't," said one of the others. "I just lost my rent. The missus is going to skin me alive."

~

Ted felt rather pleased with himself as he left the inn. He'd always been inclined to think badly of the Irkish, and especially of the nomadic types, but now he felt an increased tolerance for them. He also felt a significant increase to the weight of his pockets. On the whole, an enriching experience altogether.

Ted stumbled into a wall and leaned against it for support. The stranger had certainly been generous with his liquor and Ted had a suspicion that he would have a sore head come the morrow.

"Can I help you there, Sir?"

Ted started and looked around blearily for the owner of the voice. A young girl stood at the mouth of an alleyway. She took a hearty swig from a bottle of gin and then smiled at him coquettishly. Ted tried to focus. She was pretty. He smiled back.

"Yeah. I recon you can, dear," he stumbled over to the girl and grasped her roughly by the upper arms, forcing her back against the wall.

"Not here," protested the girl and she began to tug at Ted's arm, leading him further into the dark seclusion of the alleyway.

"Fair enough. Too many peelers around this time o'night," he conceded and let the girl lead him into the shadows, until they were out of view.

"Ere, this'll do," he said and pushed himself up against her. The girl went stiff at his touch and Ted concluded that she was more ridged than he was himself at that moment. Damn the liquor. He tried to kiss her, but she averted her face.

"Do you want my money, or not?" he growled.

The girl nodded

Ted fumbled with the buttons on his trousers.

"How much is this going to cost me?" he asked.

"Everything you have," came the curt reply from behind him.

Ted turned around unsteadily to confront this untimely interruption.

Arabella hastily backed up against the wall behind her and averted her face, her eyes screwed up tightly, but that did nothing to stop her hearing a heavy, wet smacking sound, like someone crushing a rotten potato underfoot. She felt something land on her exposed cheek which was too wet to be ash. Niall pulled a handkerchief out of his pocket and deliberately wiped the blood from the cosh.

"You alright, Arabella?"

Arabella turned to see the figure laying on the cobbles, his trousers half unbuttoned. She nodded almost imperceptibly, the shadows

109

obscuring any expression she might have been wearing. Niall stooped down and riffled through Ted's pockets, retrieving all that he found. Not a bad night's earnings, he observed. He would need every farthing if he planned to stay in Bitterend.

3rd Brevis

The day of Hans's funeral arrived without further incident. There had been no monkey attacks for the last couple of days and Claus had been very careful not to use the 'item of peculiarity'. He had spent the previous day working on the watch for Lady Drummond and making sure that the catering for the wake was in hand. He needn't have bothered as Henrietta had taken it upon herself to see to these details. The Tempest's cook had prepared a cold buffet and even some Skordian specialties. Claus had been forced to borrow quite a lot of crockery and glassware from his friends, since he and his grandfather had never really bothered to eat proper meals at home. Neither of them could cook very well and since Hans had refused to employ a housekeeper or cook, they tended to exist on snacks.

A lot of people had thought well of Hans and the shop grew warm and noisy as they congregated there after the burial. Claus was pleased to hear stories about Hans when he was young. Apparently, he had been quite reckless in his youth. He was less pleased with everyone offering their condolences, because he didn't really know how to respond, 'thank you' seemed inappropriate somehow.

Ambrose Alltard waved at Claus from behind a rapidly diminishing plate of savoury pastries and cold meats. Claus waved back and went into the office to retrieve the documents which he had read and signed the previous evening and made his way through the crowded showroom to hand them to the solicitor.

"Small print?" enquired Alltard.

"Thoroughly read." assured Claus. The small print concerning the heirloom was more or less how Alltard had described. That the watch should be passed to the eldest surviving family member. Claus could not see how this posed any problem, as he was the only surviving Vogel and

111

so he was not breaking any rules of tradition by possessing it.

"Congratulations. You are now a young man of means," beamed the solicitor. Claus tried to make covert hushing gestures to no avail. "We really should discuss some investment options!"

Claus cringed as he looked across the room to see Henry raising a quizzical eyebrow in his direction. Henry had selective hearing. He didn't seem to take any notice of what people were saying, unless it was something he wasn't supposed to hear. Claus harbored the suspicion that his friend would probably make a very decent journalist one day.

"Any luck locating the mystery watch?" continued Alltard, oblivious to Claus's discomfort.

"No," Claus shook his head. He wasn't sure why he felt the need to lie.

"Well, maybe it is all for the best." Alltard smiled.

"What makes you say that?" asked Claus with surprise.

"Um. Er. Less said, soonest mended." The solicitor tapped his nose in a conspiratorial way. "These potato rosti are really very good!"

The rosti was good, but Claus found Alltard's behaviour very confusing and was about to press him to explain himself, when he noticed that the solicitor had gone very pale and was staring across the room at someone. Claus followed his gaze and saw the man with the bright blue eyes watching them. He was smiling.

"Oh!" cried Alltard. "How remiss of me! I have just remembered that I have an appointment with a venerable lady of advanced years, who seems intent upon leaving her entire estate to her cats. Her children have implored me to make her see sense. Mind you, if I had had the misfortune of spawning such ungracious offspring, I would probably make my dog my sole beneficiary. Good day! Good day!"

With that, Alltard tapped at his mouth with a napkin, pushed his way past the other guests and vanished through the door with astonishing speed. Claus stood for a moment, staring at the empty space the solicitor had so recently occupied, before his almost occult disappearing act. Perplexed, he turned to look back at the man with the bright blue eyes, only to find that he had also disappeared. He puffed out his cheeks in exasperation and slipped into the office to escape for a little while, but no sooner had he attained his sanctuary, he heard the door open and close behind him and he sighed.

"Timesmith."

Claus turned with a start to find the old mystic woman from Katamatown.

"Why are you here?" he blurted rudely, before he could stop himself. More to the point, *how are you here?* he wondered. How had a blind woman managed to find her way into his office? And why had no one else noticed her?

"I need to talk with you about an item of peculiarity."

How does she know about the watch? I haven't told a soul, not even Henry. Claus was momentarily silent before he remembered his manners.

"Won't you sit down, Missus..." he groped around his memory, "McGrath."

He took her elbow and directed her into an armchair, although somehow, he doubted that she needed any help.

She grunted as she lowered herself onto the seat.

"Now, what is this item you mentioned?"

"Don't play coy lad. It doesn't suit you," she sneered.

Claus was at a loss as how to proceed. Should he be forthright or circumspect? Perhaps he should just deny everything?

"Missus McGrath, I don't know how you know me, nor what you

113

know about me, or what it is that you *think* you know. You speak of an item of peculiarity. Tell me exactly what it is and what you want of me."

"It *looks* like a pocket watch and I want you to destroy the accursed thing."

Claus stared at her. Perhaps she was channelling Hans from beyond the grave?

"Why should I?" he asked.

"It is an evil thing. I felt its presence the moment you used it. I saw calamities befall you in the cards."

"I don't believe in such superstitions," retorted Claus.

"Well, they believe in you," Brenna sighed. "Haven't you wondered how you can make time run backwards?"

Claus opened his mouth to reply, before he realised that he didn't know what to say.

"You're a wizard, Claus!"

Claus stared in shock at the old woman.

"What?" he managed. "Since when?"

"Nah, I'm just pulling your leg."

"Oh."

"You *are* a *Timesmith* though. Does that not mean anything to you? Did your grandfather never tell you?"

"Tell me what? What do you know of my grandfather?" Claus was beginning to feel very confused. He automatically reached for the teapot. Hans had brought him up to have good manners after all.

"Oh, for goodness sake," spat Brenna. "I can't tell whether you are being purposefully obtuse, or if you genuinely do not understand."

She gestured irritably for some tea. Claus poured her a cup and handed it to her.

"How did you know I had tea here? I thought you were blind."

"My eyes might be buggered, but there are other ways to see," she said almost enigmatically. Claus raised an eyebrow. "Besides, what kind of a person doesn't have tea ready for guests at a wake?"

"Someone obtuse?" Claus suggested.

The old woman jerked her lips in what might have been amusement.

"You are not just a watchmaker. You are a *Timesmith*. You come from a long line of Timesmiths. Your mother, your grandfather, his before him."

"I know. I wanted to be a toy maker, but grandfather wouldn't hear of it."

Brenna waved the complaint away with an impatient gesture.

"But he never got round to tell you the significance of your heritage? Not even on his deathbed? Stubborn old goat."

"No," Claus rubbed his temples. He was beginning to develop a headache.

"Timesmiths have an innate ability to travel through time. To control it."

"So…it is *me* that makes the watch…work? Some power within me?" Claus regretted his words as soon as they left his mouth. Now he could no longer deny that the item of peculiarity was in his possession.

"Yes and no. The watch has its own power, and it may have other effects upon different people, but *you* can use it to alter time. To alter events."

Claus let out a long breath which he hadn't realised that he had been holding. In truth, he felt a sense of relief to be talking about the watch

115

and its power, at least now he knew for certain that he wasn't going mad. Unless of course the old woman was mad too.

"But I don't want to use the watch to alter anything!" he protested.

"But you *have* used it."

Claus shifted guiltily.

"Yes. A little. But not to change anything of significance! The first time was an accident, the second time was to get rid of some spilt water and the third time was so that my friend had a bigger breakfast," he explained hurriedly.

If it were at all possible for a blind person to stare, then Brenna stared at him. For a moment it looked as though she were about to laugh.

"Spilt water? Bigger breakfasts? Claus, do you really have no comprehension of what it is that you have in your possession?"

"Just before my grandfather died, he spoke of an item of peculiarity hidden in the attic. He told me that it might be dangerous and that he wanted me to destroy it, but he didn't tell me why or even *what* the item was. He told me that he'd been protecting it."

"Of course. It needs protecting. Can you imagine what might happen if it fell into the wrong hands? The evil and selfish ends that it could be used for?"

"Then why did he merely dismantle it? Why didn't *he* destroy it?"

"Why haven't *you*?"

Claus pondered this.

"I don't know. I …didn't want to," he admitted. "I put it together and I felt there was something special about it. Then I found out that it had once belonged to my mother. How *could* I destroy it? I didn't see the harm."

"But now you do?"

Claus remained silent for a moment and stared into his teacup.

"I could just hide it away, like Hans did. Keep it safe but never use it," he suggested.

Brenna shook her head sceptically.

"And surely, if I'm not using the watch, it can't cause any harm. What are the odds that another Timesmith would happen upon it?" he added almost pleadingly.

"That depends whether or not another Timesmith is seeking it. These magical items have a way of attracting trouble. I've seen it before. When I was but a girl, I knew a Timesmith and he had a watch like yours."

"What happened?"

"He lost his mind, turned his own pistol upon himself and blew his brains out," said the old woman, matter-of-factly.

Claus spluttered into the tea that he'd been trying to sip.

"Because of his watch?" he demanded.

"Because he used it too often. The damn thing was full of arconian. That's what powers these watches. Every time he turned back time, he was getting blasted by arconian particle emissions. And these modern *scientists* are trying to harness its power, pah! Bloody fools don't realise the damage they could do."

"This man must have used his watch an awful lot," reasoned Claus. "I mean, it takes a very long time for arconian to drive you to insanity, surely? Take the miners for instance. They breathe in the dust for years. I know they're all a bit...laid back, but most of them seem quite rational really."

"The difference is that the miners are merely breathing in the dust. The Timesmith was exposing himself to the radiation. Every time something happened that displeased him, he would wind back time and alter events

117

to suit himself. Time travel is a very dangerous business. Combine it with arconian, the confusion of causing multiple alternate versions of yourself and the least you can expect is a shattered reality."

Claus nodded and tried to look as though he understood.

Brenna huffed.

"When you make a decision, you effectively alter your own reality."

"I suppose," Claus nodded.

"So, if you keep going back to the same point in time, over and over, making different decisions every time you are there, you are creating multiple memories of yourself and of your life," she took a sip of tea before she continued, "The human mind can't deal with that."

Claus pondered this and nodded.

"Sometimes I have trouble remembering everything I did yesterday," he mused. "If I kept going back in time, doing things differently, I think I'd be very confused."

"Of course you would. It's pointless anyway. Some things are just meant to be."

"Are you talking about destiny?"

"In a way. Imagine for a moment, that you are standing in a garden. The garden represents your life. Imagine several garden pathways. These are your choices. All the paths lead to one gate. The gate is your fate. Your destiny. Some of the paths may deviate slightly, some meander around the rose bush and some might circle the begonias, but the *destination* remains the same! You chose a path, and you stick to it! What do you think would happen if you blundered in and started pulling up the rose bushes and trampling through the begonias? Hm?"

"You'd get mud on your shoes?" Claus raised an eyebrow.

"In a manner of speaking."

"So…this Timesmith got mud on his shoes and lost his marbles?"

Brenna frowned.

"Alright, lets drop the allegories, this is making my head hurt," she said and drained the rest of her teacup in one swig. Her stomach made an unsavoury noise like a blocked drain. She held the cup out for a refill.

"So, the garden gate is our fate, where we are supposed to end up? But people change their own fate every day, as you said, just by making normal, mundane decisions," frowned Claus.

"And you've never considered that the very decisions you make will end up leading you to the exact point at which you are meant to be?"

"But that's horrible!" argued Claus. "You're saying that it doesn't *matter* what we do. Any decision we make, we'll still end up in the same place!"

"That's about the size of it," Brenna looked pleased that he was finally grasping the basics.

"So, I could go out and murder someone, but it wouldn't change my fate?"

"Do you *want* to murder someone?" the old woman asked blandly.

"No!" he spluttered.

"Well then."

Claus tried not to throw his hands up in frustration.

Brenna leaned in and put a bony hand on Claus's shoulder.

"Your life will be exactly what it is meant to be. Unless some buffoon takes it upon himself to mess around with it."

"With the watch."

Brenna nodded. "And *of course* it matters what you do in life. Being

119

a good person matters, Claus."

Claus met her unnervingly steady, pale gaze. He was certain that she could somehow see him. He heard someone from the shop making a toast to Hans.

"Yes. Being a good person matters," he agreed.

Brenna drained her second cup of tea and stood up.

"Is that why you came to warn me?" asked Claus. "Because you're a good person?"

Brenna snorted.

"You said the watch has great power," Claus persisted. "Yet you haven't come here to convince me to hand it over. Have you?" he added, suddenly suspicious.

"Dantalis give me strength. Why would I want it?" she frowned.

"Well, if you don't want it for yourself, why have you come all this way to warn me about it? I'm nothing to you. Why should you care what happens to me?"

"I'm a caring sort of woman," she growled. She slammed her cup down on the table and made her way to the door. "I must go. Mister Frampton's ointment isn't going to make itself."

"Missus McGrath…" Claus hesitated. "The tarot cards…what did they say?"

"Everything and nothing. You have too many possibilities with that wretched watch in your pocket."

With this unnerving parting statement, she swept from the room.

Claus turned to face the office window. He watched as Brenna collected her staff from where she had propped it against the wall outside. She called to her cat, and with staff and lead in hand, she made her way rapidly down the street. Her progress was unhindered as the crowds seemed to melt away, out of her path.

What had started off as a solemn day, had turned into a very confusing one. Claus felt a tug on his jacket sleeve. He looked around and was relieved to see Henry stood at his side.

"What was the witch doing here?"

"It's complicated. I'll explain later," mumbled Claus.

The pair were surprised to hear a grating, rumbling, metallic sound coming from the corner of the room. They both turned to watch the Transporter rise from the workshop in its laborious, juddering fashion. Slowly, a head came into view. The man with the bright blue eyes gave them a gold toothed grin.

"Well, that was a novel experience and no mistake!" he beamed.

Claus continued to stare. The man pulled open the door to the brass cage and stepped out onto the office floor.

"Forgive me. I was so intrigued that I couldn't help myself. I saw this device when it was first installed, but I never got the chance to use it."

"Oh, Henry, this is an old friend of Hans…" Claus began to make the introduction but realised with dismay that he did not know the man's name.

"Henry, is it? Delighted." The man with the bright blue eyes shook Henry by the hand. "Well, curiosity sated, I'd best be on my way. I have another engagement."

With that, he stalked from the room.

"Peculiar chap," said Henry lightly. "What did you say his name was?"

"I didn't. I don't actually know. I only met him the other day. He's an old friend of the family, I think."

~

121

When all of Hans's friends and associates had departed, leaving the showroom looking more like a tearoom than a watchmakers, Claus turned around to face Henry and Henrietta.

"Well, that went as well as could be expected," he said.

"There's quite a lot of food left over," said Henrietta. She began to pile the dirty crockery and glassware onto trays. "Shall I package up what you don't want and take it to the widows and orphans society?"

"Yes, that's a good idea. Don't tell them it's left over from a wake though. You might put them off."

"Not so fast!" cried Henry. "I want some leftovers!"

"Last I checked, you were neither a widow, nor an orphan," sighed Henrietta.

Henry shrugged and took a moment to peruse the leftovers.

"Just save me a little bit of everything."

Henrietta snorted.

"You're going to end up like Mister Alltard," she warned.

"That reminds me!" Henry exclaimed and spun on his heel to face Claus. "What was he saying to you, about money and investments?"

"Ah," Claus took a deep breath. "Well, he was referring to my grandfather's will. And my mother's too, actually. It transpires that she invested some money, which I was to inherit when I turned one and twenty, or before, in the event of Hans's death. Apparently the investment paid off and...well. Now I have something of a fortune," Claus finished awkwardly.

"How much of a fortune are we talking?" demanded Henry, without so much as a hint of awkwardness.

"Henry!" scowled Henrietta.

"Is that why the witch was here?" continued Henry, undaunted. "You

122

gave her money, didn't you? You're too soft!"

"No. Well, yes. I mean to say that I did give her a little money, when we first met her in Katamatown. I felt sorry for her. But that's not why she came," Claus frowned in indecision for a moment and took a deep breath. "There was something else bequeathed to me in the will, other than the money and property. A family heirloom."

He pulled the watch out from his waistcoat pocket and held it out to his friends. He might as well tell them everything now.

"She came to warn me about this."

"A pocket watch?" asked Henry.

"It's not just a pocket watch, precisely."

"It's beautiful!" admired Henrietta.

"It is." agreed Henry. "But what has it got to do with the witch, Claus?"

Claus sighed. He didn't know how to explain. He realised that his tale would sound like lunacy. He went to lock the front door and gestured to his companions to follow him to the workshop.

The trio settled around a cluttered bench and Claus scanned the work surface for the blueprints of the peculiar watch, but they were nowhere to be seen. In fact, several items seemed to be out of place. Tools were in different locations to where he recalled placing them and books were not stacked as he had left them. Claus was the first to admit that he was not the tidiest person, but there was a definite organisation to his chaos, even if other people couldn't discern it. The plans for Lady Drummond's watch were beneath the workbench and the components had been scattered around, as if someone had swept them aside. Perhaps Agatha had disturbed the items? Regardless, Claus could spare little thought for this strange phenomenon, his mind was concerned with more pressing matters.

123

"The day Hans died," Claus began, "he confided in me of the presence of, what he termed, an item of peculiarity. It was hidden up in the attic, in that old clock that never told the correct time. Remember it?"

His friends groaned. They remembered.

"He told me that he had been keeping it safe for years, but now I must destroy it, as it could be dangerous."

The siblings looked suitably intrigued.

"I thought it all nonsense, but I respected his dying wish and looked in the grandfather clock."

"And you found that pocket watch?" asked Henry.

"In a manner of speaking. I found the blueprints and the components."

"But instead of destroying it, you made it," said Henrietta.

Claus nodded guiltily.

"Well, I'd have done the same thing," said Henry, jumping to Claus's defence. "What harm can a watch do?"

"It can make you get mud on your shoes and shoot yourself in the head," said Claus.

"Er…can you elaborate?" frowned Henry.

Claus placed the pocket watch in the middle of the workbench. "It gives the term 'timepiece' an entirely new connotation. I can use it to travel back in time."

There was a moment of silence.

Henry laughed. "Oh, very good old chap. You had me going there!"

"I'm serious. I've done it. If you wind the watch backwards, time does the same."

His statement was met by another silence, but this one was louder and seemed to stretch.

"Claus, you *have* been under a lot of pressure recently," said Henry slowly, as if he were talking to someone who was mentally deficient.

"I'm not mad."

"I'm not suggesting that you are!"

"It first happened when the monkey broke through the window-"

"*What*? You were attacked by a monkey? *When*?" demanded Henry.

"Just the other night, after the incident at Beverstone's. I was sat right here. I'd been working on the pocket watch, when one of the monkeys smashed through the window. And he didn't *attack* me, as such. I think he was just in search of tea."

Henrietta and Henry both turned to look at the boarded-up window.

"Anyway, during the struggle, the watch fell to the floor and …something happened. Everything went backwards, the monkey, the broken glass from the window. At first, I assumed I was suffering some form of psychological malady. What I had witnessed was impossible after all."

"In the teashop!" gasped Henrietta. "Deja vu!"

Claus nodded desperately, willing his friends to believe him. Out of the two, Henrietta was far more open minded about things than Henry.

"You knocked over the vase when you went to pour the tea," he explained. "So, I wound the watch back and moved the vase, before you could knock it over."

Henrietta looked momentarily mortified at this allegation but rallied quickly in the face of intrigue.

"I remember you moving the vase," she nodded slowly. "I *knew* something felt wrong."

"*I didn't*," said Henry, who raised his eyebrows. "But this is marvellous! Think of the possibilities!"

125

Claus smiled, relieved that his friends seemed to believe his unbelievable story.

"You mentioned that Hans said it was dangerous," said Henrietta, glaring sidelong at her brother.

"That's what he said. And Missus McGrath too."

"Missus McGrath?" frowned Henry.

"The mystic woman. Otherwise known as Madam Nimueh."

"Well, what does she know about it?" asked Henry.

"Honestly, brother," sighed Henrietta. "She's a seer. Those people know about occult things."

"She certainly seemed to," agreed Claus.

Henry snorted in derision.

"She seemed to know Hans too. It was all very singular. Then she told me that I am a Timesmith."

"We already know that!" spluttered Henry. "Bit bloody obvious, since we're sat in a watchmaker's shop!"

"No, I mean…Apparently a Timesmith is different from a watchmaker. It's an ability to travel through time, it's passed down from generation to generation. She said she'd met a Timesmith long ago and that he'd owned a watch just like this one. It seems as though he abused the power and ended up going mad. He shot himself."

Henrietta put a hand to her mouth.

"Claus, I think you should dispose of this watch immediately," she said urgently.

Claus looked into her earnest eyes.

"Perhaps you are right."

"No!" exclaimed Henry. "That would be scientifically negligent! You could write a paper on you experiences! Present your findings to the Bitterend College of Science!"

"I think The Occultist's would be more interested than the BCS," mused Henrietta.

"Huh. Rumour has it that they're nuttier than a Matis Day pudding," sneered Henry.

"They're a commendable organisation!" snapped his sister.

"I'm not writing a paper about anything!" retorted Claus. He suddenly felt overwhelmingly tired and rather irritable. "Now, if you'll both excuse me. I need to make some tea for the monkey," he stood up abruptly, entered the Transporter and wound the lever with as much dignity as he could muster.

Henrietta rounded on Henry. "Now see what you've done," she hissed.

~

Ten minutes later, teapot deployed, and temper regained, Claus re-joined his friends in the workshop. He brought a plate of sandwiches and some shortbread with him.

"Claus, I don't mean to question your judgement..." said Henry carefully, "But did you say you needed to make tea for the monkey?"

"I leave a pot outside. Ever since he broke through the window."

"Won't that just encourage him?"

"I don't know. I haven't had any problems as yet. He just drinks the tea and leaves."

"Which reminds me, what are we going to do about Cordage?"

"It was in the paper today, about his death," piped up Henrietta. She slapped a hand to her mouth and looked ashamed.

"Which paper?" Henry demanded. "Not ours! That was *my* story!"

"News like that travels fast," said Claus, not unsympathetically.

"But we were the first on the scene! Who wrote it?"

"Peter Longscroft of The Bitterend Gazette," said Henrietta.

"Ferrety little slime ball!" cried Henry. "He's nothing but a jackleg hack!"

"Take heart Henry. You could still unravel the mystery of the marauding monkeys," said Claus with sincerity.

"And you did say that Lord Cordage had a monkey butler who just happens to fit the description of the escaped creatures," said Henrietta. "There has to be some connection, although it doesn't explain why there is a whole *troupe* of them on the loose."

"You're right!" exclaimed Henry, never one to stay discouraged for long. "We need to talk to this Todorovich bloke."

"Todorovich?" Henrietta frowned and she reached for the short bread. "Surly you don't mean Nikola Todorovich?"

"He *did* sign his letters N Todorovich," shrugged Henry. "Why? Do you know him?"

"Honestly! Don't either of you *read*?"

Henry and Claus looked at each other. Henrietta made an impatient sound.

"He's an inventor, a mathematician and an engineer!"

"Really? That must keep him busy," Henry smirked.

"Very! He discovered the internal energy of arconian, amongst other things."

"Oh!" Claus snapped his fingers. "He was involved in the notorious AA/DA war!"

"Indeed."

Henry frowned. "Is he the chap that kept arconizing animals to prove his point?"

"No, no," Henrietta shook her head. "That was the other one-" she stopped abruptly and frowned at the boys. "*What letters?*"

Claus scanned the cluttered workbench and began to collect the stolen missives. One of the envelopes now sported a brown, circular stain from the bottom of a teacup.

"There was this strange machine in the room where Cordage died. It looked rather like a sideboard and I *accidentally* set it off," lied Claus.

"Set it off? Exactly how does one *set off* a sideboard?"

"It made a lot of noise and lights," Henry shrugged.

"We think it might be the device that Todorovich warns about in these letters." Claus passed them over to Henrietta, who read them all in quick succession.

"You got these from Lord Cordage's home?" she asked and glared at the boys, who silently nodded in unison.

"You removed evidence from a crime scene?"

More nods.

"I despair, I really do."

"We need to talk to Todorovich," said Henry undeterred.

"Hm," Henrietta looked thoughtful. "There's an exhibition on at the museum of science. He's displaying one of his inventions. Perhaps we might get a chance to speak to him there? Although, he's a quiet man, by all accounts."

"Then we'll whisper," suggested Henry.

Henrietta smiled before turning her attention to Claus.

129

"Now, Claus," she said, in a business-like manner. She turned and fixed him with a very forceful stare. Her resemblance to her father could be quite striking at times. She even linked her fingers together and leaned forward slightly over the workbench. Claus half expected her to address him as Mister Vogel.

"You *will* remember to get rid of this peculiar pocket watch of yours, won't you?" Her question was more of a command than a question.

Claus nodded without hesitation. Her tone brooked

no argument.

"Good. It's probably for the best."

There was a sound like crockery on cobblestone outside the window. All three of them turned instinctively to look at the boarded-up window, even though they couldn't see out of it.

6th Brevis

A small boy strolled casually past a costermonger's cart and picked up a carrot as brazenly as if he had paid for it. An unusual item for a young boy to filch one might think, especially given the fact that there was a quantity of sweet apples nearby, but ever since an unfortunate incident, whereupon an onion was mistaken for an apple and bitten into with expectant relish, the boy had a firm aversion to the fruit. Consequently, he snacked predominantly upon carrots and other such items, which could not be easily mistaken in the gloom of early morning as anything other than what they were. As a result of his eating habits, the boy had earned himself the name Rabbit amongst his peers. Rabbit would have preferred an edgier moniker, such as The Fox, or some other predatory creature, but his friends placated him by insisting that 'Rabbit' suited him on account of his speed and uncanny ability to avoid getting caught by the peelers.

Rabbit leaned nonchalantly against a wall and chewed thoughtfully upon his stolen breakfast. The man whom he had been set to tail was making his way ever closer to one of the establishments owned by Rabbit's employer. He kept his eyes upon the man as he walked past The King's Ransom and turned into a side alley. Convinced of the man's intention to pay his employer a visit, Rabbit tossed aside what little remained of his carrot and sped off, taking a route that was undoubtedly faster but potentially hazardous to anyone who had not made the journey a thousand times before. He climbed to the top of a wall, the crumbling masonry providing handy footholds, and heaved himself up onto the roof of a tumble-down building. He made his way with a light step and all haste over the rooftops, towards the rookeries which lay behind The King's Ransom.

Click Clack the Locust made no sign of alarm or surprise when the young boy swung himself into the second story room through the

131

window.

"Ere, you know that fella what you told me to keep an eye on?" said Rabbit without wasting a breath with a word of greeting, "He's on his way here."

"Well, you best go and find out what he wants," replied Click Clack with unconcern, as he finished his task of counting the previous night's spoils.

Rabbit shrugged and made his way down the rickety staircase. He would have preferred to go along the rooftops again. It was safer.

He found the man with the bright blue eyes stepping through the doorway of the 'fabric manufactory'. He seemed to be conducting a careful appraisal of his surroundings but by no means looked as if he was interested in placing an order for cotton.

"What can I do for you, Mister?" asked Rabbit.

"I want to find the Locust," said the man with the bright blue eyes. "I was told to come here."

Rabbit frowned. People who knew of Click Clack did not generally tell strangers where to find him.

"And what might be your business, Sir?"

The man with the bright blue eyes seemed to be amused by the suspicious tone of the small boy's question.

"I heard that he was a man who could... procure things."

Rabbit appeared to mull this over for a moment, but in truth he was just buying Click Clack time to prepare for this visitor.

"Alright. This way," he said at length.

Rabbit led the stranger up the stairs, with many a cautious backward glance.

"Mind your step," he warned, although it couldn't be said for certain whether his comment referred to the dilapidated steps or to the man's impending introduction to Click Clack.

They entered the upstairs room to find Click Clack half reclined on a musty old chaise lounge, which might have been upholstered in green velvet once upon a time, puffing on a long stem pipe and sipping green tea.

"Good morning," he said affably.

The man with the bright blue eyes nodded in greeting.

"I was told you might be able to help me."

"Was you now?" Click Clack's eyes shifted very briefly towards Rabbit, who shrugged. "And what could I, a poor old cripple far from home, possibly help you with?"

The man with the bright blue eyes smirked a little as if he thought that, although diverting, Click Clack's pretense of incapacitation was egregiously unconvincing. He pulled a rolled-up piece of paper from the inside of his coat and stepped forward. He held the paper out, but Click Clack didn't bother to move, instead Rabbit darted forward to intercede it. He didn't read it, although Rabbit *could* read, all of Click Clack's 'boys' could. Click Clack saw to that. He shook it open and passed it to his master, along with some reading spectacles which lay on a nearby dresser. Click Clack donned the half-moon eyeglasses and held the paper at arm's length to peer at it. He took several sips of tea before he made any comment and was pleased to sense his visitor's patience begin to fray.

"These are plans for a pocket watch," remarked the man with the bright blue eyes.

"I can see that, me old cocker. Why don't you stop wasting both of our time and take it to a watchmaker?"

"I can make it myself," said the man irritably. "What I need is the components. They are unusual."

133

"But not illegal."

"Hard to come by. I've made a list of what I need," he said as he produced another piece of paper. Again, Rabbit took it from him and passed it deferentially to Click Clack, as though he were some sort of king of the ragamuffins.

Click Clack squinted at the grubby list. He disapproved of the man's hurried, untidy scrawl.

"These are magical items. Not my forte at all. Might I suggest that you take your list to a mage or a witch?"

"Well then, can you at least point me in the direction of one?"

Click Clack appeared thoughtful for a moment.

"No. I'm afraid I can't."

The man with the bright blue eyes clenched his fists. For a brief moment he looked as though he might be inclined towards bodily violence, but all of a sudden, he seemed to decide against it and merely nodded and took his papers back. He tipped his hat, turned and left the way he had come without further comment.

"He's a bad'un," frowned Rabbit. "You want me to keep on him?"

Click Clack moved a moldering cushion on the chaise lounge and retrieved his pistol which he had concealed beneath.

"Yes, and I might be inclined to join you. I think I want to keep an eye on this one myself."

~

Claus felt like a bit of a fraud as he stood in the Bitterend Museum of Science, waiting for Todorovich to give his demonstration. It wasn't as though he wasn't interested, there was nothing *uninteresting* about the bizarre, metallic, conical shaped apparatus which stood before him, nor the exceptionally tall, thin, black haired man, who looked uncomfortable with garnering so much avid attention. It was more the fact that all those who surrounded Claus were science fanatics and Claus was merely a time travelling watchmaker, investigating a murder and an errant monkey horde, and there under false pretenses.

The science museum veterans were jostling for position upon the wooden benches which were arranged in rows, facing Todorovich, his blackboard and his extraordinary machine. Claus, Henry and Henrietta raised their eyebrows at one another and found seats near the back.

Todorovich was softly spoken, but the dome shaped, capacious interior was designed much like an

amphitheater, the acoustic effect enabling his voice to be carried to every eager ear.

"Ladies and gentlemen. Thank you for coming. This..." Todorovich gestured somewhat needlessly to the obtrusive device, "Is the Cone."

Claus noticed several people around him nodding their heads, as if they already knew what that meant. He turned his focus back to Todorovich and tried to concentrate on what the scientist was saying. He picked out various words and phrases, such as 'Arcon frequency emitter' 'high vibrational power' and 'internal arconian accelerator' but he failed to determine how these terms fitted together to make a coherent sentence.

After a while Henry leaned in towards Claus. "Do

you understand any of this?" he whispered.

"Shh," hissed Henrietta.

Todorovich turned to the blackboard and drew some indecipherable shapes upon it, which produced much murmuring and nodding from the audience. Henry and Claus exchanged a puzzled look.

As much as he was intrigued by the machine, Claus really didn't have any notion as to what Todorovich was talking about. He tried to concentrate but his mind seemed determined to wander. After what felt like a few hours, he was rudely brought back to the present moment, as Todorovich demonstrated his machine. Someone had dimmed the lights without Claus noticing and he wondered what on Cellanor was going on. There were a few shouts and shrieks from the audience, despite the scientist's prior warnings of an imminent loud noise. Claus could feel his ribs vibrating. There was a dreadful, grating noise and he covered his ears along with all the other spectators. What could only be described as lightning began to fork out from the machine in great, red crackling arcs. Claus had to admit that it was rather spectacular, although after a few minutes he began to feel quite lightheaded and he noticed a strange smell in the air.

After Todorovich had deactivated his machine, everyone clapped before getting up and breaking away into small factions to discuss what they had learnt. Todorovich was approached by a few serious, *scientific* looking men, who sported very serious looking moustaches.

"Now's our chance," said Henry, craning his neck to keep Todorovich in view.

"Wasn't that amazing?" Henrietta beamed.

"I have a headache," stated Claus.

"But aren't you amazed?" persisted Henrietta.

"Yes," said Claus, without enthusiasm. "I am amazed."

"It was pretty good. But what's the point? Just to make a bunch of loud noises and sparks?" Henry seemed to realise what he'd said and looked significantly at Claus. "Sound familiar to you?"

"*A bunch of loud noises and sparks?*" spluttered Henrietta. "Weren't you even listening?"

"Yes, I was listening, but he might as well have been speaking in ancient Katamese for all the sense it made to me," shrugged Henry.

"You just saw the future of arconian development!" Henrietta was almost hopping up and down on the spot.

"You can explain it to us in layman's terms later, but for now we have to interrogate Todorovich. I mean, *engage him in conversation*," Henry added hastily upon seeing the look on his sister's face. "Claus, perhaps you should show Todorovich your remarkable pocket watch while we're here? He is a scientist after all. He'd probably be terribly interested. He might even be able to shed some light about how it works."

"But Claus has already destroyed the watch," Henrietta gave Claus a sharp look. "Haven't you."

Claus raised his eyebrows innocently and nodded.

"Hm," said Henrietta, entirely unconvinced. "*I* will talk to Todorovich."

Despite affecting the appearance of one who is dreadfully put upon, she couldn't disguise her excitement. She sashayed over to the scientist who immediately gave her his undivided attention, regardless of a number of gentlemen, trying desperately to engage him in conversation. Henry and Claus followed in her wake and exchanged a grin.

"It's like having your own secret weapon," whispered Henry.

"It was terribly interesting," Henrietta was enthusing, as the boys joined her. She smiled and tugged upon one of her dark, glossy ringlets.

"I'm so glad to have amused you, Miss?"

"Tempest. Oh, this is my brother, and our friend, Mister Claus Vogel."

The men exchanged hat tipping's.

"Vogel the watchmaker?" asked Todorovich.

"Indeed," nodded Claus, amazed that the scientist had heard of him.

"I've always wanted to own one of your timepieces, Mister Vogel."

"Pop by the shop any time, Sir. You can find me at Sovereign Street."

"A family run business, is it not?"

"Er, it was. My grandfather recently passed away. Now it's just me."

"Oh. I'm very sorry to hear that," said Todorovich. He looked as though he meant it.

"We heard you had suffered your own bereavement recently," said Henrietta with a sympathetic look. Todorovich looked taken aback. Henry tensed.

"Yes," said Todorovich. "How did you know?"

"Oh, you know the press," shrugged Henrietta. "Oh, I'm so terribly sorry, perhaps I ought not to have mentioned it?" She widened her large almond shaped eyes and nibbled on her bottom lip.

"No, no. Don't distress yourself, Miss Tempest. Lord Cordage's death has struck me a hard blow, I'll admit. It was so unexpected."

Henrietta touched his arm. The scientist blushed. Henry relaxed.

"You were friends," Henrietta nodded sympathetically, she artfully moved him surreptitiously away from the other gentlemen. Henry and Claus followed at a discreet distance. Claus thought that perhaps Henrietta would get more information out of Todorovich if the two of them were left alone, but he knew that her brother wouldn't hear of it, nor would Claus for that matter, they had Henrietta's good name to consider after all.

"It wasn't a particularly long acquaintance," said Todorovich. "But Lord Cordage was such an amiable sort of chap, one couldn't help but like him. We had a mutual interest in science. I even designed and constructed a new piece of equipment for him."

Claus and Henry held their breaths and strained their ears.

"Oh really? What was it?" Henrietta attempted to maintain a demeanour of polite interest.

"The Amplificator. It was supposed to intensify things, but I could never get it to function properly."

Henrietta raised her eyebrows. "What sort of things?"

"Are you familiar with the Cordage's Re-flavourment Tea Leaf Strainer?"

Henrietta nodded.

"Well, it's similar to that. Only on a much larger scale. It renders The Re-flavourment Strainer somewhat obsolete of course. William wanted to invent a blend of leaves that could be used over and over, without losing the flavour or intensity. The blend would be quite expensive when first purchased, but the longevity of the leaf would far outweigh the initial outlay."

"How does it work?"

"Well, you would place the blend you had chosen to intensify inside compartment 'A', set the MSG to the desired level- sorry, that's an abbreviation of 'molecular strengthening gauge', then activate the arconian charge. Arconian light particles would travel through the object, enhancing its flavour and the finished result would pop out of compartment 'B'"

"And what would happen to the original blend?"

"Oh, that would remain unchanged. The Elorian's are sticklers for tradition after all. The original blends will still be available."

Henry couldn't help but pipe up at this point.

"So basically, what you're saying is, you pop something in this machine, turn it on, blast it with arconian and wait for a stronger version of whatever it is, to appear from the other side?"

"Erm. Yes. Essentially."

Henrietta tried to appear nonchalant. "So…theoretically, this *Amplificator* could be used to enhance not only tea leaves, but other things too?"

"Theoretically, yes. Well, anything that one could fit inside compartment A, that is."

"And could you use it to make multiple copies of one object?"

"Indeed. William wanted to produce vast quantities for commercial sale. I've studied arconian for years. It's fascinating and I don't think we've yet discovered half of its potential. Did you know that it grows? I've seen it under the microscope. It divides and duplicates itself, more like a single celled organism than a mere lump of rock."

"Could it be used to enhance something living?" Henrietta ventured.

"Oh no! The molecular complexities of a living subject would be far too great for the device to handle. I can't imagine what the end product would be, but I doubt it would be good!"

Henrietta made an attempt to turn her grimace into a smile.

7th Brevis

"**S**o, we all agree that Todorovich is responsible for unleashing the hyperactive monkey horde?" Henry asked.

"Inadvertently, I suppose," shrugged Claus. "It's too much of a coincidence that Lord Cordage received this flavour enhancement machine and now there just happens to be multiple Dahljeeling's running amok."

"But that's hardly Todorovich's fault," said Henrietta, jumping to the scientist's defence. "More than likely the monkey took it upon himself to investigate the Amplificator and inadvertently activated it."

The three were sat in the office at the printers at Brisk Street. Henry had stayed up all night to write his report.

"The maid did mention that Dahljeeling liked to hide in small spaces," said Claus. "Cupboards and the like."

"That doesn't explain why his 'enhanced' versions are ransacking Bitterend," Henry frowned. "You'd think they'd all just want to find somewhere small to hide."

"But the machine has enhanced *all* of Dahljeeling's characteristics," Claus reasoned. "Yes, he's agoraphobic, but he's also a tea addict. Perhaps his drive for tea has forced his duplicates out into a world that they can't cope with. And we know that his original self is a little…erm, highly strung."

"Highly strung?" Henry stared with incredulity at his friend. "He flings his own feculence around when he doesn't like the tea!"

Henrietta wrinkled her nose and peered over her brother's shoulder, where he was sat at a desk.

141

"No, you can't write that!" she snapped, as she pointed towards the bottom of the article. "It sounds as though you're accusing Todorovich of murder."

"Only indirectly."

Henrietta scowled.

"I don't see how Todorovich's invention could have caused a fatal head injury."

"No, but we've seen what a troupe of Dahljeeling's can do. Need I remind you of the mess they made at Missus Beverstone's?"

"But they didn't actually harm anyone!" protested his sister.

"One of them *attacked* Claus!"

"Erm, technically he didn't attack me. He was just scared," said Claus "Perhaps it was an accident."

"Accidental death, due to monkeying around," Henry smiled. "What we need is the actual police report."

"And how on Cellanor do you intend to get your hands on that, dear brother?" Henrietta folded her arms.

Henry looked thoughtful.

"No!" Claus almost shouted. "If you're considering breaking into, or infiltrating Moarland Yard, you're on your own!"

Henry huffed.

"I could try to get more information out of Todorovich," suggested Henrietta.

"Really?" her brother brightened again. "How would you manage that? You'll probably never see the man again."

"Actually, I'm having dinner with him tonight, at Eldarn View."

"Dinner?" exclaimed Claus.

"Eldarn View?" cried Henry. "Good grief. What has mother to say about this?" he demanded.

"Oh, she was the one who told me I ought to go. Don't look like that, brother. I'm a big girl."

"You only just had your coming out ball!"

"Precisely. I've *had* my coming out ball," Henrietta smiled coquettishly. Henry looked down and muttered something uncouth into his chest.

"I think the butler did it, in the parlour, with the teapot," Claus suddenly remarked in an attempt to prevent any more bickering. It had the desired effect and the twins laughed.

Henry omitted the paragraph that implied Todorovich was guilty of murder, or at least manslaughter, with a large black cross. He looked thoughtful before speaking carefully.

"Eldarn View though. He must be trying to impress you."

"Well, it worked," smiled Henrietta unashamedly. "Don't fret so, brother. We'll be surrounded by other diners. What's the worst that could happen?"

~

One of the benefits of having a wealthy newspaper owner as a father and being the only daughter of a fashion-conscious mother (aside from having a large allowance) was the effect it had on one's wardrobe. Henrietta owned a good many high-quality dresses.

It wasn't that she particularly wanted to impress Todorovich, although she did think that he seemed like an agreeable fellow but going out for dinner somewhere as prestigious as Eldarn View warranted wearing something special. As she stepped into the foyer, she realised that her instincts had not led her awry. She practically matched the décor.

143

The dress was quite simple, a silvery, grey coloured silk, patterned with black velvet applique. The skirt was narrow and had one of the ultra-modern smaller bustles and fell into a short train at the back. It was sleeveless, which was a tad risqué for a chilly brumail

evening, so Henrietta had donned a pair of long cream gloves to cover her naked arms. The dress was perhaps a little too sophisticated for a girl of her age, but she received many admiring looks as she removed her fur trimmed cloak.

The foyer was tastefully decorated in black, grey and cream. The floor was tiled with a black and white chequerboard design. The towering columns which held up the ceiling were carved into elegant arches. The walls supported vast mirrors which reflected the light from the huge crystal chandeliers. They dazzled the eye as they cast tiny rainbows all over the room.

Henrietta finished her appraisal of her surroundings and turned to face Todorovich, who also seemed to be a little dazzled, although he wasn't paying much attention to the chandeliers. She smiled and offered him her arm which he took readily, and the pair made their way into the dining room.

An orchestra was playing at one end of the room. Henrietta wasn't sure if this was an advantage or a hindrance. It might make private conversation difficult, as they would have to raise their voices, on the other hand, it could make their words hard to follow for anyone who had a mind to listen in. Not that Henrietta thought that anyone would want to eaves drop. Todorovich was famous, but only in certain academic circles.

They received no particular attention as the waiter showed them to their table and went to fetch them some wine. Henrietta drank little and noticed that Todorovich showed the same restraint. She wondered if he was naturally a man of moderation, or whether he just wanted it to appear that way for her benefit. She was inclined to believe the former.

He was rather thin. She wished he *would* drink more, that way he might be more inclined to discuss the misadventure of Lord Cordage.

After much pleasant small talk and a bowl of turtle soup, Henrietta steered the conversation towards Todorovich's inventions. Or to one invention in particular.

"I've been meaning to ask you about that enhancement machine you invented. Do you think you'll patent it?"

"The Amplificator? Why? Do you want to buy one?"

Henrietta smiled. "I can't imagine what I'd use it for. I suppose if you had a really wonderful pair of shoes that you were afraid of wearing out, one might use it to strengthen the fabric or heels."

Todorovich chuckled.

"Other than that..." Henrietta trailed off and shrugged.

"Surely you wouldn't want to wear the same pair of shoes two seasons in a row, Miss Tempest. They would be outmoded."

"I'll have you know it's a difficult thing getting a good pair of shoes these days," Henrietta smiled.

"Well, aside from shoes, I thought that it might be useful for other items. Medicine perhaps. One could enhance the healing properties of certain compounds. Think of the lives that could be saved."

Henrietta nodded. "Yes, I can see how that would be helpful. But what about alcohol and narcotics? What if someone decided to strengthen the effects of arconian dust, or the Katamese weed? They'd make a fortune and get their customers addicted faster than they might ordinarily. You said that you could enhance *anything* that would fit in the Amplificator."

Todorovich sipped his wine, as if contemplating whether or not to speak what was on his mind. "Miss Tempest, if I may be so bold, you are shrewder than you let on. I believe your mind isn't half as preoccupied with shoes as you'd lead others to believe."

"There are times when it comes in useful if people think that your head is full of nothing but taffeta and frills."

"I for one, am glad that it is not," laughed Todorovich. Henrietta decided he was really quite handsome when he wasn't so serious all the time. "But you've stated the very reason why I could never patent my design. I'm familiar enough with the human nature and its propensity for self-gain. The Amplificator must be destroyed. I worry that it has already fallen into the wrong hands now that William is…gone."

"But you mentioned that you could never get it to work properly."

"That doesn't mean that someone else couldn't."

"Forgive me, Mister Todorovich, but if *you* can't get your own invention to work, I fail to see how anyone else could. What was wrong with it anyway?"

"It had a habit of enhancing the wrong flavours. We experimented a lot with various leaves, but the resulting beverage was always undrinkable, far too strong with a bitterness that set your teeth on edge. Not useful at all, but I'm still anxious to get it back."

"Can't you go to the police? Tell them that it's yours and that you want to collect it?"

"I already asked. The only proof I had that I designed The Amplificator was within the letters that I exchanged with Lord Cordage, but apparently they are nowhere to be found."

Henrietta felt a horrible swooping sensation of guilt in the pit of her stomach.

"Anyway, Lord Cordage paid for it. That makes it his. Or his successors. Unless I break into his house and steal it, I've really got no hope of getting it back."

"Oh dear."

The waiter arrived with saddle of mutton in red currant jelly for Henrietta and poached salmon for Todorovich. Henrietta didn't, or rather couldn't, stand on ceremony. She sliced into a boiled potato without delay.

"I have an idea..." she said, once she had swallowed. "My brother has... a knack for getting into places others can't."

"He has contacts, you mean?"

Henrietta laughed and shook her head as she cut into her mutton. "Not exactly. What I meant was, there may be a chance that Henry could gain access to Lord Cordage's house. If you described to him how to dismantle The Amplificator, it would no longer pose a threat."

Todorovich looked hopeful. "You really think he could gain access? I believe the house may still be deemed a crime scene."

"All the better. Makes it more credible that he would want to be there."

"Why?"

"He's a journalist. Or he's trying to be."

Todorovich frowned before clicking his fingers.

"Henry Tempest. I knew that I had heard the name before! I'm deducing that your brother is Henry Tempest Junior and that the pair of you are the issue of Henry Tempest, owner and chief editor of The Tempest's Eye?"

"Issue?" Henrietta giggled. "That's one way to put it, I suppose."

"And you think that Henry might be able to infiltrate a crime scene, just because he works for a newspaper?"

"Oh, he doesn't work for a newspaper."

Todorovich looked confused.

"Not yet. He will though. Eventually," she added in an attempt to ease her dinner companion's evident uncertainty. "Papa is very particular about who writes for his paper. He wants Henry to work his way up from the bottom, so to speak. He wants him to learn the business properly, instead of having it handed to him on a silver platter."

"Your father sounds like a wise man," nodded Todorovich.

"He has his moments. I happen to agree with him. Needless to say that Henry does not."

"So, what are you proposing, Miss Tempest?"

"Henry enters the house under the pretext of interviewing the servants, or the police, about- forgive me- the mysterious death of Lord Cordage-"

"But what if they don't want to talk?" Todorovich interrupted.

Henrietta smiled and shook her head. "Really, Mister Todorovich. People *always* want to give their opinion about murder or suspicious incidents. Including the police," she speared a green bean on the end of her folk and coated it in gravy before continuing. "So…Henry distracts the police by talking to them-"

"Even though he's not a proper reporter."

"They won't know that." assured Henrietta. She noticed how empty her plate already looked in comparison to Todorovich's.

"And then what?"

"Either Claus or I will accompany Henry into the house, then while he presents a diversion, one of us will slip in and disable The Amplificator. Simple."

Todorovich leaned back in his chair with an air of bewildered anxiety.

"I don't want any of you to do anything rash. Not on my account."

"Oh, no need to worry about that. We're old hands at being rash. If we weren't doing something rash on your account, it would be on our own."

Todorovich still looked uneasy. "Well, discuss it with your brother. And I will do whatever I can to repay the kindness, if you decide to proceed."

He dabbed his mouth with his napkin, evidently finished with his meal. Henrietta concluded that he was definitely a man of modest appetite. Not something she was accustomed to, having spent her life taking meals with her twin. She chased her last remaining dumpling around her plate in an attempt to soak up the rest of the red currant gravy.

"You could always grant him an interview. The Tempest's Eye is not a scientific paper, of course, but I think our readers would be interested in you. 'The man behind the machines.' And to be honest with you, Henry could do with the practice," she grinned.

"Certainly. That's the least I could do."

Henrietta took a deep breath before addressing the next issue.

"Do you know anything about Lord Cordage's monkey?"

"Dahljeeling? He's a capuchin. They're highly intelligent. He made me tea whilst I was visiting. Quite remarkable. Why?"

Henrietta hesitated. "There seems to be an epidemic of Dahljeeling's, ransacking greater Bitterend."

"Dahljeeling's *plural*? You mean…"

"We think he somehow ended up in The Amplificator and made several *enhanced* versions of himself," Henrietta nodded as she finished Todorovich's sentence for him.

"Good grief. Who knows what ramifications this could have?" Todorovich's voice rose in distress.

"They *have* been causing quite a stir and they seem to be rather dangerous. With violent tendencies."

149

"But Dahljeeling is such a gentle creature," Todorovich shook his head. "I can't imagine that he would hurt a fly. Unless…" he trailed off.

Henrietta looked at the scientist sharply.

"You said The Amplificator made the tea unpalatable. It strengthened the undesirable qualities. Could that also affect personality traits?"

"I've no idea, but if Dahljeeling's doppelgangers are dangerous, that may well be the case." Todorovich looked resolute. "The Amplificator *must* be destroyed, before it can do any more harm."

"I agree. Oh look," smiled Henrietta. "Pudding!"

~

Ambrose Alltard was a man who appreciated the finer things in life. He maintained the opinion that a man could suffer all manner of hardships, as long as he had a few creature comforts to sustain him. He was fantasising of these creature comforts as he walked in through the front door of his home in Heartfelt. A seventeen-year-old bottle of single malt whiskey to be exact. His man servant, Edward Tibbs, took his master's coat and hat from him and Alltard inquired upon the whereabouts of Missus Alltard. The man servant answered that she had gone out to dine with her sister.

"Abandoned once again!" lamented the solicitor, in a profound tone of despair. He quickly rallied. "Very well. Tell Cook to rustle me something up for supper. Nothing too heavy, I already ate at the club. Maybe just a slice of game pie and some roasted potatoes. And perhaps some beef loin with dripping and some bread."

Tibbs the manservant nodded and turned to make his way down the hallway towards the kitchen.

"Oh! And a bit of stilton!" Alltard called to the retreating man's back. "No! A selection of cheese and biscuits! And just one or two of those excellent pork suet dumplings!"

Satisfied with his supper choices, Alltard passed through the front parlour and into his study to drop off his paperwork. The sooner he sorted out his documents from his day of toil, the sooner he could relax, as a man of his age ought to do. Upon opening the door to his study, he discovered several peculiarities that rendered relaxation impermissible. The room was not an exceptionally large one and in consequence it was always rather warm, especially when a cheerful fire burned in the hearth, as it did now. But lo and behold! Some unthoughtful person had left the sash window wide open and the room was quite frigid. Alltard's paperwork, that was always put away neatly in his filing cabinet, or in the leather-bound ledgers which sat tidily upon the bookshelf, was strewn across the floor.

A handsome mahogany writing desk took pride of place opposite the chimney breast. There was a matching chair before it, which was currently occupied by a man who was not Ambrose Alltard.

"Who in the mines of Rothgar are you, Sir?" enquired the solicitor with a most affronted air. The man in the chair looked around and smiled. He was holding a document in his hand.

"You!" gasped Alltard.

"I would have thought you might greet me a little more cordially after all these years, old man," Niall looked the solicitor up and down appraisingly. "You're even fatter that I remember."

"Why are you here?"

"Here in your study? Or here in Bitterend?"

"Either! Both! I shall send for the police!" Alltard would have fled from the room if he had been foolish enough to believe that he could outrun a man half of his age and half of his weight. "You will leave my house this very instant!"

"I am here for my inheritance," Niall's bright blue eyes were as cold and penetrating as a Skordian gale as he waved the papers he clutched in his hand.

"What are you talking about?" demanded Alltard.

"I thought that you wanted me to leave?"

Alltard made a daring grab for the documents and to his utter surprise, his adversary relinquished them. The solicitor tore his gaze from the other man's face and glanced down at what he held.

'The last will and testament of Hans Vogel.' He read, then said aloud. "This is no concern of yours."

"Oh, but it is. It states that the eldest surviving member of the family has claim to an heirloom. I only want what is rightfully mine."

"It isn't rightfully yours. You have no rights. You saw to that when you murdered poor Eva!"

"You aren't still harping on about that are you?"

"Scoundrel! Cur!" Alltard forgot his fear and became quite emboldened in his fury. "The gallows are too good for you! I'll see you thrown over the Northwall! *Tibbs!*" he bellowed.

Niall sprang out of the chair and pinned the solicitor against the wall. Alltard saw a flash of silver appear and felt the cold pressure of steel against his cheek.

"I should have brought a longer knife," hissed the assailant. "To cut through all this blubber." The blade pressed into Alltard's cheek and a droplet of blood ran down his face and onto his collar. The man with the bright blue eyes seemed to take great pleasure in watching the colour drain from Alltard's face. "Now, you are the executor of the will, are you not?"

"I am," Alltard breathed heavily.

"Then it is law that you see to it that Hans's wishes are carried out."

"Even if I do, you will not get what you want," gasped Alltard. "You are not the eldest surviving member of the family!" The solicitor seemed to regret his words the moment they left his mouth.

Niall frowned momentarily before he laughed belligerently.

"That's not what I heard. I should have known. The old witch is still alive," he stared at the solicitor with a suspicious countenance. "What did she do? Falsify her own death? Changed her name, I suppose? And how would a lowly old woman achieve that? She must have had help from someone with legal knowledge. Someone just like you, I don't doubt."

"W-what are you going to do?" stuttered Alltard. The man with the bright blue eyes grinned and Alltard felt the need to vomit.

A staccato clacking sound could suddenly be heard upon the floorboards of the room beyond and a brief moment later the study door was thrown back with such force that, if Alltard had not been in such a desperate situation, he would have worried for the wellbeing of his wallpaper.

"I say old chum," said the Katamesian man, who had just burst into the room. "That ain't no way to give a respectable gent a shave. You want one of these!" He brandished a pair of long, silver razors with ornately carved ivory handles.

Niall stared for a moment at the blades and then at the Katamesian with the crazed gleam in his eyes who held them. He seemed to way up his options momentarily, before releasing Alltard and making a hasty escape, by means of the open window through which he had gained entry.

Alltard stumbled over to his chair and fell down upon it.

"Pray, Sir," he gasped, his hand pressed over his racing heart. "If you have come to kill me then do it quickly. I don't think my heart can take much more excitement."

"I ain't here to kill you, Mister Alltard. I been tracking that shifty little bastard for days." Click Clack the Locust waved one of his evil looking weapons towards the window, or rather at the man who had just left via it.

"*Please*, put those away," Alltard begged, looking at the razors.

"Oh. Sorry." Click Clack snapped the razors closed and put them in his pocket. "Don't mind if I sit down, do you? Me feet are killing me," he sat down in the chair by the hearth without waiting for an answer.

Alltard stared at his rescuers wooden legs and uttered a slightly hysterical laugh. He retrieved the bottle of single malt from the cupboard beneath his desk and poured out two glasses, handing one to his guest.

"I am in your debt, Mister…"

"Yusheng Chow, but everyone calls me Click Clack. Cheers," he took a sip of his drink and seemed to approve.

"My name is Ambrose Alltard."

"I know."

"Oh. Yes," Alltard said, and shook his head as if to clear it. "You seem familiar to me, Mister Chow. Have we met before?"

"Katamesian," shrugged Click Clack. "Ain't you heard? We all look the same."

Alltard was quite certain that the man before him looked nothing like anyone he would encounter under normal circumstances.

"Why have you been following that man, Mister Chow?"

"Favour for a friend. She wanted to know his whereabouts. I don't recon she'll be pleased that he's here in Bitterend, nor that he's threatening innocent people, like your good self."

"May I ask, whom is the woman?"

"Madam Nimueh."

"You mean Brenna McGrath!"

Click Clack nodded.

"That's it!" Alltard snapped his fingers. "I recall now, you were lingering outside her shop. You must go to her at once, Sir! I fear that vile man means to do her great harm."

"Fat chance!" scoffed Click Clack.

"He's very dangerous," insisted Alltard.

"Not half as dangerous as Nimueh, I'd wager." Click Clack looked up and noticed the obvious look of concern upon the solicitor's face. "Don't fret. I'll look after her," he added.

"He's killed before," warned Alltard, in an attempt to impress a sense of caution into this peculiar man.

Click Clack shrugged.

"So have I," he said casually.

Alltard could not think of a suitable reply to this and so remained silent and sipped his whiskey.

"Who is he anyway? She didn't say," said Click Clack conversationally. "I mean, she told me his name, Niall McGrath. Black sheep of the family, I take it?"

"He's Brenna's son."

8th Brevis

"There have been occasional times in my life, when I have felt the need to question my sanity. This is definitely one of those times," said Claus, unhappily.

He stared at the flint stone wall, at the moss that lined the cracks and the ivy that clawed at the stone. Ivy was supposed to climb walls. Respectable watchmakers were not.

"It's all for a good cause," said Henry and he clapped his friend on the back. "Anyway, this was your idea."

"Only because I didn't want you to cause unnecessary explosions. Speaking of which, what if I can't disarm the cabinet? What if I do something wrong? What if I blow it up?" Claus felt himself begin to perspire, despite the frozen air.

"Just...don't," advised Henry.

Claus unfolded and scrutinised the piece of paper for the tenth time. Todorovich's instructions were very clear and simple and Claus would not have thought

twice about carrying them out had he not seen Todorovich's Cone in action. His palms were clammy as he stuffed the note back in his pocket.

"Ready?" asked Henry. He interlinked his fingers before him and crouched down a little, in order to give Claus a boost.

"No," frowned Claus, who put his foot into Henry's hands and experienced a sudden sensation of elevation. The wall around the Cordage house seemed a lot taller when one was hanging from the top of it. Claus scrabbled his feet a little and managed to haul himself to the brink. He felt about eight years old again, nothing much had changed it seemed. A pigeon which had been sitting quietly in the silver birch tree next to the wall cried out indignantly at his sudden appearance and flapped away. Claus gazed at the pale house and wondered if entering and breaking was as bad as breaking and entering.

"I'll run round to the front and meet Henrietta," Henry stage whispered. "Give us five minutes."

Claus nodded and watched Henry hurry off to the front of the house.

Earlier that day, Claus, Henry and Henrietta had gathered for afternoon tea and cakes at the newly reopened Beverstone's Tea Shop, where Henrietta disclosed the events of the previous evening's dinner with Todorovich.

"You're not coming with us," Henry said to his sister at once.

"But he's *my* acquaintance!" protested Henrietta. "I might even go as far as to say he's a friend!"

"She has a point," said Claus.

"Why do you always side with *her*?" complained Henry.

"I'm just thinking that Henrietta might be a better distraction than me."

"Oh, I see," Henrietta put on an affronted voice. "You just want me to come along and sweet talk the policemen."

"In a nutshell," grinned Claus. "You two keep them busy, while I sneak past into the parlour and destroy Todorovich's machine."

Henry looked troubled. "I know that we Tempest twins are diverting company, but I'm not sure how you're going to sneak past unnoticed."

Henrietta bit her lip. "He's right. They're going to notice you, even if I throw the most monumental fainting fit. We'll have to somehow get them away from the door long enough for you to enter the parlour."

"What about a small explosion? That would work," suggested Henry.

"No! No," Claus shook his head vehemently. "No explosions. I'll go over the back wall. The parlour had a glass door leading out into the garden, I'll enter that way, while you two distract the police, break The Amplificator and leave."

"Simple. Straightforward. I like it. Perhaps we should have a code word though?" mused Henry. "Something to indicate that you should get out of there fast. You know, in case something goes wrong, or it looks as if someone might enter the parlour while you're still in there."

"Dahljeeling?" suggested Henrietta.

"What if the subject of the monkey butler arises when you're talking to the policeman?" said Claus. "No, it's got to be something that you wouldn't say by accident or coincidence. Something out of context, but memorable."

"Spotted dick," announced Henrietta, looking down at her plate.

~

Perched atop the wall, Claus took his watch out and timed five minutes. After said time had elapsed, he twisted around and carefully lowered himself down the other side of the wall. There was still a four-foot drop, even with his arms fully extended. He landed rather heavily and felt a sharp pain in his ankle.

"Blast it," he hissed. He crouched low and made his way awkwardly across the sprawling garden, stopping at intervals to hide behind topiary and marble statues depicting Denalian gods. He looked up into the face of a particularly surly looking deity, who seemed to glare disapprovingly down at him.

As if trespassing wasn't enough, Claus was forced to limp over the perfectly manicured grass. He felt like an out and out criminal, but the pathways were made of gravel and would have been too noisy. He made it to the rear of the house without incurring any attention, other than the austere gaze of the statues, and he leaned against the brickwork and took deep, calming breaths. At least he didn't feel too exposed with the wall at his back. He took a brief moment to compose himself, then ducked down below the level of the windows and crawled on hands and knees through the flower beds towards the Bonancian doors of the parlour. The mid-brumail foliage was nothing but sharp branches and snagging twigs that caught in his clothing and scratched his skin. He was painfully aware that his trousers would never be the same again.

The broken windows had all been boarded up, apart from one, which had survived the atrocity. Claus peeked over the window ledge, to make sure that no one was in the parlour. The coast seemed to be clear, so he reached out and pulled on the handle of the Bonancian door. It moved without resistance and Claus realised that he had been holding his breath. After all, there had been no guarantee that the door would be unlocked. It suddenly struck him as strange that this door would be left unfastened, but then who would be stupid enough to break into a house that was currently occupied by the boys in blue? Apparently, Claus would.

It was at that moment that Claus heard the barking. He looked around in time to see a dog, the size of a small horse, baring down upon him. He stood up and instinctively shielded his head with his arms before the full weight of the guard dog sent him flying through the unopened glass door. The dog didn't maul him, but it wouldn't let him move either, so Claus could do nothing but lay amongst the shattered glass and splintered wood of the doorway as the parlour door crashed open and a policeman ran into the room, closely followed by the Tempest twins, who were both shouting the words 'spotted dick' at the top of their voices.

~

Niall frowned at the spread of cards which lay before him. He was

159

undoubtedly better at reading the tarot than playing poker, but it was impossible to glean the future when an idiotic whelp kept playing at being a Timesmith.

"Afternoon," said Arabella, as she entered their rented room with a basket hooked on her arm. It contained fresh bread, cheese, ale and a mutton pie. In her other hand she held a bunch of daisies. She observed Niall's expression and occupation before enquiring in a casual tone,

"Good grief. The look on your face. Is somebody going to die?"

Niall merely grunted in response.

"Well, we certainly won't be dying of starvation any time soon," continued his stepdaughter, as she hunted around the room for a jug in which to put the flowers.

Niall grabbed her by the waist as she bustled past and pulled her down to sit on his lap.

"What's all this then?" asked Niall, indicating the basket of food and bunch of flowers.

"Well, we have to eat. And I thought the flowers would brighten the place up."

"We don't have money to waste on flowers."

Arabella scowled.

"Arcon's arse, don't make that face at me, girl. It's like your mother's come back from the grave."

"I didn't waste any money. I didn't pay for them."

"Arabella! You didn't steal them, did you?" Niall looked incredulous. "What about the Eleven Edicts of Piety that your grandfather was always harping on about?" he laughed.

Arabella used the distraction to break free from his grasp. A look of pain cast a shadow on her face at the mention of her grandpapa, and she quickly turned her back on her stepfather to conceal it.

"I didn't steal them. The flower seller gave them to me. We got chatting."

Niall's fists clenched upon the tabletop. "Oh, I see. Giving you the eye, was he?"

"It was a woman," Arabella responded calmly, as she retrieved a spare water jug.

"Oh."

"She seemed to notice that I wasn't local, and I ended up telling her about Furthermoor and how the daisies reminded me of the gardens around the parsonage. Anyway, she said they wouldn't last another day and that I may as well have them if they made me smile."

"You shouldn't be telling strangers about yourself," chastised Niall.

"Oh, for goodness sake, she was merely being friendly. Besides, I was lonely. Don't you want me to have any friends?"

Niall failed to respond, so Arabella began to arrange the flowers in the jug.

"The ale was free too," she added, before a frown creased her brow. "People are strange in this city."

"People are strange in every city," nodded Niall, who'd turned back to glare down at the tarot cards.

"Do the locals speak their own language in Bitterend?"

"They have lots of languages here. On account of all the foreigners. But generally, most people speak plain Elorian, same as the rest of the country."

"Hm. It sounds silly, I know, but it almost seemed like the man in the ale shop was talking backwards."

"Backwards?" Niall asked sharply, his attention now fully focused on

161

his stepdaughter.

"Perhaps it was just my imagination. I'd had a bit of a funny turn after all. Maybe that's why he gave me the money back for the ale," Arabella shrugged. "Anyway, what did you mean when you said, '*we don't have money to waste*'? Business has been good since we arrived here."

"Changed your tune a bit, haven't you? I thought you didn't like Bitterend?"

"Don't change the subject," she frowned. "What's going on?"

Niall sighed and reached for the bottle of ale.

"I might have to speculate to accumulate."

"More than usual? Big game is it? Are you planning to rip off a toff? You'll have to get a new set of clothes, if you want to fit into that sort of society."

"No. No, that's not it," Niall hesitated as he watched his stepdaughter arranging the flowers. "You like nice things, don't you?"

"I do, if I'm given half a chance," Arabella grinned.

"I want better for us, Arabella. I'm tired of playing the game. We can't keep doing this forever. There's going to come a time when we get caught and then what? It'll be the gallows for me and Dantalis knows what'll happen to you. I promised your mother that I would take care of you."

Arabella sat down at the table and reached for his hand. He looked tired and careworn; his customary devil may care attitude gone without a trace. She'd rarely seen him look graver.

"I have relatives, here in Bitterend," Niall continued.

"You told me you didn't have any family," frowned Arabella.

"Distant relations. Not worth mentioning. A half uncle. Anyway, he died recently."

"Oh. Is that why we're here? Did he leave you something of value?"

"Well now, that's the rub. Seems all of the family's assets and the estate has passed to my uncle's grandson."

"I see," Arabella nodded with dawning comprehension, all too familiar with the workings of her stepfather's mind. "And you mean to relieve him of it."

"Indeed. The money, the property. All of it. There's a few loose ends I'd have to see to first, but if the boy were to die, I would be the only surviving member of the family. Legally, I would be entitled to the lot, regardless of our estrangement."

"Then, the boy is your cousin?" Arabella frowned as she tried to decipher the familial connection. "You intend on *killing* him?"

"*Half* cousin," Niall corrected her. "Half second cousin, to be precise."

"Still…" Arabella shook her head.

"I need to get close to him. I need him to trust me. There is an item I want, more than the money or property. An item which would change our fortunes forever."

"It must be worth a very great sum!" Arabella raised her eyebrows.

"It's priceless."

"Well, wouldn't it just pass to you along with the rest of the fortune, if the boy was…" Arabella paused uncomfortably before finishing her question, "dead?"

"Not necessarily. Not if it was lost, or hidden, or destroyed. I can't afford to take that risk."

"So, you mean to get close to the boy and take this…what is it?"

"A pocket watch."

Arabella burst into derisive laughter.

163

"A *pocket watch*? I thought perhaps it was the Despair Diamond, the way you're carrying on!"

"It's no ordinary pocket watch," snapped Niall, irritably.

"What then? Is it made of solid gold?" Arabella teased.

"Better. I told you, it'll change our fortunes."

"Well, you're on your own. I'm not going to help you. I'll not conspire to kill some innocent boy. Your own *cousin*," Arabella stood up from the table, her temper riled. She needed a tot of gin. Niall grasped her by her wrist and yanked so hard that she had no choice but to sit back down heavily upon the chair.

"You'll do as you're told, my girl," he growled.

~

"Claus, why are you limping?" frowned Henrietta.

"I missed a step on the way down to the showroom," replied Claus rather shortly.

He wasn't usually one to sulk, but he was feeling a bit sorry for himself. His ankle had a mild sprain, it was quite sore but more of an inconvenience than anything. His back was the predominant cause of his aggravation. He'd had to employ a physician to extract the shrapnel from the broken Bonancian door. It had been costly, time consuming and very painful, and of course he'd had to lie about what had happened. He was also annoyed that he'd been forced to use his watch again, but he couldn't really see any other way to resolve the situation. The reversal of time hadn't cured his injuries, but at least he wasn't in jail.

Claus, Henry and Henrietta entered Beverstone's and Clause resigned himself to listening to the same conversation he had already heard. He tried to remember everything he had said and to say it at the right time. He wanted to change things as little as possible, the thought of muddy shoes and bullets to the head prevalent in his mind.

"Spotted dick," said Henrietta.

"I think I might have gone off it," huffed Claus.

"Well, we can use something else if it really bothers you?"

"No. Better stick with that."

"What's wrong with you? You've been like a bear with a sore head all afternoon," said Henry.

"I'm fine."

"You're not. And don't take this the wrong way, but you look strangely lumpy," observed Henry, frowning at the irregularly shaped bulges protruding from beneath Claus's jacket.

"Hindsight," said Claus, which offered no explanation at all.

The twins exchanged a look.

~

Claus sat atop the wall (for the second time that day) and watched Henry disappear. He didn't bother to wait for five minutes as instructed but began to unwind a long length of rope which he had wrapped around his torso, hidden beneath his jacket. He swung one end over the nearest branch of the tree and caught it. He knotted it around the branch and pulled on it to test his weight, before climbing down its length to the ground below. It didn't change the fact that he had a sprained ankle, but at least now he didn't have two. He left the rope hanging there, so that he could make a quick exit if necessary. In hindsight, their initial plan was terrible. They hadn't considered personal injury or on-site security, nor even made an emergency exit plan. Claus hoped that this was on account of all three of them being decent, law abiding people, who were inexpert at gaining illegal entrance to a property, and not simply just because they were stupid. Well, this time Claus was better prepared.

He made his way towards the back of the house, again, this time keeping an eye out for the guard dog. He crawled beneath the windows of the parlour and peered over the sill to make sure no one was inside. He was wearing his least favourite trousers.

He reached the door and pulled a small can of oil from an inside pocket. He made sure that the hinges were well oiled and so the door made no noise when he opened it and darted inside the house, before the monstrous canine appeared. He pulled a brown paper package out from another pocket and unwrapped the lamb's livers, which he'd laced heavily with the laudanum that the physician had given him to ease the pain in his ankle and back. He tossed the meat out of the door, onto the grass.

"Right," he whispered to himself, satisfied with his precautions.

He lit a lamp and took out Todorovich's instructions. He could hear the muffled sounds of the Tempest twins talking outside the parlour door. Claus felt his mouth go dry in anticipation of hearing the words 'spotted dick' and he came to the conclusion that he would probably have to avoid that particular pudding for the rest of his life. He strained his ears but there was no mention of the dreaded dessert and so he got to work on The Amplificator.

He used the small pliers and wire cutters which Todorovich had supplied, along with his instructions. It was fairly straight forward - despite Claus's recurring mental images of forked lightning- unscrew this nut, remove that metal plate, and cut such and such wire. Claus completed the task with relative ease, which surprised him. He wasn't scientifically minded in the slightest, but he supposed that years of tinkering with watches and clockwork had given him a steady hand and a precise mind when it came to delicate engineering. As instructed, Claus pocketed a strange looking copper coil which Todorovich had drawn and labelled 'conductor' along with the fist sized lump of faceted arconian. Mission complete, he allowed himself to breathe and turned to make his exit.

Dusk had fallen in earnest beyond the Bonancian door, and Claus could see nothing but himself and the room in which he stood, reflected in the dark glass. That, and a small brown face topped with a fez.

"Dahljeeling!" Claus hissed. He and the monkey stared at each other for a moment. Claus had just made up his mind that he would rather face the monkey butler than the chaps of Moarland Yard, when Dahljeeling suddenly turned away and was lost in the darkness. Claus opened the Bonancian door warily. The last thing he wanted was to be thrown through it again. He looked around but there was no sign of the primate, so he slipped out into the gloaming, relieved beyond measure to be out of the house. He felt as if he'd spent far too long in the parlour, his anxiety had made the time drag.

He started to make his way across the lawn when a strange, sonorous noise caught his attention. It sounded like someone slowly sawing through a large chunk of wood with a blunt saw. In the darkness, and in his haste to get away, Claus almost stumbled over the source of the noise. The guard dog was sprawled on the lawn, fast asleep and snoring. All the liver had gone. He tiptoed around the creature and hastened away across the lawn in a strange, hunched over manner, which he hoped could be deemed a stealthy type of sprint.

Claus reached the wall and climbed the rope. Hans had been a firm believer in manual labour, so hauling himself up was no great task, but his cuts and bruises protested at the physical exertion. He sat atop the wall for a moment and breathed deeply before he gathered up the rope and used it to lower himself down the other side. He noticed that one of the cuts on his forearm had begun to bleed again, the blood soaking through to his white shirt cuff. He wrapped his handkerchief around the wound, leaned against the wall and waited for the twins to join him. As his heart rate returned to its normal speed, he started to shiver and was convinced that his sweat soaked clothes were beginning to freeze. If the

167

twins didn't hurry up, he would soon become as rigid as the Denalian garden statues.

Thankfully, Claus didn't have to wait long before Henry and Henrietta re-joined him. As soon as he got home, Claus climbed the stairs and got into a hot bath. He resolved to stay there until his muscles stopped aching, or the water grew cold. As he wallowed and slowly began to thaw, his mind turned to Dahljeeling. Something about the monkey's eyes had struck him as being so terribly sad. He made a mental note to brew some tea as soon as he got out of the tub.

He placed a hot flannel cloth over his face and sank further into the depths of the copper bath. A banging sounded from overhead. He took no notice. Sometimes Agatha visited the vacant floors upstairs. He didn't mind, as she kept the place clear of rats and mice. A louder thudding made him remove the flannel and gaze upwards at the ceiling as if staring hard enough would allow him to be able to see through floors.

"Agatha!" he called.

The door was pushed slowly open and the cat slipped into the room, her head tipped to one side in a questioning manner.

The thudding continued.

Claus groaned. He stood up and dried off hastily, wrapped himself in his dressing gown and pushed his feet into his slippers. He made his way to the stairs, shivering after being immersed in the heat of the water. He paused at the bottom. He was wary of what he might find waiting at the top and decided to venture into his grandfather's room to retrieve the pistol which he had kept hidden under a loose floorboard, beneath the bed. Claus had never had anything to do with firearms and he had no idea how to use the weapon, but he felt a little more confident with its cool weight in his hand. He crept up the stairs as silently as he could and peered into the darkness.

"Hello?" he said quietly, praying that there would be no reply.

There was a sudden blur of movement from the other end of the shadowy passage. A small dark shape hurtled towards him at breakneck speed. He instinctively slammed himself back against the wall and felt the air rush past him as the shape sped up the stairs. Claus grimaced and swore and took off after the intruder.

He chased the figure along the top hallway and saw that it was making its way towards the attic. He raced after it and flung himself up the ladder just as the attic door swung closed in his face. He burst through and came to an abrupt halt, panting with adrenalin more than physical effort.

"I have a pistol!" he yelled. At this point, he thought that offence might be the best defence. He only hoped that the intruder wouldn't notice the tremor in his voice.

"You are trespassing! Show yourself!" He heard a faint whimper from the corner of the room. He edged closer towards the sound, holding the pistol in both shaking hands before him. What little moonlight that managed to penetrate the clouds and smog, shone through the windows, illuminating little square islands of silvery light upon the dusty floorboards. Outside, it had begun to snow. One of the glass panes had been smashed and flakes drifted lazily into the attic, settling on the floor momentarily before they melted.

Claus's ears hurt as they strained to detect the slightest noise. He almost jumped a foot in the air when he heard a slight rustling. His heart was beating so hard that he could feel its reverberation in his skull. He stalked towards where he thought the rustling sound had come from. He peered slowly around the corner of an old wooden tea chest. One of its sides was missing. A pair of moth-eaten curtains had been bundled inside and amidst the folds of fabric sat Dahljeeling.

"What in the mines of Arcon are you doing here?" frowned Claus.

The monkey didn't answer. His eyes were huge, and his arms were wrapped around his torso. He shook from head to tail. He looked so pathetic that Claus lowered the pistol. The monkey suddenly began to scream and pointed towards the broken window behind Claus, who spun around to see another Dahljeeling, this one with strangely ill-formed features and extravagant teeth, appear at the window, followed by another and then four more. The doppelgangers pointed and shrieked in a gross mimicry of their original and began to pile in through the broken glass, seemingly unconcerned about personal safety. The Dahljeeling in the tea chest screamed and bolted further into the dark depths of the attic. The other monkeys didn't seem interested in Claus, other than the fact that he was stood in their way. They hissed at him threateningly. He realised that it would take just one monkey to decide that he was bold enough to attack, to incite the rest of the mob. With this in mind, Claus raised the pistol and squeezed the trigger. Luckily, he hadn't been aiming to hit anything, because the shot went widely askew. His whole arm was thrown backwards, and the bullet lodged somewhere in the rafters. But the sudden, deafening noise was enough to scare the primates. They screamed and retreated through the window and disappeared into the snowy night. Claus took a moment to collect himself.

Now he had another window to board up.

"Dahljeeling?" he called and squinted around in the darkness. He heard a muffled little cry and walked forward until he saw the monkey cowering beneath the dress maker's mannequin.

"You were hiding from your duplicates?"

Dahljeeling made a quiet squeak sound.

Claus held his hand out, and after a little hesitation, Dahljeeling reached out and took it.

"Come on. I don't know about you, but I could do with a cup of tea."

"Squeak," said Dahljeeling and scampered up Claus's arm to sit on his shoulder.

Claus took the monkey down the stairs and into the parlour, where he sat Dahljeeling on a foot stool, gave him a blanket and built the fire high. After he'd finished his task, he turned to look at his guest, who was staring with a look of bafflement at the stuffed monkey toy with its symbols.

"Why were they after you?" murmured Claus. "Poor little chap."

He stood up and went to make the tea. When he turned back, Dahljeeling was snoring quietly. Claus picked him up as gently as he could and carried him through to his grandfather's room, where he tucked him into the bed. He didn't know what else to do with him. He sighed and made his way to his own bed where, despite his mind being full of thoughts and questions, he fell asleep as soon as his head touched the pillow.

9th Brevis

laus opened his eyes and stared at his bedroom ceiling for a moment. He enjoyed a few blissful seconds of sleepy amnesia, not a care in the world, before memory returned and all of his thoughts and worries descended upon him in one great, heavy, groan inducing cascade.

He would have to board up the broken window in the attic, and maybe he should do all of the other windows too, while he was at it. What if the mad monkeys returned? And what was he to do with Dahljeeling? He didn't have the heart to take him to the Bitterend Zoo but turning him out on the street was unthinkable. His doppelgangers had clearly intended to do him harm and Claus felt an obligation to keep him safe.

Perhaps he should try to disguise Dahljeeling?

He suddenly remembered that he had promised to have lunch with the twins, and he snatched at his watch, which ticked sedately upon his bedside table. He breathed a sigh of relief to see that he had an hour until his appointment. He sat up in bed and realised that the light was wrong. His room seemed overly bright for the month of Brevis. Reluctantly he climbed out of bed and shuffled over to the window. He pulled the curtain back to see that Sovereign Street was covered in a sooty, grey blanket of snow and shivered.

A light tapping sound from the bedroom door made Claus turn and stare in bemused wonder, as Dahljeeling entered with a tea tray balanced on his head. He moved forwards and offered up the tray. Claus hastened to relieve the little monkey of his load.

"Thank you."

Dahljeeling bowed and scampered out of the room. Claus felt uncomfortable seeing the little fellow bob at him in such a subservient manner. He was not accustomed to being waited on and certainly not accustomed to anyone bringing him tea in the morning. Although he probably could get used to the idea. He poured the tea and milk into the cup and sipped. He felt the warmth coursing down his throat and felt just a little better about the world in general.

~

"I'm sorry, Sir. You can't bring that in here," said the proprietor of the third eating establishment that Claus and the twins had tried to enter. Evidently monkeys were not welcome anywhere in the city of Bitterend. They hadn't even bothered to try Beverstone's, concerned about what effect seeing a primate might have on Missus Beverstone, after her recent misfortune.

"He's terribly well behaved," assured Henrietta.

"I'm sorry, Miss."

Henrietta sighed. Henry's stomach grumbled.

"Perhaps we should take him back to the shop, Claus. We could lock him in?" he suggested.

"Nonsense!" protested Henrietta. "That would be cruel. And from what Claus has told us, potentially dangerous. What if his duplicates come after him again?"

"That's why I didn't want to leave him," frowned Claus. "And he looks so forlorn."

The three turned to look at the monkey, who gazed back at them with huge, sombre eyes.

"I want to get some new clothes," said Claus. "For Dahljeeling. He needs to look different from the other monkeys. Do you think there would be any tailor willing to dress a monkey?" Claus caught sight of Henry, who was giving him desperate looks and frantically shaking his head from behind his sister.

173

"Of course!" exclaimed Henrietta. "I know just the place! I think we should go there right now and then head back to ours. Cook could rustle us up some lunch without a fuss."

Henry gave Claus a commiserating look which plainly meant, 'You don't know what you've let yourself in for.'

~

The group turned back and walked through the gently falling snowflakes, towards Opal Road. The mixture of ash and the high volume of human and equine traffic had turned the snow on the ground into an unattractive blackened slush.

Henrietta brought them all to a halt outside a particularly fashionable looking tailors. Claus chewed his bottom lip nervously.

"Do you think that they'll let us in?" he wondered.

"Pshaw," Henrietta waved her hand in an unconcerned manner. "I'm on good terms with the owner," she strode forth and pushed open the door, making the little bell tinkle.

"Meese Tempest!" smiled a dapper, dark haired, mustachioed man, who was measuring a gentleman's collar. "Have you convince-ed your brother that he needa to update heese wardrobe again?" he asked, with a Denalian accent that was as smooth and thick as melted treacle.

"Not my brother, Mister Abano. May I present my good friend, Mister Claus Vogel, and Dahljeeling, his monkey butler."

Mister Abano stared at the monkey for a second before his face split in a wide grin.

"Wonderful! Let me finish up weethe Meester Grant here, and I will tend to you personally. Roberto!" he cried over his shoulder, towards a room at the back of the shop. "Some wine!" he demanded, before turning his attention back to his customers. "Meese Tempest, you know thee drill." Abano waved his hand towards an area of the shop which

174

was decked out like a particularly fashionable parlour. There was a low table set before two large and well-padded armchairs, a sofa and even a potted fern.

Henrietta winked at the tailor, to the disapproval of her brother, and they each settled themselves into the plush seats by the window.

"You shouldn't go around winking at strange Denalian men," Henry hissed.

"I know, brother, but Gianni has such an immaculate moustache, I just can't seem to help myself," she answered in a guileless manner.

They didn't have long to wait before Gianni Abano practically pounced upon them.

"Hmm. Wella now. What can I do?" he seemed to be directing the question more to himself than to his customers.

"You tell us, Mister Abano. Claus here needs an entire new wardrobe-"

Claus began to choke but Henrietta raised her voice over the interruption.

"-and his monkey needs a new suit or two, as quickly as possible."

Mister Abano pulled Claus up out of his seat and looked him over with a scowl, then did much the same to Dahljeeling.

"Yes, I can see theese is an emergency. The monkey, he no problem. Meester Claus..." Abano raised an eyebrow and pulled around at Claus's jacket lapel. "Might take a leetle longer."

"We were thinking maybe something in aubergine velvet for Dahljeeling," stated Henrietta.

"We were?" Claus raised his eyebrows.

"Wonderful!" cried Abano. "I have some offcuts of a bronze and chocolate brown jacquard that would make a splendid leetle waistcoat.

175

Meester Claus…I think also thee darker tones would suit you best. Natural colours, nothing too garish weethe your fair hair and pale complexion. Jewel tones are *out of the question*! You'd looka like a corpse!"

Claus nodded in bewilderment as the Denalian whipped out his tailor's measure and began wrapping it around various bits of Claus's anatomy.

"Black would be striking, especially weethe ash blond hair," he continued.

"Black?" Henrietta frowned. "Might that not make him look like an undertaker?"

"No, no. We put leetle hints of colour in, moss green velvet for thee waistcoat, for instance," he grabbed a swatch of fabric from a nearby table and held it up to Claus's cheek.

"Ooh! Brings out your eyes, Claus," beamed Henrietta.

Claus made some sort of noise, which he hoped sounded positive. He looked over at Henry for assistance, who shrugged and returned a sympathetic expression. When Abano had taken all of Claus's measurements and decided upon a colour theme with Henrietta, he got to work measuring Dahljeeling, who actually behaved more stoically than Claus. After an hour of picking out fabric samples, most of which got a tut and a head shake from Henrietta, Claus decided to sit down with a cup of tea and let the tailor and his new personal wardrobe assistant get on with it.

"Was it this bad when you came here?" he whispered to Henry. Henry tugged at his gold and raspberry coloured cravat.

"Raspberry?" he hissed. "You think I wanted *raspberry*?"

"I suppose it might match your eyes after a few too many glasses of brandy."

Claus had heard from Henry about the peculiar phenomenon which occurred when one went shopping in the company of Henrietta Tempest, although he'd never witnessed it firsthand before. Henrietta insisted that they walk back along Opal Road, instead of hailing a cab, claiming that a walk in the snow was good for the constitution. It seemed to Claus that they would only travel a few yards down the street before they were inevitably sucked into another shop, where the staff and proprietor were practically on first name terms with Henrietta, and Claus would suddenly find himself relieved of a quantity of money. Apparently he needed new shoes and new gloves, handkerchiefs, cufflinks, a couple of hats and an umbrella. This was a revelation to Claus as he stumbled along the street with his arms full of packages and a confused expression on his face.

"Can we get a cab *now*?" he asked.

"Of course!" Henrietta looked over the packages with glee.

"I don't know why you look so happy. You didn't get anything."

"No, but shopping for others is very nearly as satisfying as buying for oneself."

"That's because you're not the one paying for it..." Claus trailed off as Henrietta waved her hand at an approaching cab, clearly not paying attention to a word he was saying.

"What? You think she actually pays for stuff herself?" asked Henry incredulously.

~

"Do you really think the other Dahljeeling's will come back?" wondered Henrietta aloud, as she tucked into her smoked salmon and quail's eggs. The group had finally made it to Brandish Way, to the Tempest residence, for what had turned out to be a very late lunch indeed.

177

"I really hope not, but they seemed intent upon getting at him. No, thank you, Dahljeeling," Claus waved his hand as the monkey offered him a jug of hollandaise sauce. Dahljeeling kept trying to serve Claus's food, much to the bemusement of the Tempest's staff.

"But why do they want him?" said Henry, with his mouth full. "And how do we know that this is even the original Dahljeeling? It could be part of some dastardly plot."

Claus and Henrietta laughed.

"To what end?" grinned Henrietta. "To serve tea and wash Claus's dirty undergarments?"

Claus chose to ignore this comment.

"This *is* the original Dahljeeling," he insisted. "He looks different from the others. Plus, he's not murderous."

"The maid at Cordage's has probably reported him missing to the police by now. It's not going to take long for them to put two and two together and realise that he is behind the tea raids," said Henry. "They'll be looking for him. You'll be harbouring a wanted monkey. How will you explain his presence in your establishment? Cordage's death is under investigation Claus, it could make you a murder suspect."

"Then what should I do?" Claus sighed.

"Look, let us not get ahead of ourselves," said Henrietta cheerfully. "Usually when the police put two and two together, they come up with five. If the maid reports a missing monkey, it will be a monkey wearing a garish red coat and a ridiculous hat- no offence, Dahljeeling," she added.

Dahljeeling squeaked.

"Not a stylish frock coat, with contrasting waistcoat and velvet top hat-"

"Top hat?" interjected Claus.

178

"-Furthermore," she continued, undaunted. "The attacks were made by *multiple* monkeys, ergo the police will be looking for more than one. *We* only know that Dahljeeling is the root cause, because we found out about Todorovich's Amplificator, and he isn't about to tell anyone anything. The only evidence that ties Dahljeeling to this whole business are the letters which are in *our* possession- which I recommend we burn, by the way- and the only other person who knows anything about any of this is Lord Cordage, and I'm quietly confident that he will remain silent about the whole affair."

The boys felt slightly mollified.

"The sooner we can get Dahljeeling his new clothes the better," said Claus.

"I couldn't agree more. If there *were* to be any arrests, it would be for crimes against fashion. Gianni booked us in for a fitting next Thursday."

Claus groaned.

"Oh, and Todorovich wants to take us all out to dinner when he has the time, to show his gratitude. A good excuse for you to show off your new evening attire Claus."

Even though Henry was already eating at that precise moment, his countenance brightened at the notion of a free meal

10th Brevis

Claus pulled his coat collar up around his ears against the cold. He would not have admitted it to Henry, but he was eagerly anticipating the completion of his new brumail coat as he trudged through the snow laden streets.

The thought of hailing a cab and going back home was quite attractive, but he had come this far. Sometimes Claus found that a walk would clear his mind and his mind certainly felt rather cluttered of late. Without prior intention, he seemed to be making his way towards Blacktemple. He'd had no notion of where he was going when he left The Emporium that afternoon, but at some point, the idea of paying a visit to Madam Nimueh had entered his head. He wanted to find out more about this 'Timesmith' business. He'd accepted that he could turn back time. He had very little option other than to accept it. He had beheld the evidence with his own senses, but that didn't make it any less peculiar. The Blind Seeress of Katamatown seemed like a woman well versed in peculiarities.

Having grown up in Bitterend, with a grandfather who viewed the concept of an allowance as some sort of alien notion, reserved for the children of aristocrats who were 'idle malingerers', Claus knew of a great many shortcuts to get about town, because he'd rarely had the money to hire a cab. He went to turn down one of these shortcuts, when the overwhelming sensation of being watched made him glance around. He'd felt as if he'd been followed ever since he left The Emporium, but each and every time he looked over his shoulder there had been nothing to affirm this suspicion. No one was watching him. No one of note was nearby. Indeed, there were very few people around at all, now that the sun had set. He gave a mental shrug and proceeded down an alleyway.

He walked at a brisk rate, mainly in a bid to keep warm, but partially because of his growing sense of unease. He thought he heard a low whistle from some undeterminable direction, when his progress was abruptly hindered by a man who stepped out in front of him. A large man.

"You got the time gov'nor?"

"All the time in the world," replied Claus, without thinking.

The large man didn't seem to find this statement very helpful and so signalled for his equally large friend to join him.

Wonderful, thought Claus. It seemed very likely that this pair were robbers. He would have to protect the Item of Peculiarity, regardless of what they did to him. He couldn't let it fall into anyone else's hands, even if that meant he had to sustain a beating. Unfortunately, he was already in bad shape from his misadventure at Cordage's.

The brawny duo advanced, herding Claus so that his back was to the wall, cutting off his means of escape. Claus felt somewhat outraged at this turn of events. He had enough to deal with at the moment. Perhaps if he whipped out his watch now and wound it back, the pair of thugs would loom their way in reverse and this encounter would never take place. It was unfortunate that Claus imagined the ruffians lumbering backwards, because the mental image struck him as rather humorous. If ever there was an inopportune moment to laugh, it was when one was outnumbered in a dark alleyway by a pair of thugs.

The first man seemed somewhat put out and shoved Claus hard against the cold brick wall, where he pinned him by the throat with one hand and produced a small blade with the other.

"Funny, is it?" he growled.

Claus noted that the man's breath was rank with the stench of stale alcohol and the sulphuric odour of arconian dust. Though the man's personal hygiene was of little consequence, Claus was concerned that if the assailant had been imbibing liquor and narcotics, he would be more likely to use his weapon, not having the mental coherence of sobriety to moderate his temper.

Claus debated answering the mugger, unsure if he should try to defuse the situation, but then perhaps anything he said at this point would only rile the man further, and so he remained in silent indecision.

"Oi!" came a shout from further down the alleyway.

A hand seemed to materialise out of the darkness and gripped the thug by the wrist. There was a stomach curdling cracking sound and the blade clattered to the ground. The thug cried out in agony, released his grasp on Claus and bent over, cradling his broken wrist against his torso. His friend rushed forward to aid him and received an elbow squarely in his face. He ricocheted backwards from the force and lost his footing on the treacherous snow laden ground. He landed on his back where he writhed and screamed, clutching at his face, blood running freely over his lips and chin. Claus's rescuer wasted no time in administering a well-aimed kick to the thug's ribs.

"You broke my wrist, you maniac!" yelled the first ruffian.

"Aye! And I'll break more than that if you don't piss off right quick!"

The pair needed no further encouragement to flee and made a hasty and somewhat shambolic retreat from the alleyway.

Claus stared at his saviour and let out the breath he'd been holding.

"You alright there, Claus?" smiled Niall.

"Better than them," Claus nodded in the direction that the thugs had departed in. "Thank you."

"No trouble. Shall we see about getting you home? I could hail you a cab?"

"I feel I owe you a drink at the very least," Claus eyed his new friend with wonder. He didn't seem the least bit troubled about this event.

"Unfortunately, I have a prior engagement tonight, but I might take you up on the offer in the future."

The pair turned and made their way back down the alleyway to the main street, the opposite direction that the thugs had taken.

"Where were you off to anyway?" asked Niall.

"Oh, I had a mind to pay someone a visit."

"A girl?" grinned Niall.

Claus laughed. "No. Well, a woman."

Niall glanced sidelong at him and smirked.

"No honestly, it's nothing like *that*. She's about two hundred years old."

"Oh. A relative?"

"A witch actually. I had a mind to ask her about…a problem."

"I wasn't aware there were any witches around here."

Claus was surprised by his companion's reaction. He'd half expected his admission to be met with scorn or scepticism, but the man at his side looked genuinely interested.

"Madam Nimueh. She has a shop in Blacktemple. She makes potions for ailments and does fortune readings. Tarot cards, tea leaf reading and the like."

"I may well pay her a visit," smiled Niall.

"You don't consider it tosh then?"

"Not at all. I dabble with the tarot myself."

Claus raised his eyebrows in surprise.

"What?" asked Niall. "Do I not seem the type?"

"Is there a type? I never really gave it much credence before, but lately…"

"I understand," Niall met Claus's gaze with such forceful

comprehension that it made Claus flinch and instinctively place a protective hand over the watch in his pocket.

"You must miss you grandfather terribly," continued Niall. "I don't believe that when someone dies they are truly gone. Why not seek out the help of a medium to communicate with them?"

Claus relaxed. "Indeed."

Niall waved at an approaching hansom and the cabbie brought his horse to a halt.

"You know, you should meet a friend of mine," said Claus. "I think you and her would have a lot to talk about."

"I'll come by the shop some time," Niall opened the cab door and Claus mounted the step. "Sovereign Street, driver," he called up to the man on the dickie box. "Do you need money for the fare?"

Claus waved the offer hastily away.

"You've already done more than enough."

He settled himself in the cab and Niall closed the door. The cabbie clicked his tongue at the horse, and they began to move. A sudden thought entered Claus's head which filled him with horror.

"I've just realised! I still don't know your name, Sir!" he called.

"You can call me Patrick. Patrick O'Connor," laughed Niall.

Niall watched the cab until it was out of sight and then turned in the direction of the nearest alehouse. He wanted to check on Arabella, but first he must conclude some business.

The alehouse was teeming when he entered. Some of the patrons were getting rowdy, some stared miserably at their drinks with unseeing eyes, and some had already fallen asleep. The pair he sought were sat in a corner, looking morose, nursing cups that were filled with something stronger than ale. They reminded Niall of a pair of stray dogs who'd lost a fight and dragged themselves off to hide in shame and lick their wounds.

"Well. Would you look at the state of you two?" remarked Niall.

"You've got some nerve. Showing your face!" spat the first thug.

"What's your problem?"

"My *problem*? You broke my damn wrist, you cracked bastard!"

"You drew a knife on him!" hissed Niall. "I told you to scare him, rough him up a bit if you had to. Not cut him up!"

"You broke by bose!" complained thug number two. He was holding a bloodied rag to his face.

"I had to make it look convincing."

"We want the rest of our money," the man with the broken wrist said, in a tone which brooked no argument.

"Be bant extra! Be bant combensation!"

Niall looked from Broken Nose to his friend.

"Honestly, I can't understand a word he's saying. You might need to translate," he said earnestly.

Thug number one stood up abruptly and made to grab Niall, who raised his hands in a placatory gesture. "Let's go outside. I'll recompense you most handsomely, but I need to fetch the money. I don't carry too much coin about my person. There are thieves and brigands everywhere these days."

"We want double what we agreed."

Niall nodded amiably. "You'll get your due."

The thugs glanced at each other and followed Niall out of the alehouse and along the darkened street. There wasn't much in the way of lighting in the poorer parts of town. Niall walked quickly, heading in the direction of The Pretty Penny.

"Where's this money then?"

"At my digs."

"How far?"

"Not much further. We'll cut through here," Niall didn't wait for a reply, but turned a corner and disappeared down the side of a disused building. The rats hurried out of his path as he slipped quietly through the darkness. He wished the other two men would hurry up. Arabella would begin to fret if he wasn't home soon.

He glanced around himself and decided that this was as good a place as any. He came to a halt and span on his heel to face the pair that were rushing to keep up behind him. The first man had barely a second to register what was going on. He obliged Niall by practically running straight into the cosh which was all but invisible in the dense shadow. Niall laughed when he realised it was the man with the broken nose. Oh well, if a job was worth doing…

The second thug tried to pull Niall off his comrade, but his broken wrist was a terrible hindrance, and he could do little more than watch as his friend was bludgeoned over and over until he lay silent and still in a puddle of filth blackened slushy snow that was quickly turning red.

Niall straightened up and turned around to look at the second man, who had ceased his futile efforts to help his companion, and all the fight seemed to have left him. He shook his head mutely and backed away, a look of absolute horror upon his face. Niall said nothing, but advanced slowly. There was no shred of emotion on his face, his eyes seemed oddly blank, as if he were looking at, but not really *seeing* the other man. It was as if this was all some boring task which he must get done before he could go home for his supper. The thug realised that there was no point trying to appeal for his life. No point in pleading or supplicating or attempting to parley with this man. The thug wasn't even entirely sure if this *was* a man or some demon coughed up from the mines of Arcon. His natural instinct for self-preservation took over and he turned to flee, but he didn't get far. He hadn't noticed that a beggar was sat in the shadows. He tripped over the vagrant's outstretched legs and went sprawling face-first to the ground. He didn't get the option of standing up again.

Business concluded; Niall wiped his face with his handkerchief. He didn't want to go home covered in blood. His stomach rumbled and he realised that he was hungry. If only he hadn't made such a mess of his clothes, he could have popped to get some supper to take home to Arabella. Still, she was good at making a meal out of next to nothing.

Niall riffled through the men's clothing and pocketed anything of worth, before turning to look at the vagabond who was sat on the ground, his back propped against the wall. He squatted down beside the man, who had probably died of exposure or starvation, and prised a bottle from his ridged hand. He smelt the contents and then took a swig.

"Waste not.".

11th Brevis

Click Clack glanced around to make sure that no one was watching him, before he fumbled with the loose brick beneath the window sill. He extracted the key which was hidden in the gap behind the brick and inserted it into the lock.

The bell above the door tinkled solemnly as he entered the dark and silent shop.

"Brenna?"

He stumped towards the back room and peered around the curtain. The tarot cards were laid out on the table along with a long-forgotten cup of tea.

Click Clack felt an odd tightening sensation in his stomach, and he clattered up the stairs two at a time. He paused briefly when he saw the old woman lying motionless upon the bed. The large grey creature, which could loosely be described as a cat, was curled up at her feet. He opened his orange eyes and yowled. Click Clack crossed the room in a couple of strides, took Brenna by the shoulders and shook her vigorously.

"*What? What?*"

"Praise Dantalis," Click Clack breathed out and then swore. "It's me, Yusheng."

"I know it's you, you damn fool. Who else is going to break into my home and make such a racket?"

"You're all right then?" he asked, ignoring the insult.

"Why wouldn't I be?" Brenna demanded, as she sat up.

"The boy told me that the shop's been closed for days and that you ain't left it."

"Boy? You've had one of your scallywag's watching me?"

"Well…" Click Clack faltered.

Brenna huffed and climbed from the bed and pulled on her dressing gown.

"Go and make yourself useful and put the kettle on," she snapped. "Barging in uninvited. Lucky I didn't have a heart attack, being woken up like that."

Click Clack raised an eyebrow but did as he was told.

"I ain't seen you since I told you your son was at large in Bitterend. That's why I *barged in uninvited*. I thought you might be…I don't know what I thought," Click Clack shrugged.

"What date is it?" asked Brenna, as if she hadn't been listening.

"Shop all locked up and dark," he persisted. "You in your bed in the middle of the day. What was I supposed to think?"

"I'm an old woman. Why shouldn't I go to bed when I'm tired?"

Click Clack snorted sceptically and took a pair of clean cups from the dresser.

"I *am* tired," Brenna insisted. "I've got a lot on my mind."

"Your son?"

"Aye. And my nephew. I'm worried the silly bugger is going to be tempted to reset time."

"Reset-?"

"Time, aye. And I don't mind telling you, Yusheng, that's no laughing matter when you're in my line of work. Seeing to Missus Hardy's haemorrhoids or Mister Shipperton's in-growing toenail once is enough

189

for me, but the thought of having to do it over and over ..." Brenna sighed. "There should be an inner circle of The Underworld reserved for that sort of thing."

"Um..." said Click Clack in confusion.

"Well. You might as well know everything. Since you seem determined to poke your nose into my business," Brenna sat down at the small table. "I'm starving. Grab that cake and sit down."

Brenna was pleasantly surprised at how quickly Click Clack cottoned on to the theory of time travel. Most people seemed to have problems grasping the concept.

"So, you, your nephew, your son, you're all *Timesmiths*? And if one of you uses the watch to go back in time, you can all feel the effects?"

Brenna nodded. "It isn't a pleasant sensation."

Click Clack bristled and stood up.

"Well, I'm going to march round there and demand the damn thing! Then I'll chuck it in the river!"

"It won't do any good. This isn't an ordinary watch, Yusheng. It's a lot harder to get rid of than you might imagine. Besides, only someone with magical abilities could destroy it."

"But you're a Timesmith. I'll send some boys round to mug the kid, and then *you* can break it."

Brenna shook her head.

"I'll make sure they only rough him up a *little* bit," assured Click Clack.

"No. The last time someone tried to take that watch by force, a good woman died. Claus's mother."

"Oh." Click Clack sat back down. "I have a funny feeling that this is where your son comes into it."

190

"He killed Claus's mother because he wanted the watch."

"But why? Why does he want it so badly? Surely any idiot would realise owning something like that is dangerous?"

"He was desperate. His father died when he was small. I was left on my own to bring him up. It was hard times. The hardest. We left Irkland in search of a better life and wondered the land for years. We took up with the travelling folk, as you already know, but eventually ended up back in Irkland. Anyway, Niall was always dreaming up ways to get money. As he got older, he got tough. Started thieving, small stuff at first, just to get by. Then one day he robbed a jewellers. Him and his pal Patrick O'Connor. They didn't consider the owner might have a blunderbuss behind the counter," Brenna shook her head sadly.

"Patrick got shot. Tore a great hole in his leg. Niall ran for it. Well, the police arrested Patrick. They would have hanged him too, if he hadn't died first. The police physician tried to patch him up, but he bled to death in his cell. He never mentioned Niall.

After that, we left Irkland for good. I knew I had a half-brother here in Bitterend, so we came here to find him. The family were good to us. Took us in. Claus was very small. One day, me and Hans got to talking about our father and the whole Timesmith business. It was a sore subject, seeing as how he went mad and killed himself. My niece, Eva had the watch. Hans said he didn't trust himself to keep it, but Eva was a sensible girl. Anyway, Niall overheard all this and asked if he could borrow the watch. He wanted to go back and save Patrick."

"Really?" Click Clack couldn't keep the surprise from his voice. "So, his intentions were *good*?"

Brenna grunted.

"You know what they say about good intentions."

Click Clack nodded.

"At first he just wanted to save Patrick, but when Eva refused to lend him the watch something changed in him. He'd always had a certain darkness within, but it grew and consumed him. The presence of the watch can do funny things to some people. Influence them. Or maybe that's just something I like to think, to make it all easier. Maybe he's just an evil little bastard and always was."

The pair sat in silence for a while. Bodkin brushed against his mistress's leg.

"So…now Niall has felt the presence of the watch and come back to try to claim it. And we have to protect Claus?" said Click Clack.

"I failed to protect his mother. It's the least I can do."

"But Claus doesn't know that you're his aunt?"

"Hans never told him. He didn't want anything to do with me after…what happened."

"We'll see the boy right. Don't worry. I think you should tell him the truth though."

"Oh aye? I'm sure that would go down well. 'By the way, I'm your long-lost great aunt. My son murdered your mother, but you know how families can be.'"

~

Arabella tiptoed past her sleeping stepfather, who merely gave a snore and noticed the clothes that Niall had discarded to the floor the night before. She sighed in disapproval and bent to retrieve the garments. They were heavily soiled and would need a wash. Arabella froze when she realised what the stains were. There was too much blood for it to have come from a knuckle fight or tussle. Too much blood for someone to lose and live. She had half a mind to throw the items into the fireplace, but she wasn't sure if the impulse arose from a desire to protect her stepfather, who had clearly done something dreadful, or just out of sheer horror. Her entire life seemed to be a blood-soaked question mark these days and she longed for simpler times.

She gazed over at Niall, who slept peacefully. He looked almost angelic in his slumber. Almost. But he'd changed since Mother died. Everything had.

He had returned the previous evening in high spirits and Arabella had spent the time of his absence drinking gin, so she hadn't noticed the state of his clothing. She might have confronted him about the bloodied garments had she thought he would tell her the truth.

Niall stirred and sat up.

"Morning."

"It's almost evening, actually."

"Is it now?" Niall was entirely unconcerned about the hour.

"Are you staying in tonight? Or do you have more *business*?"

Niall either chose to ignore or didn't notice the little inflection in his stepdaughter's question.

"A bit of both. We need to pay a visit to my cousin."

"We?"

"I told you that you were going to help me. Help *us*," he corrected himself.

"And I told you that I wouldn't."

"We're not going round to murder him. Don't be so dramatic girl."

"So, what's the plan?" Arabella asked with trepidation.

"I told you, I need to get close to him. I rescued him from a pair of thugs last night."

Arabella felt dizzy with relief. Niall hadn't committed some dreadful murder, he'd merely acted in self-defence, caught up in a brawl which was nothing to do with him.

"Now he views me as his saviour. A hero. He owes me."

"Were you hurt?"

Niall laughed.

"Hardly. They weren't about to attack the man that hired them."

"Hired?" Arabella felt her stomach plummet once more.

"Aye. I hired them to scare him. We need to go and visit him, all beaten up. Tell him the bastards that tried it on last night tracked us down to exact their revenge."

"All beaten up," echoed Arabella, through numb lips.

"We appeal to his good nature. Get you inside and then you can get the watch."

Arabella shook her head.

"I don't understand. I don't even know what it is I'm supposed to look for! A watch in a watchmaker's shop? That's like looking for a needle in a haystack. And anyway, how am I to 'get inside' as you put it?"

"I'll deliver you to his door, the worse for wear. The watch we're after is likely the one he keeps upon his person at all times. You set yourself up in his house, charm him as only you can, and when he's eating out of the palm of your hand, you take the watch."

"You want me in his bed?" Arabella's voice was monotone. Something inside her had gone cold and hard.

"No! I'm not a whoremonger. Just flatter him. Pay him attention. There's no need to touch him."

"I won't do it," Arabella turned her back upon her stepfather and wrapped her shawl around her shoulders. She needed some fresh air. She needed to be anywhere but here.

She sensed Niall advancing on her from behind, he moved with an almost eerie silence, but the old floorboards moved with the distribution of his weight. She turned to confront him but before she could do anything, he had struck her across the side of the face.

Niall sprang forward to catch Arabella before she fell to the floor. He walked back to the bed before laying her carefully down and kissing her gently on her closed eyelid that would probably swell.

He went to the washstand to freshen up and then proceeded to dress in a leisurely manner. The clothes he had worn last night were out of the question, but after quick deliberation, he decided to don the shirt that he had been wearing. There was blood around the collar, and a few drops down the front, which would make the whole effect more visually arresting.

He walked over to face the wall, standing a small distance away from it, leaned back and then lunged forward, smashing his head against the plaster. He repeated this action until blood trickled over his brow. Then he went to check his appearance in the glass. Happy with how he looked, he swept his insensible stepdaughter up into his arms and headed out, via the dingy back staircase, to avoid being noticed.

~

Claus made his way over to the door of The Time Emporium to turn the sign from *open* to *closed*. The light from the shop reflecting in the windows made it impossible to see out into the darkness of the street outside. Therefore, he sprang away from the door in surprise as it was thrown open with force, setting the little bell which was hung above it to jangle alarmingly. Niall staggered his way into the shop with a young lady draped across his arms.

"Mister O'Connor!" Claus was very pleased to be able to address the man by his name at last, though less than pleased that his new friend had come to pay him a visit under such circumstances. His forehead sported an angry looking swelling that oozed with blood.

"Mister Vogel. I'm afraid I must ask a favour of you," said Niall.

195

"Of course. What has happened?"

"Those pair of thugs that set upon you last night. I must have rubbed them up the wrong way."

"They did this?" asked Claus, horrified that Mister O'Connor's intervention on Claus's behalf had caused such violent repercussions.

"They must have seen me and followed. We were out to get some dinner and they appeared out of nowhere. My daughter. Arabella," Niall nodded his head, somewhat redundantly, towards the girl in his arms. "I did my best to protect her, but they caught me unawares."

Claus looked at the young lady who had apparently feinted after some unmentionable ordeal. She was very pale and had a pronounced bruise covering her left eye, which seemed to be darkening by the second.

"My first thought was to get her to safety and I'm afraid that this was the closest place to hand."

"My grandfather's bedroom," Claus gestured upstairs "It's quite comfortable and there's a fire burning. She can rest there while I send word for a physician."

"I have my own physician. I can go and fetch him, if you don't mind looking after her for a short while?"

Claus nodded and led the way to the second floor.

Niall laid Arabella on the bed and Claus stoked the fire.

"Is she alright?" frowned Claus. "I mean...other than the bruise?" He was loath to say what was in his mind.

"Yes. I might have been caught off guard, but I soon rallied, do not fear. They got more than they bargained for."

"I don't doubt it," said Claus earnestly. He had a vivid recollection of Patrick O'Connor's impromptu savagery. He certainly wasn't the type of man you would want to get on the wrong side of.

"I hope this isn't too much of an imposition?"

"No. No of course not. It's the least I can do after you came to my aid."

"Are you sure?"

Claus waved the question away, but inwardly he wondered how one looked after an unconscious person.

"Much obliged. I'll come back as soon as I can."

With that, Niall put his hat back on and swept from the room.

Perhaps he should call upon the twins for help. It didn't seem entirely proper for this girl to be alone in Claus's house with him. He didn't even have a housekeeper who could act as chaperone.

He located a blanket from the trunk, at the foot of the bed and carefully laid it over her. On closer inspection he realised that she must be around the same age as he himself. Her skin was as white as porcelain, her red hair had come loose and spread across the pillow. She looked like a tragic heroin from a painting.

A shuffling sound from the doorway made Claus tear his gaze away from the young woman's face, albeit reluctantly.

Dahljeeling gave the girl a quizzical look.

Claus shrugged in response.

"Perhaps some tea?" he suggested, without any real conviction. She didn't look as though she were in any condition to enjoy a hot beverage. Claus debated sending Dahljeeling to the Tempest's with a note requesting their company, but he was worried about sending his furry friend out alone, in case his demonic doppelgangers came after him again.

He heard the sound of feet ascending the stairs and remembered that he hadn't locked the shop door. He couldn't imagine that Mister O'Connor was back from his errand already, he'd only just left.

"Claus! Cooee! It's only us!"

The twins bustled in from the landing.

"We just saw Han's Irkish friend coming out of the shop. He told us what had happened," said Henry.

"Your timing is impeccable."

"We were coming round to tell you about the note that I received from Nikola," said Henrietta. "He's taking us all to The Edenia on the Eighteenth," she pushed past the boys as she spoke and hastened over to the unconscious girl on the bed. "Gosh, how *could* they?" she exclaimed, aghast as she examined Arabella's swollen eye. "The brutes!"

"What's worse is that I'm responsible," said Claus miserably. "If it wasn't for me, this wouldn't have happened."

"What do you mean, old boy? It's not like *you* punched her in the face," frowned Henry.

"Mister O'Connor came to my aid yesterday evening. A pair of ruffians had me cornered in an alleyway. I don't know whether they intended to rob me, or give me a thrashing, but they were in a sorry way by the time Patrick was done with them. It seems that this is their revenge."

"Patrick O'Connor," said Henry. "A name at last."

"What?" Henrietta's voice was shrill in her agitation as she cut across her brother's words. "Cornered by ruffians? Why are we only just hearing about this?"

"I haven't had the chance to tell you!" protested Claus. He was painfully aware that his eyes kept wondering back to Arabella, as if some magnetic force had control over them. "Anyway, they didn't do me any harm. They didn't get the chance thanks to Mister O'Connor. I am in his debt. Do you think Todorovich would mind if I brought him along for dinner? Arabella would have to come along too, of course."

"Of course," smirked Henry and he winked.

Claus frowned at his friend in confusion.

"I assume you were out wandering the streets last night then?" snapped Henrietta.

"I was hardly *wandering*. I was going to Katamatown to pay a visit to Missus McGrath."

Arabella's eyes flew open, startling Claus who had once again returned to his occupation of staring at her.

"McGrath?" she almost shouted. The twins jumped in alarm.

"You're awake!" Henrietta sat on the edge of the bed. "How're you feeling, my dear?" she asked with concern. "Your father left you here while he went to fetch a physician. Claus is a friend of his."

"Missus McGrath?" Arabella repeated, staring at Claus, who had become strangely tongue-tied and merely nodded in affirmation. "Do you know anything about her?"

Claus and the twins glanced around at each other.

"Brenna McGrath? Erm, not much. She's an Irkish mystic who has a shop in Blacktemple. She reads fortunes and sells ointments," Henrietta shrugged. "Tarot cards and tea leaves. Things of that nature."

Arabella looked confused and somewhat stricken. She fell silent and her eyes went out of focus, as if her mind were somewhere else.

"I think she must be in shock," whispered Henrietta. She reached out slowly and laid her hand on Arabella's arm. "Do you remember what happened to you?" she asked kindly.

Arabella shook her head. The firelight shining on her cascading hair seemed to sparkle and flash like gold and rubies. Marsh lights to lure an unwary traveller to his doom. Claus shifted uncomfortably and cleared

199

his throat.

"Do you remember your name?" persisted Henrietta. She'd read quite a lot about the subject of head injuries and the short-term memory loss that a concussion could cause.

"Arabella Mc-" she paused, but only for a heartbeat. "O'Connor."

"How about a cup of tea, Miss O'Connor?" asked Claus, not knowing what to say or do. He felt a desperate desire to leave the room and, perversely, an equally strong desire to remain.

Dahljeeling darted forward in glee, eager to be of assistance.

Arabella almost fell backwards off the bed in shock at the primate's sudden appearance.

"Oh, don't worry!" exclaimed Henrietta. "He's not one of those feral creatures who've been terrorising Bitterend. You've no doubt read about it in the papers."

Arabella nodded. "He can make tea?"

"Most adeptly," smiled Henrietta.

Dahljeeling puffed his chest out in pride.

"That would be lovely," said Arabella. "And I don't suppose I'll ever get the chance to drink tea made by a monkey again." There was the vaguest hint of amusement in her tone.

"Lovely," echoed Claus, somewhat dreamily.

Henry hastily turned his laugh into a cough.

"Tea, please, Dahljeeling, if you'd be so good?" said Henrietta. "And you boys go and find something to put on Miss O'Connor's eye," she instructed.

Claus and Henry looked flummoxed.

"What sort of something?" asked Claus.

"A steak!" replied Henrietta, with impatience.

"I don't have any steak!"

"Something cold to take down the swelling!" she snapped.

The boys looked at each other and scampered out of the room. There was a slight tussle at the door as they both tried to exit at the same time. Henry won due to his advantage in weight.

"Something like steak," said Claus, as the pair searched through the meagre contents of the cabinets.

"What about this?"

"Henry, that's a tin of tuna."

Henry glanced at the item he held in his hand.

"It's cold," he said reasonably.

Claus shook his head and carried on searching.

"I've never seen you blush, by the way," grinned Henry.

"What? What? I'm not blushing! What are you talking about?" bristled Claus. He stuck his head further inside the cabinet. "There's nothing in here that's remotely steak-like."

"She's very pretty."

"Who is?" asked Claus vaguely.

"*Arabella*."

"Is she? I hadn't noticed."

"In fact, *pretty* doesn't do her justice. I might be inclined to call her *beautiful*. Wouldn't you agree?"

"I couldn't comment. If you're so taken with her, why don't you try to court her?" snapped Claus hotly.

Henry sighed and shook his head.

201

"Oh, there's nothing here!" complained Claus. He looked around the room in vain and shrugged. Then he glanced at the window and snapped his fingers.

"What?" frowned Henry.

"Something cold, she said," he moved over to the window and slid the pane of glass upwards.

"Genius!" Henry smiled. "There's not much that's colder than snow."

"Indeed. And it's soft."

Henry joined Claus at the window and proffered his handkerchief.

"I'll use my own, thank you," Claus said.

Henry detected a definite 'tone' in his friend's words, and he bit at the insides of his cheeks to prevent himself smiling. He watched as Claus very carefully ruined one of his best handkerchiefs by filling it with snow

When the pair returned to the bedroom, it was to find Arabella sat up sipping tea and talking with Henrietta.

Claus offered the snow filled handkerchief and Henrietta nodded in approval.

"It's *my* handkerchief," said Claus. "Not Henry's."

Henrietta raised an eyebrow.

"I really don't care who the handkerchief belongs to, Claus. As long as it's clean."

"It is!" He looked at Arabella. "All of my handkerchiefs are very clean. Definitely. Apart from the snow. Which was my idea. And I don't mind getting snow on it. Why would I?" Claus was painfully aware that he was waffling, but he couldn't seem to control himself. He could feel the eyes of the twins upon him. "It's my handkerchief after all."

"Yes," Arabella nodded. "You said that."

Oh Dantalis, she thinks I'm an idiot, thought Claus. *But she did smile at me,* he reasoned with himself, before a nasty little voice in his head said: *she's smiling at you in the same way someone smiles at the village idiot.*

"Er...I have to go and..." *kill myself.* He gestured in no particular direction and fled from the room.

~

Claus paced up and down the workshop. This was a nightmare. Where on Cellanor was Patrick? It was almost midnight. As he stared at his watch, he contemplated winding it back so that Miss O'Connor wouldn't think him such a fool. Perhaps he should wind it back far enough so that she was never attacked in the first place. But if he did that then he would never have met her. In truth it was worse than that, because he *would* have met her. He'd know that she was somewhere in Bitterend, but she wouldn't even know that he existed. Something about that scenario appalled him. He was also appalled and guilt-ridden at his own selfishness and the fact that he was even debating not using the watch to heal her injury.

The sound of the transporter in use pulled him back to his surroundings and he looked around to see the twins.

"What is wrong with you?" demanded Henrietta, as she disembarked.

"I needed to put the cat out."

"Is it that time already?" asked Henry. "Good lord. How time flies when one is having fun."

"You're not *leaving*, surely?" Claus squealed.

"And leave you alone with Miss O'Connor?" Henrietta raised her eyebrows in scandalised horror. "Of course not. I'll stay with her. In any case, she shouldn't be left alone with a head injury. I can nap in the chair if needs be. Henry can sleep in the parlour."

203

Henry scowled at his sister but didn't argue.

"I wouldn't dream of leaving the poor girl alone with you. You'd probably start ranting about your handkerchief again. Honestly, it's as if *you've* had a blow to the head, not her."

"I…I…" Claus stammered.

"You are acting like a lunatic. Just calm down and be yourself," advised Henrietta in a kinder tone. "You're not going to impress her by babbling like a buffoon."

"I'm not trying to impress anyone. I don't care what she thinks of me," Claus noticed that the twins were giving him exactly the same look:

Pity.

12th Brevis

Henry smiled as he made up his make-shift bed in the parlour. He felt sorry for Claus, of course, but there was something hilarious about watching his friend squirm. He would give him some advice about woman in the morning. Claus had never really had much to do with the fairer sex after all, apart from Henrietta, and that hardly counted. Henry had harboured the suspicion that perhaps one day, his best friend and sister would wed, but that seemed very unlikely now. He would have liked to have had Claus as his brother-in-law, but they were already as good as family. Better really, as they actually liked one another. A loud banging from downstairs interrupted his thoughts and he joined Claus and Henrietta on the landing.

Henrietta leaned over Arabella, who seemed to be sleeping soundly. She was a little worried as she was certain that she had read something about concussion victims being made to stay awake. She didn't have the heart to wake her though. Black eye or not, she looked so careworn and exhausted, that Henrietta had a suspicion that her recent ordeal with the brutes who had attacked her, was merely one piece of a very distressing puzzle. A loud banging from downstairs interrupted her thoughts and she joined Claus and Henry on the landing.

"That must be Mister O'Connor, back with the physician," she guessed.

"It's about time!" Claus complained and he hastened down the stairs two at a time.

Henrietta strained her ears and heard the shop bell jangle, followed by the sound of male voices, one of which unmistakably belonged to Patrick O'Connor. She turned and went back into the bedroom. Miss O'Connor would need a chaperone if the physician intended to examine her.

Arabella was propped up on one elbow when Henrietta re-entered the room. Her eyes were wide with fear.

"I believe the physician is here," said Henrietta and went to sit in the chair. Arabella clutched at her arm as she passed.

"Just the physician? Alone?"

"Well, I believe your father is with him," Henrietta was shocked at the strength of the other girl's grasp. Perhaps she was frightened of physicians? Many people had aversions to anything of a medical persuasion after all. Henrietta took Arabella's hand and sat on the edge of the bed.

"Don't fret. I won't leave you on your own with him."

"I don't want to see him!"

"Now, now," soothed Henrietta. "I'm sure he'll just want to check your head wound. It's a nasty bump you have."

"Not the physician. Him! My *father*!"

"Oh!" Henrietta raised her eyebrows. She stared at the other girl. Her face, which was already a pale shade of alabaster had turned ashen, the dark circles under her eyes appeared livid against the white. "Alright," Henrietta nodded.

"Send him away, Miss Tempest! Please!"

Henrietta nodded again and squeezed Arabella's hand before she got up. She closed the bedroom door behind herself and leaned her head against it for a moment in contemplation. Miss O'Connor was scared of her father. No, not scared. Terrified. The sound of footsteps upon the stairs caused her to turn.

Claus preceded Mister O'Connor and someone Henrietta could only assume was the physician, onto the landing.

"Henrietta, this is Doctor James," Claus indicated the man.

Henrietta nodded briefly and looked at Mister O'Connor.

"Your daughter would rather you stayed out here, Sir."

"That's unexpected," smiled Niall. "Why would she want that?"

"She was most insistent," Henrietta hadn't moved away from the bedroom door and in consequence blocked their access to the patient.

Niall stepped closer and loomed over Henrietta. She remained rooted to her post and tilted her head back so that she could maintain eye contact. The hairs on the back of her neck seemed to prickle.

"I merely wish to see how she fares."

"*She was most insistent,*" she repeated.

"Mister O'Connor, why don't we go into the parlour for a brandy? It's been a very long evening after all," said Claus.

Niall looked away from Henrietta and nodded, his demeanour transforming at once to one of benign affability.

Claus glanced at Henrietta as he held the parlour door open for his guest, a look of perplexity on his face. Henrietta stared mutely back at him before he disappeared through the doorway.

"Doctor James," she said. Her voice wavered slightly, and she cleared her throat. "Shall we?"

"Lead on," said the physician.

Henrietta tapped lightly on the bedroom door before opening it a fraction.

"Miss O'Connor? It's just myself and the physician."

Arabella seemed to sag back into the pillows in her relief.

Henrietta stood back from the door to allow Doctor James entrance to the room. As he passed by her, she caught the unmistakable odour of strong liquor upon him and he seemed to stagger a little. She hastened over to the bed to stand guard over her charge.

"Your father told me what happened. How do you feel?" Doctor James slurred.

Arabella seemed to consider this question briefly and then gave a small shrug. The physician bent down and looked at her head wound.

"Well, I suggest you rest for a week. You seem well looked after here, in any case." Doctor James looked up at Henrietta. "I'm assuming she can stay here. I don't think she should be moved at any time soon."

"Of course. But I thought she might have a concussion?"

"Oh. Oh yes, very likely," he nodded.

Henrietta frowned.

"But surely you should check?"

"Check? Oh. Yes, I suppose I should." Doctor James stared at Arabella for a moment before reaching for her wrist and checking her pulse. He looked grave. "Yes. Definitely a concussion."

"Perhaps you should ask her if she has a headache. Or Nausea?" Henrietta snapped.

"Very well," he looked at his patient. "Do you?"

Arabella shook her head.

"Well, that settles it. Definitely a concussion."

Henrietta stared in bewilderment at the physician. He looked as though he hadn't shaved in days.

"She should stay here in bed for a week, get plenty of rest and she should be as right as rain. That's my diagnosis."

"You mean your *prognosis*."

"Yes, that too."

~

Henrietta waited until Mister O'Connor and Doctor James had departed before she let her guard down.

"I've never heard such a load of tosh in all my life!" she raged.

The boys stared at her in confusion.

"There's something seriously wrong," she continued.

"With Miss O'Connor?" Claus demanded.

"No. No, she'll be fine. Physically."

"What do you mean, *physically*?" asked Claus, aghast. "Has she sustained some sort of lasting mental impairment?"

Henrietta glanced towards the stairs and put her finger to her lips to indicate they should lower their voices, then ushered them into the office and closed the door.

"Miss O'Connor is in full control of her mental faculties," she assured Claus. "*Doctor* James on the other hand…"

"What are you saying?" frowned Henry.

"I'm not convinced that he was even a real physician," Henrietta flopped down in one of the chairs, exhausted. "He reeked of alcohol."

"He'd probably been *drinking*. It is half past one in the morning, don't you know?" reasoned Henry. "Poor chap could be forgiven for enjoying a drink at the end of the day."

"He was unshaven," continued Henrietta.

"Maybe he's growing a beard for brumail," shrugged her twin.

"He was incompetent. I'm not convinced that he knew what a concussion *was,* let alone how to treat one. He didn't even know the difference between *diagnosis* and *prognosis*."

"So, what exactly are you implying?" asked Claus. "That Mister O'Connor is being duped by a fake physician?"

"I doubt that Mister O'Connor has ever been duped by *anyone*," she replied darkly.

"Then what? He deliberately employed the services of a fraudster?" Claus looked incredulous. "To what end? Why on Cellanor would anyone do that?"

"Any decent person wouldn't, but I suspect that your new friend isn't a decent person."

"What makes you say that?" bristled Claus. "We've no reason to doubt him. He came to my aid, didn't he? Who knows what might've happened if he hadn't intervened? He may well have saved my life. I owe him."

"Yes. I'm sure that suits him very well."

Claus shook his head and turned to leave the room.

"Claus…" Henrietta took a deep breath and tried to calm herself. "What do we actually know about this man? He suddenly showed up out of nowhere after Hans died, claiming to be an old friend. Miss O'Connor was adamant that she didn't want him anywhere near her-" she held her hand up in anticipation of interruption "-and before either of you dismiss her actions as the confused ramblings of an assault victim, she seems perfectly compos mentis in my opinion. She was terrified of him, and when I told him he couldn't see her, I can understand why."

Henry sat down in the chair next to his sister.

"What do mean?" he asked anxiously.

"There's something about him. Something…" Henrietta shook her head slightly, trying to find the right word. "*Predatory*."

"You felt afraid of him?"

"His very proximity made my blood run cold."

Claus was beginning to feel quite unwell. Seventeen years of experience had taught him to pay attention to Henrietta's 'female intuition'. Not to mention she'd always been an excellent judge of character in the past. She tended to notice the little things that other people did not.

Claus chewed on his lower lip.

"What do you suggest we do?"

"I haven't the vaguest notion," she rubbed at her forehead as though she were developing a headache. "I'll talk with Miss O'Connor once we've all had a sleep. I'm too tired to think about anything properly now. I'll get to the bottom of it though, eventually."

Claus didn't doubt it. It seemed that the journalistic blood flowed in all the Tempest's veins.

~

Breakfast was a strange affair that day. No one rose from their slumber until mid-afternoon. With nothing in the house to feed any of his guests, and Miss O'Connor's infirmity, Claus had little option but to venture forth to retrieve supplies. He struck upon the idea that he could visit a teashop, order enough food for four people and one monkey, and then take it home with him. With glee, he saw that Beverstone's was open for business again, although Missus Beverstone was nowhere to be seen. Ordering for himself and the twins was easy, as was feeding Dahljeeling, who didn't seem to mind what he ate, as long as it was washed down with a cup of tea, but what should he get for Miss O'Connor? What if she hated coconut? Or had an aversion to currants? Or deeply mistrusted marzipan? To solve this dilemma, Claus ended up buying one of everything. The young woman who worked in the teashop looked at him curiously as she packed all the cakes and pastries into a large box.

211

He struggled the short way back to The Emporium, only to be met by the twins, who were waiting impatiently at the door. The delicious smell that was emanating from the box was evidently too much for them, and they practically jumped upon him in their excitement. They briefly fought over who would carry the box upstairs, before realising that this would only prolong their starvation. Claus was reminded forcefully of a pair of dogs (pedigree, of course) and he grinned. Wisely, he kept this thought to himself.

"Are you going to lay a tray up for Miss O'Connor?" asked Henrietta, with her mouth full.

"I was hoping *you* would," admitted Claus. "I can't very well take it to her, can I? She's in bed!"

"Oh, I suppose you're right," Henrietta patted her lips with a napkin and began to fill plates with huge quantities of food.

"Blimey!" exclaimed Henry. "She's not going to eat all that!"

"No, this is for me."

Henrietta made her way upstairs and did her best to tap upon the bedroom door, which was no small accomplishment, given the weight of the tray she held.

"Good morning!" she smiled. "Well, afternoon I suppose."

Arabella looked up with puffy eyes and Henrietta noted that the swelling seemed less to do with her black eye and more to do with the fact that she'd obviously been crying. She set the tray down upon a chest of drawers and moved across to the window to open the drapes.

"I've stayed too long," said Arabella.

"Nonsense. I've brought you some breakfast, well, desert, by the looks of it. It's not very elegant I'm afraid, but it is tasty."

"Thank you. You're very kind."

Henrietta waved her hand in an airy manner.

212

"Claus went out and fetched it. There's no housekeeper or cook here. Can you credit it?"

"Claus."

"Yes, do you remember him? You were in a bit of a state last night, if you don't mind me saying?"

"No, no. I remember him," Arabella nodded.

"Well, quite," grinned Henrietta. "He's not usually as odd as that."

"He eats cake for breakfast, has a monkey butler and a preoccupation with his handkerchiefs," said Arabella. "No. Not at all odd."

Henrietta burst out laughing and Arabella smiled in spite of her circumstances. Henrietta's mirth seemed to be contagious.

The pair ate in companionable silence for a time and Henrietta observed that Miss O'Connor must be very hungry if the way she seemed to inhale her food was any indication. She decided to let the other girl eat her fill before she broached any subject that might upset her.

"So, Miss O'Connor..."

"Call me Arabella, please."

"Very well. Then you shall address me as Henrietta. Your accent isn't the same as your father's," Henrietta noticed the darkness creep back into Arabella's eyes at the mere mention of Patrick O'Connor. "Where do you come from?"

"A small village in Furthermoor. It's of no consequence to any but those who reside there."

"You miss it," stated Henrietta.

"Terribly. I miss my grandpapa too."

"Not your mother?"

"Yes, although she passed away a year ago."

"I'm sorry," frowned Henrietta.

"As am I," Arabella smiled sadly. "I miss the wide-open spaces of back home. You know, if I went to the top of the hill, I could watch the sunrise. Bitterend is so crowded. So many buildings and people. And this accursed ash and smoke which never seems to shift. You can barely see the sun in the sky, let alone watch it rise. I wonder how you can stand it."

"I've never known anything else. Father runs his business here. He's the owner of a local newspaper, *The Tempest's Eye*," Henrietta shuddered at the pun. "What does your father do?"

"He…gets by. My grandpapa is a holy man."

"Oh, you see now I'm imagining some quaint little thatched vicarage, surrounded by green pastures and poppy fields, and a well-meaning but ultimately annoying verger, who has very dubious taste in bonnets."

Arabella burst out laughing.

"Am I correct in my assumption?"

"Yes and no. The verger *was* annoying though."

"Bad bonnets?"

"Bad *everything*. Apparently, he once proposed marriage to my mother."

"Do you have a beau back home? I would have thought you'd have many a suitor."

"No," she said in a lifeless tone. "We move around too often for me to form any sort of friendships."

"Why?"

"There was a…spot of bother. A disagreement within the family. We left the village after my mother died. We travelled around a lot, trying to

214

find somewhere to call home."

Henrietta patted the other girl on the hand sympathetically. "Do you want to go and visit your father later? If you feel up to it? I'm sure he would like to see you."

"No!" Arabella touched her swollen eye. "No, I don't really feel well enough."

"Well, there's no rush. He knows you're in safe hands here, I'm sure." Henrietta tried to sound indifferent and changed the subject. "Will you go back to see them at some point? The rest of your family, I mean. Your grandpapa?"

"I shouldn't think so. I doubt that I would be welcome. In any case, he probably wouldn't recognise me now."

"It isn't my house you understand, and you'll have to put up with Dahljeeling sleeping in the bedside cabinet, but I'm sure I can speak on behalf of Claus, when I say that you're welcome to stay here as long as you need to," Henrietta smiled. "Lord knows someone should speak for Claus. What do you intend to do about your clothes and personal items? I could send someone round to collect a few things from your lodgings, if you'd like. Maybe get your father to-"

"No!" Arabella hesitated and took a deep breath. "No, it's fine. I don't really have much in the way of personal items."

"Well, you'll need some clothes at the very least," Henrietta suddenly beamed. "We'll have to go shopping!"

Arabella looked embarrassed. "I don't really have much money."

"Oh, pish posh! Let me worry about that."

"I really couldn't."

"You really must. Honestly, it would be my pleasure," Henrietta stood up and pulled Arabella to her feet. She turned her around on the spot and looked her over with an appraising eye. "Hm. You can borrow some of my clothes in the meantime. We're of a similar height and I can always nip in a few seams to make some of my dresses smaller. As for personal items, I have far too many. You'd be doing me a favour if you took some, and I won't take no for an answer."

~

Henrietta imparted the information she'd extracted from Arabella to the boys as she made ready to return home to collect some clothes and various other items that a young lady shouldn't go without.

"You are coming back, aren't you?" asked Claus with an imploring tone.

"Yes, of course. But Claus, you're going to have to speak to her at some point. And not about handkerchiefs. She thinks you've got some sort of problem."

Henry let out a hoot of laughter.

"And you really ought to do something about your hair. And about employing a housekeeper. Arabella can't very well stay here without another female in the house. It's unseemly."

"What's wrong with my hair?" Claus asked sullenly.

"Nothing a good brush wouldn't sort out."

"And who said anything about Miss O'Connor *staying* here?" he frowned while doing his best to smooth his hair with his hand.

"Oh, you'd send her back to her creepy father, who she's clearly terrified of?" Henrietta raised her eyebrows.

"Well, no. Of course not."

Henry snapped his fingers as a thought occurred to him.

"Father is always harping on about how we have too many staff. Do you think Hattie would accept a position here? She doesn't get on with mother's lady's maid and she did admit that she found our household a little dull after working for vampires, or whatever they were."

"If she can cope with vampires, then I see no reason that she would turn her nose up at a time traveling watch maker and his monkey butler," reasoned Henrietta.

Claus stood mutely between the twins as they arranged his life for him. He did feel a bit put out being compared to a vampire. Surely he wasn't as peculiar as all that?

"We'll talk to her when we get home," nodded Henry.

"What?" spluttered Claus. "You're leaving too?"

"A chap's got to change his clothes and freshen up! We won't be long."

~

Claus watched from the window with a morose expression as his friends climbed inside a hackney carriage. He was stood in the office and had a sudden and overwhelming desire to descend to his workshop and fix the wheel on one of Agatha's clockwork mice. He made himself a cup of tea (all the while knowing that he should go upstairs and offer one to his guest) and got to work.

It felt good to be back in the workshop. It was his domain. His lair. His sanctuary, blessedly devoid of bossy friends and mysterious young ladies who seemed to have some occult power that turned him into a babbling idiot. There was order here. There were cogs and wheels, there were springs and sprockets. There was the unmistakable sound of the transporter in use.

"Forgive me, I didn't realise anyone was down here," said Arabella.

She pulled the metal bars aside and disembarked.

"Mha," answered Claus. He hastily removed his goggles, painfully aware that they made him look like a giant insect.

"Oh, don't let me interrupt you! I was merely being curious. This contraption is amazing! What is it called?"

"Er, it doesn't really have a name. Not a patented one at least. We just refer to it as the transporter," Claus mentally checked the words that had just come out of his mouth. No babbling, no strange syllables which weren't really words and not one mention of handkerchiefs. "My mother wanted a safer way to transport the clocks up to the showroom. It's like what they use in the mine shafts. Handy when we have a delivery of wood too."

"I can imagine. It's marvellous. Are you making a watch? Please don't let me disrupt your work."

"Oh. Well. It's not really work. I'm just playing if truth be told," he tried to conceal the mouse as Arabella drew closer. Was it considered odd for a grown man to play with brass mice?

"May I see?"

"Er, yes. It's for my cat, actually," he hastened to explain. "She's terribly good at catching rats. So good in fact, that she's run out of things to chase and so I made her some clockwork mice to play with." Why could he talk like an actual *human being* when he was tinkering down in his dingy basement? He felt scared to say too much, in case this was just some momentary lapse of lunacy.

Arabella peered at the mouse.

"This is beautiful. Have you ever considered selling clockwork toys?"

Claus stared at her for a moment. "Yes. Yes, I have. My grandfather thought it rather foolish."

"Hmm," she frowned and leaned over his shoulder to get a better look at what he was doing. Her hair smelt like lemons. "Oh, I see, the wheel is damaged. But shouldn't you use a Point Three spindle to reattach it?

218

Then it might not wobble about so much."

"Hmah," replied Claus.

13th Brevis

Arabella heard the clocks in the shop below chime One o'clock. She blew out the candle and snuggled further beneath the eiderdown. She tried not to remember what Henry had disclosed that evening: that Hans Vogel had taken his last breath in the very same bed. For the first time in what seemed an age, she felt safe and secure. Dinner had been quite a jolly affair, mercifully devoid of anything sweet. The Tempest twins had returned with hot food from their own kitchen, along with an array of clothing items which Arabella secretly considered too fine for her to wear. Henrietta's idea of a 'walking dress' was a far cry from Arabella's own. She hadn't mentioned this of course, not wishing to seem ungrateful or risk hurting her new friend's feelings.

Her thoughts turned to Claus, who slept in the room next to hers. Perhaps he wasn't asleep yet. Maybe he was lying in bed, staring at his ceiling, consumed by his own thoughts just as she was. He seemed as though he thought a great deal about things. His countenance took on a certain aspect at times, as though physically he was in the room, but his mind was elsewhere. He was nothing like what she had imagined when Niall had first mentioned the existence of a cousin. What had she imagined? She wasn't entirely sure. A young boy perhaps? Someone who looked like Niall. Someone who *acted* like Niall. They were related after all. A spoilt fop with a large inheritance, maybe. What she *hadn't* imagined was a kind, softly spoken, strapping young gentleman with snowy blonde hair and the keen light of a sharp intellect burning behind his green eyes.

He was a little odd, to be fair, but most creative people were, and she found it endearing rather than disturbing. He seemed a bit more at his ease this evening in any case. The group had discussed the recent monkey attacks and debated upon where the creatures might be hiding to evade capture. Claus spoke eloquently about his business and inventions and once Arabella had admitted her ardent interest in clockwork and mechanisms, he'd become positively talkative, with barely a stutter. Arabella allowed herself a clandestine smile.

A sharp tapping sound from the other end of the room interrupted her pleasant, if somewhat guilty, train of thoughts. She peered over the edge of the blankets but could see nothing in the darkness. The sound was repeated, and she scrabbled for a match to light her candle. Blessed light filled the room and momentarily blinded her. She blinked to let her eyes adjust to the sudden illumination before squinting around the room. Was it the ghost of Hans Vogel, angry that she was in his bed? Perhaps he had come to chase her out of the house. Spirits knew everything after all. He would know that she was an imposter. A liar.

If Hans Vogel was haunting her, she couldn't see him.

She opened the bedside cabinet door and peered inside to see if Dahljeeling was fidgeting, but the little monkey was sleeping peacefully.

Another tapping sound made her turn her head in the direction of the window. She slipped from the bed and shivered in her borrowed nightgown, which was rather less substantial and far prettier than the nightwear she was used to. Wrapping her arms around herself, she tiptoed to the window and twitched the fabric of the curtain aside, just as another stone hit the glass. She let out a small shriek and ducked instinctively below the level of the windowsill. After taking a couple of deep breaths, she collected herself and stood up. She peered through the glass and saw Niall standing on the cobbles below. For a moment Arabella feared that her dinner was about to make a reappearance. He beckoned to her to come downstairs and she shook her head. He repeated his gesture impatiently and fearing whatever action he might resort to in the face of such disobedience, she hoisted the window open.

Freezing air rushed into the room.

"Any luck?" he whispered.

"None at all."

"You should look in his bedroom, when he's asleep. What in the creator's name are you wearing?"

Arabella self-consciously wrapped her arms more tightly around herself.

"My friend lent it to me."

"I don't like it. It makes you look like a slattern."

"I don't care what you like. Leave me alone."

"What's the matter with you girl?" Niall asked in an offhand manner.

"The *matter*? You walloped me!" she hissed, suddenly quite emboldened in her anger.

"Not really. I told you, it was part of the plan," he said reasonably, as if they were discussing the weather.

Arabella's mouth fell open, but such was her appalled astonishment, she couldn't summon any words.

"Leave me alone," she choked. "Go away and never return."

Niall looked as if he were about to speak, but Arabella pulled the window shut with a smart thump and almost ripped the curtain in her ferocity as she pulled it closed.

~

It was Jack's first day on the job. On any job, come to that. Technically, it couldn't be considered 'day' as it was getting on for midnight. This was the sort of work that needed round the clock attention.

Jack had been offered the chance to join the elite. To become a hero.

To earn some real cash for a change, not to mention the respect and veneration of those around him.

He had been offered this opportunity whilst in the tavern and it had seemed like a really good idea at the time to accept. Now that the effect of the ale had worn off, Jack was starting to realise that sobriety and hindsight were the co-conspirators of regret. He had heard tell of these 'recruitment' agents, who went around conscripting young men to work in the mines, but he'd never dreamed that he would be stupid enough to except their damn coin.

He'd been down on his luck. He'd been skint. He'd been drunk. Now he was an arconian miner and he had to work for a year because he'd taken the money. Everyone said that if you could get through the first year, it didn't seem so bad after all. Jack suspected this might be because by the time you'd spent a year below surface, breathing in arconian dust, you were dancing to your own tune that only you could hear.

Jack had grown up in Northwall. In the cold Brumail months, he had slept upon the ground to keep warm, so he'd understood that the mines below the city would be hot. What he'd failed to understand was that the heat of the mines was incomprehensible. The heat was immense. It was searing. It snatched at your lungs when you tried to breathe. Sweat beaded upon his brow and trickled into his eyes, causing his vision to blur. His thin linen shirt stuck to him like a second skin and he didn't even want to contemplate his dwindling chances of fatherhood. Many of the older miners worked naked but Jack really didn't feel that this was for him. He noticed a lot of scar tissue on the men. Old burns from working with the volatile substance. He also noticed a lot of vacant expressions. He couldn't believe the rumours that some people lived in the older, unused parts of the mines. It was unthinkable.

Jack put the rubber pipe into his mouth and sucked down a couple of lungfuls of oxygen. The pipe was attached to a bellows-like contraption that was strapped to his back.

"Easy there, son," said Donnal. "You'll be out of air by breakfast time at that rate."

Donnal was an older miner who had been paired up with Jack. Miners always had designated 'buddies' that they would work with. It was the sort of job that required you get to know, and preferably trust, the man at your side, just in case you ran into difficulties. Or caught fire. Or went stark raving mad.

"Why don't *you* have a bellows?" asked Jack. He looked around and noticed very few of the miners carried the breathing apparatus.

"Too heavy. Too hot. Anyway, I'm used to the arconian now. And if it gets too dusty, well, I've always got my kerchief here." Donnal indicated the piece of cloth which dangled limply around his neck like a scarf.

Jack followed his buddy through the labyrinthine corridors of rock, hewn by the labours of men long dead. They'd walked for what felt like miles and descended even further. He stared at the map he'd been equipped with but at this point it would be more useful to mop the sweat from his brow than to pinpoint his location. He imagined being lost down here and shuddered. He prayed to Dantalis that he wouldn't have to go much further below ground, half convinced that he would bump into Arcon himself at this rate.

There was not much call for lamps in the active parts of the mine, for fear of starting any new fires. In any case, arconian glowed from within, an angry orange-red luminosity that was adequate to see by. Every so often, Jack and Donnal would pass by the mouth of what was termed a 'Dark Tunnel'. This was not just a description of the lighting conditions. Dark Tunnels were the ones that had been abandoned, either due to the fact that all the arconian had been mined from them, or that the tunnel was particularly troublesome and had claimed too many lives to warrant anyone working in them.

Jack peered cautiously at the Dark Tunnels as he walked past. There were so many tales about the mines which he'd heard as a young boy. The ghosts and hauntings, the curses, the so called 'Lost One's' who were the people that had nowhere else to go and lived in the abandoned mines and became mad, subterranean hermits.

Something moved in the darkness.

Jack blinked and tried to rub the sweat from his eyes. He stared into the mouth of the Dark Tunnel.

He could make out many silhouettes of...*things* travelling at speed past the tunnel's opening. He came to a halt to watch in horrified fascination.

Jack realised that his buddy hadn't noticed that he'd stopped, and he ran forward to catch up with him.

"Donnal! You won't believe what I just saw! A horde of little brown monkeys, all wearing matching red jackets! They're in that Dark Tunnel, back there!"

Donnal smiled.

"That's nothing. When I first started working here, I saw a troupe of dwarfs, all dressed up in studded leather harnesses. One was playing the maracas and one had a squeezebox."

"I don't think it was an arconian dust dream. This was really real!" protested Jack.

Donnal patted his buddy on his shoulder.

"Don't you worry lad. You'll get used to it. Best to have a suck on your air pipe if you're feeling anxious."

"Good day, Hattie," smiled Henrietta as she walked through the door into The Time Emporium. "How're you settling in?"

The Tempest's maid had jumped at the chance to become housekeeper for Claus. Not only did she receive a substantial pay rise with the promotion, but her living arrangements had also improved dramatically. She had her own bedroom and sitting room on the fourth floor.

"Just fine, Miss, but between you and I, this place needs a lot of work. You can tell that bachelors have been living here."

"Is it too much for you?"

"Not at all, Miss. You know how I like to keep busy. Anyway, I have Mister Dahljeeling to help me."

The newly instated housekeeper was very impressed with Dahljeeling and not at all discomforted by the fact that he was a primate. If anything, it merely increased the esteem in which she regarded him. She insisted upon referring to him as *Mister* Dahljeeling, as though he were head butler in some grand household.

"Has Claus got you minding the shop?" asked Henry. "Has he gone out?"

"I'm just keeping an eye on things while Mister Vogel is in his workshop. He and the young Miss seem quite absorbed."

Henrietta noted that the housekeeper diplomatically neglected to expand upon what the pair were absorbed in.

"Tinkering again are they?" asked Henry, with a somewhat petulant tone to his voice. He wasn't used to sharing his best friend. "They're always tinkering. I came to visit yesterday, and Claus sent me away! He

226

said he was too busy!"

Henrietta exchanged a glance with Hattie and had to hide her smile from her brother.

"Well, we'll have to drag them out today. Claus has his final fitting at Mister Abano's," she said, as she made her way into the office.

The twins entered the transporter and Henry began to wind the handle. Henrietta silently praised the Creators that the contraption made such a racket when in use. The last thing she wanted to do was sneak up unannounced on the pair in the workshop.

In hindsight, Henrietta thought that a brass fanfare might have also been necessary, as neither Claus nor Arabella seemed remotely aware that they had company. They were sat with their heads together at the workbench, pouring over some new design that Claus had come up with. Henrietta was intrigued at how they managed to get any work done when they sat so close to one another. There certainly wasn't any elbow room. She cleared her throat pointedly and the pair looked up. Claus sprang up out of his seat.

"Hallo you two!" he almost sang the greeting at them.

Henry raised his eyebrows and Henrietta giggled.

"Sorry to interrupt, but you have an appointment with the tailor, Claus."

"Oh! I'd forgotten all about that."

"Yes, I suspected that you might have."

Claus merely nodded and grinned like a mad scientist. The goggles did nothing to dispel this comparison. Arabella stood up on her tiptoes and gently pulled the eye apparatus from his face, which only meant that his attention was once again fully focused on her. She carefully smoothed his hair out of the way of the rubber head band and smiled at him indulgently.

227

"I think I'm going to be sick," muttered Henry. "Can't we just leave them here and fetch the damn clothes ourselves?" he whispered.

Henrietta trod on his foot.

"Arabella, I found a dress you could wear for dinner tomorrow evening. I took the liberty of nipping it in a bit. I think it will suit you very well."

"Oh, Henrietta. You've already done too much!" Arabella shook her head disapprovingly. "I was going to wear one of the other dresses you gave me. They're all so beautiful."

"But they're *day* dresses!" exclaimed Henrietta in horror. "I won't hear of it."

Todorovich had happily extended his invitation to include Arabella.

"Shall we go then?" asked Henry impatiently. "I'm sure Hattie is more than equal to the task of minding the shop for an hour."

"She's a gift from Dantalis," nodded Claus. "I don't know how I ever coped without her. She made us a three-course dinner last night. I don't know how, as we don't even have a proper kitchen!" Claus and Arabella began to giggle as if this was terribly amusing.

"Oh my," sighed Henry. "Let's get this over with."

~

A final fitting at Abano's was always a jovial affair, especially for Mister Abano, when a customer spent as much as Claus had. The tailor made sure that the wine kept flowing and so the group was rather squiffy by the time they left the premises. Claus and Arabella linked arms and tottered in the direction of home with the twins bringing up the rear.

Suddenly their progress came to a halt as Arabella stopped walking. Henrietta almost barged into the back of her and reached out to steady herself. She clasped onto her friend's shoulders and realised that she had gone ridged.

"Arabella?" Claus looked at her in confusion. She'd turned deathly pale and her eyes were wide. He followed her gaze.

"Arabella, what's the matter?" asked Henrietta. "Are you unwell?"

"Was that Patrick?" asked Claus. He couldn't be sure of the man's identity, but he was certain that there *had* been a man watching them from a distance. Arabella went limp and Claus was forced to hold her up by the arm which was linked through his.

"I'll hail a cab," said Henry

~

By the time they had travelled the short distance back to The Emporium, Arabella was steadier, but still very pale. She allowed Claus to carry her upstairs to the parlour as she didn't quite trust her legs to support her weight.

"Do you think it's the head injury?" whispered Henry to his sister. They were stood around her as she sat on the sofa, unsure of what to do for the best. "You said that the physician was incompetent."

"She's a lot hardier than she looks," Henrietta whispered back. "Look how quickly her bruise healed."

"It was Patrick," stated Claus, not bothering to keep his voice low and Arabella jumped. "He was following you. I'm right, aren't I? What has gone on between the pair of you? Why are you so terrified of your own father?"

Arabella stared up at him.

"Patrick O'Connor is dead. The man you've met is actually called Niall McGrath."

"Why should he lie about his name? And why would he follow you

229

around?"

"He's not following me," she wailed. "He's following *you*."

Claus was nonplussed. He sat down on the sofa next to her.

"And why is he so interested in Claus?" ventured Henrietta. She followed Claus's example and lowered herself into the armchair. Henry felt rather silly standing around like a spare part, so he perched upon the footstool.

"He's Claus's cousin," Arabella whispered.

It was Claus's turn to go pale.

"Cousin? How? All of my family are gone!"

"No." Arabella shook her head. "He's your half second cousin."

"I knew it!" cried Henrietta in triumph. "I knew there was more to all this."

"I didn't," said Henry in bafflement. "Your father is actually Claus's *half second cousin*, using some dead chap's name? Is anyone else confused?"

Arabella didn't answer. She hadn't taken her eyes from Claus. He returned her gaze as if frozen in time.

"He lied. You both lied to me," his voice was barely audible. "Why didn't I know about him? Why didn't Hans tell me I had other relatives?"

"I don't know."

"Oh!" Claus turned ashen. "Then that means that you and I are related!"

"No. He's my stepfather."

"Hang on, one thing at a time! Can we go back to the part where he's Claus's cousin?" protested Henry.

"Arabella," said Henrietta as she leaned forward. "Just tell us everything from the beginning."

"I may need a drink," she smiled weakly. "Is there any gin?"

"If there is, I think I'll join you. Boys?"

Claus and Henry nodded, and Henrietta got up to peruse the top of the sideboard. She located the brandy and a bottle of gin and returned, pouring each of them a glass of their preferred beverage.

Arabella drank hers in one swallow.

"Leave the bottle."

Henrietta shrugged and handed the other girl the gin.

"I didn't *mean* lie to you," said Arabella earnestly. "I was put in a…position against my will and I just didn't know how to tell you the truth. I'm afraid you will cast me out when I tell you."

Henry raised his eyebrows and nodded as if this was a reasonable assumption, to which his sister cast him an icy glare.

"Go on," she encouraged.

"It was true, what I told you about my home. I was born in a small hamlet in Furthermoor. My real father died when I was quite young, but not young enough that I didn't mourn his passing. Something…happened to me. I'm not sure if it was caused by shock, or grief, but I started to experience strange things."

"What sort of strange things?" asked Claus, ashamed to ask such an indelicate question, but curiosity had the better of him.

"I could sense things that I couldn't before. I knew when it was going to rain. I knew when animals were unwell and what was ailing them. I could feel other people's emotions. And I could talk to the dead. I could see the spirit of my father."

Henrietta leaned forward in her seat. "You mean…"

231

"I'm a witch." Arabella nodded. "I didn't realise though, until I confided these peculiar happenings to my mother. She had suspected as much. She was a witch too, you see. She began to teach me, in secret. Witchcraft had been outlawed in the village.

The years passed by and we became accustomed to our quiet little life, just mother and I, but we were terribly poor without father's income. Grandpapa suggested that we come and live with him, which we did, although we had to be very careful about my witchcraft lessons.

Mother was very beautiful and attracted a great deal of attention from prospective suitors, one of which was the verger." Arabella gave Henrietta a significant look at this point. Henrietta nodded in recollection.

"Mother wanted nothing to do with him. Regardless of the man's general lack of appeal, she had already met Niall McGrath, or Patrick O'Connor, as you know him. He was travelling through the village and my grandpapa thought it only decent to let him stay in one of the barns, even though the rest of the villagers had a deep mistrust of the nomadic folk. Niall repaid my grandpapa by doing odd jobs. We had some livestock. A few sheep and a couple of horses that he would tend to. Anyway, he and mama fell in love." Arabella refilled her glass and drank from it as quickly as she had the first time. "They married in secret, as everyone was opposed to the match, although no one was quite as opposed to it as the verger. He seemed obsessed with mama, he would follow her around all the time and watch her and bother her. In the end mama and Niall decided they would leave.

The spying verger got wind of their plans. He must have been watching us all the time, as he knew my mother had been practising witchcraft. He informed the beadle, who searched our rooms and found enough evidence to convict her to the gallows."

Henrietta gasped and turned pale.

"Gallows?" exclaimed Claus. "What sort of people hang witches?"

"The people of Crookford," Arabella shrugged. "Mama made Niall promise to take care of me. The villagers were already suspicious of me and it would have only been a matter of time before I felt the noose around my neck. It was impossible to stay in the village. Especially after Niall had paid a visit to the verger,"

"When you say, 'paid a visit'..." Henry raised an eyebrow, "I'm assuming you don't mean he popped round for a cuppa and a slice of cake?"

Claus and Henrietta stared at Henry with matching looks of incredulity.

Arabella made a noise somewhere between a snort and a laugh.

"No."

"Oh, hold on!" blustered Henry. "Are you saying we've been fraternising with a murderer?"

"Shh," snapped Claus and Henrietta as one.

"We fled Crookford," continued Arabella, "travelled around the countryside for a while. I fancied myself some wild, free creature, roaming where I pleased. When brumail came it wasn't always so pleasant. We ended up in Bightport Town. I thought it immense and feared I would get lost. Silly really, when I now compare it to Bitterend! We stayed there for almost a year and I grew accustomed to it. I liked to be close to the sea. Niall seemed to make enough money to keep us in relative comfort, I didn't really question him about his business, although I suspected that he gambled. I didn't know for certain until one night, when I was so bored and lonely, I went to find him. One of the men he'd been playing cards with took a shine to me and said something that Niall didn't approve of. Niall hit him so hard, that he fell senseless to the ground. I always assumed he had a vicious streak, after what had happened with the verger, but I suppose I was glad he'd killed him, in a way. It seemed like justice for my mother, however ashamed that makes me feel to admit."

233

"I think most people would want some sort of revenge," said Claus. "I lost my own mother when I was young. She fell down the stairs, but if someone had killed her, I think I would feel the same as you."

Arabella smiled slightly, grateful that Claus didn't think her a monster.

"Niall searched the unconscious card player. He went through his pockets where he lay. Robbed him of everything he'd won at the card table. Anyway, my stepfather thought that this was an excellent way of making money and brought me along to every card game from then on, to 'distract' the winner."

Henrietta put her hand over her mouth, appalled. Claus sprang up from the sofa in agitation.

"He forced you to-"

"No," interrupted Arabella, keen to dismiss his fears. "I didn't have to touch them. Merely *look* as though I wanted to."

"That's disgusting," spat Claus.

"I used to get quite drunk before I had to play my part," Arabella nodded.

"Why on Cellanor did you stay with him?" asked Henrietta.

"I had nowhere else to go. I had no one else to turn to. Better off with a man who would protect me than on my own."

"Only just," frowned Henrietta.

"Anyway, just last month he suddenly turned to me one evening and announced that we were leaving for Bitterend the very next day. He wouldn't tell me why. Ever since that night, he's been agitated and on edge. We hadn't been in Bitterend long, but I think he actually murdered a man right in front of me, it was dark, and I'd been at the bottle, but..." Arabella shuddered slightly at the memory. "Eventually he told me he had a cousin, here in Bitterend, but only because he wanted my help. He said that there was a family fortune that was rightfully his. He seemed obsessed with getting his hands on some pocket watch. He said it was a family heirloom and that it would change our fortunes forever. I think he might be quite unhinged."

Claus, Henry and Henrietta exchanged a dark look.

"He told me that we needed to gain your trust. He hired some men to come after you, Claus. Just so that he could intervene and win your friendship. Then he hit me in the face and brought me to you. He wanted me to search the house for this stupid watch while I convalesced here. I've had nothing to do with him since, but I see him watching," she shuddered.

Claus glanced at Henrietta. She might have looked smug in any other situation. Her intuition had been correct, but she looked far from pleased at the revelation.

"McGrath," mused Henry. The others stared at him. "Oh, come on! Brenna McGrath the Irkish witch. Niall McGrath the Irkish..." He sought for the right word. "Bastard. There must be a connection. *She* knows about the watch. *He* knows about the watch."

"So, there *is* a watch?" frowned Arabella. "What's so special about the damned thing? Can it make a cup of tea? Do a dance?"

"Ah," said Claus. "You might want to pour yourself another gin."

~

It was late by the time the twins decided to call it a night.

"What do you think will happen?" asked Henry, as they stood outside to wave down a passing cab. They turned and gazed up at The Time Emporium. The only soft illumination in the otherwise dark building came from Claus's bedroom.

"I don't think I need to paint you a picture," smirked Henrietta.

"No! I mean... Patrick-Niall, whatever his name is. He's going to be

235

trouble."

"Yes, Henry," sighed Henrietta. "I fear you're right."

18th Brevis

Claus's new wardrobe, or at least a portion of it, was delivered directly to his door that afternoon by Mister Abano's errand boy. It was not a moment too soon, as Claus, Arabella and Dahljeeling were due to attend dinner and a show that evening, at The Edenia Theatre with the twins, courtesy of Todorovich.

Claus selected himself an ensemble fit for evening wear, while whistling a merry tune and turned to gaze into the looking glass. He felt a little silly and overdressed, but at least he didn't look like a shop boy. On previous occasions, when the need for formal attire had arisen, Claus had borrowed clothes from Henry, but that was no longer an option. Claus had always been quite small and skinny for his age, but over the past year he'd suddenly shot up, as if his body was making up for lost time. He now stood three inches taller than his friend and he was also a good deal broader across the shoulders, due to manual activity. Not to mention (and Claus was always very careful *not* to) Henry was used to being waited upon and fed four meals a day. In consequence he carried rather more weight than Claus, who would probably look quite comical if he were to borrow any of Henry's clothes these days.

The reflection of Arabella appeared in the looking glass behind him. She had borrowed one of Henrietta's evening gowns and she looked anything but comical wearing it. Claus's breath got stuck in his throat as he tried to speak.

"Do I look passable?" she asked anxiously.

Claus turned to face her. He didn't trust himself to speak, so he nodded emphatically instead.

The multitude of clocks in the showroom struck Seven. Arabella pulled a fur lined cloak around her shoulders and they descended to the shop.

Claus had never actually been inside a theatre before. Apparently the play they were going to see was some new version of Rattlepole's *Avanti*. Henry had been able to convince the manager of the theatre to permit Dahljeeling entrance, with a promise that both the play and the food would get a glowing review in The Tempest's Eye.

Claus and Dahljeeling loitered on the street outside and shivered until Claus spotted a hackney and signalled for the driver to pull up. He waved a hand at Arabella through the shop window, where he'd insisted that she stay in the warm. He'd neglected to add that he didn't want her waiting around on the street in case her stepfather was lurking in the darkness. She joined them outside and Claus locked up behind them. He'd told Hattie that she must not answer the door on any account, no matter who the visitor proclaimed to be.

Claus pulled his new greatcoat tightly around himself. Dahljeeling also had his own greatcoat, an exact replica of Claus's own, only in miniature. Henrietta's idea no doubt. He had to admit that Dahljeeling looked rather dapper in his new clothes and they certainly helped him to stand out from his demonic doppelgangers.

They walked arm in arm carefully over the cobbles, which were now glazed with a treacherous layer of soot blackened ice. Dahljeeling didn't seem to have the same problem with balance as his human companions, but he was not enjoying being outside, even though he had been cooped up for days. Claus was loath to let him out, for fear his doppelgangers might reappear and attack, but the agoraphobic monkey was more than happy to stay inside.

Claus took another quick glance around to check that there was no sign of Niall McGrath or the marauding monkeys, feeling a bit like a paranoid, yet woefully inexperienced bodyguard, and handed Arabella into the carriage.

The sky was clear, and the air was so cold that it almost hurt to take a breath. Despite their warm clothing, both monkey and humans shivered all the way to Threefold Square.

They met the others who were shivering outside the theatre.

"Dahljeeling?" gasped Todorovich. "What's he doing here?"

Henrietta made hushing sounds and the group entered The Edenia with all haste. The theatre was warm and full of bright lights and colours and Claus immediately felt himself begin to thaw. Now that they were out of the biting cold, Claus exchanged a more cordial greeting with Todorovich and introduced Arabella.

"And you've already met Dahljeeling," said Claus.

Todorovich nodded with a look of intrigue and motioned that Claus and his friends should follow him to the restaurant. It was terribly comfortable, with interesting works of art adorning the walls.

Henrietta tugged at Claus's arm, pulling him slightly away from the rest of the group.

"Did you go to visit Madam Nimueh?" she asked in a low voice.

Claus shook his head.

"Arabella was exhausted after yesterday's revelations. We're going tomorrow."

"I don't know how you can stand the suspense. Aren't you interested in finding out about this supposed estranged cousin of yours?"

"Exceedingly, but I dare say waiting another night won't change his diabolical plans."

"I must say, you're taking all of this very calmly."

"Am I?" Claus chuckled mirthlessly.

Henrietta frowned in concern, and the pair re-joined their party who were being shown to their table.

As soon as they were seated Todorovich began to thank them all for their help with disposing of The Amplificator. Claus felt a little less grumpy about the injuries he had sustained when faced with such earnest gratitude. The wine helped too.

"And now, you must tell me how you came by William's monkey," Todorovich lowered his voice.

"It was the evening that we disabled your machine," said Claus.

Todorovich looked apprehensively towards Arabella.

"We can speak freely in front of Arabella, do not fear," Claus reassured the scientist. "I saw Dahljeeling while I was at Cordage's. It seems that he followed me home but-" Claus frowned, "He was pursued by his doppelgangers, who appeared intent upon doing him harm, though we cannot work out why. He's living with me now. For the time being at least," he added, not willing to convey how attached he had become to his fury friend.

"Why would his duplicates want to harm him?" frowned Henry, directing his question at Todorovich.

"I've no idea, although The Amplificator was never designed to augment a living subject. Even inanimate objects proved difficult to enhance to a satisfactory standard."

"They're certainly proving difficult to round up," said Henry

Conversation turned to the subject of food and they each began to peruse the menu. Claus became dimly aware of raised voices from the foyer before the restaurant door burst open and a horde of red coated monkeys poured in.

The primates screamed along with most of the diners. They charged around the restaurant and jumped up upon the tables, sending half eaten plates of food crashing to the floor. They picked up bottles and wine glasses and threw them across the room, they swung from the chandeliers and ripped paintings from the walls.

"Dahljeeling!" gasped Henrietta, looking desperately at Claus, who managed to break free of his shocked paralysis. He gathered the terrified monkey up and held him tight against his chest under the cover of his dinner jacket.

"We have to get out of here!" cried Henry above the din. Everyone else seemed to have the same idea and a veritable stampede towards the exit ensued. The hitherto elegant diners had turned into a panic-stricken mob, all thoughts of decorum and manners set aside. People were pulling and pushing each other out of the way. Sharp elbows were jabbed into ribs. Clothing was torn. They congregated en-mass at the doorway and the more souls who endeavoured to exit, the fewer got out through the door. Claus tried to keep track of his friends, but they were quickly lost in the throng. He could just about hear Henry over everyone else's screams and shouts.

"Claus, run!"

Claus employed his full strength upon forcing people out of the way. The doorway was like a bottleneck and when he finally squeezed his way through the aperture, he shot out onto the street like a sparkling wine cork, stumbling partially from his own momentum as well as from the force of those around and behind him.

Pedestrians going about their own business in Threefold Square stopped and stared at the great outpouring of screaming people emerging from the doors of The Edenia. Claus quickly picked himself up off the cobbles, afraid that he would be trampled to death and looked desperately around for his friends. Had the maniacal monkeys turned up in pursuit of Dahljeeling, or was it mere coincidence? Henry had told Claus to run, and as much as he would have liked to, he couldn't leave without the others. He knew the monkeys might come crashing through the doors at any moment, but he remained rooted to the spot, holding his breath as he searched the faces of the screaming crowd. Then he caught sight of Arabella and managed to breathe again. She was closely followed by Henry and Todorovich. Henry was carrying something. His

241

face was deathly white. Claus stared at the bundle in his arms. Todorovich was running towards him and shouting something indiscernible.

"A cab! Damn it! Get a cab!" Todorovich didn't wait for Claus to respond but ran out into the road with a red face and flailing arms.

Henry stumbled closer and Claus heard his own heart thudding even louder than the cries of the people around him. Henrietta hung limply in her twins embrace. Her blood looked too red as it flowed over the whiteness of her face.

"I tried to keep hold of her hand, but I couldn't," Henry spoke as if he didn't understand his own words, as if he were contemplating a particularly difficult mathematical problem. "She tripped and fell to the floor and no one stopped. They just ran over her." He stared at Claus with unblinking eyes. "I tried to keep hold of her hand," he repeated, as if he needed Claus to understand that.

"Here!" shouted Todorovich from behind them. A carriage had drawn up and it seemed that the scientist was having to fight other people for its hire. Claus helped support Henrietta's weight and the pair laid her across one of the seats in the cab. Henry got in beside her and cradled her head in his lap. The blood was starting to coagulate in her hair, the colour blending in with her dark tresses. Claus felt absurdly upset about that. Henrietta was very particular about her hair. She wouldn't want it messed up like that.

"Is she breathing?" asked Todorovich.

Henry nodded.

"Do you have a family physician?"

Again, Henry nodded.

"Brandish Way! And hurry!" Todorovich yelled at the cabbie.

~

There was a cream and blue striped velvet sofa in the hallway. It faced a wall upon which hung a painting by Hamish Sergeant. It depicted a lonely windmill and a sullen, stormy grey sky. There was something rather depressing and forlorn about it. A remoteness. An expectancy of an imminent deluge. At one end of the hallway was a window. It was tall and narrow, and the glass was divided up into little diamond shapes, the ones closest to the frame had coloured glass with pictures of bluebells. There were fifty-seven of them in total.

Claus knew there were fifty-seven of them, just as he knew that there were one hundred and fifteen tassels at each end of the carpet by his feet. He knew this because he had just counted them. Twice.

He was sat on the sofa between Dahljeeling and Arabella, who was holding his hand. Every now and again Henry would emerge from his sister's bedroom to give them an update on her condition which had, as yet remained the same.

The physician had arrived with alacrity, horses snorting with exertion, steam rising from their flanks. He had not yet left Henrietta's room. The remaining Tempest's had each dealt with the situation in his or her own way, leaving Claus and Arabella alone and feeling as if they were intruding on the family's grief. Henry would leave his twin's side only to make brief reports upon her health in a muted, dead tone which matched the glazed look in his eyes, before he hurried back into the room. Whenever the door opened, Claus could hear Missus Tempest quietly sobbing from her daughter's bedside. Mister Tempest could be heard stamping around the house. He would ascend the stairs, stand for a moment beside the door, pace back and forth across the landing and then go back down the stairs. Claus knew him to be a decent sort of man, who loved his family dearly, but he was accustomed to getting things done by either throwing large amounts of money around or by shouting very loudly. As neither of these things could fix his daughter, he was at a loss. Claus had just begun to count the stripes on the sofa when he became aware of a glass of whiskey being held beneath his nose. He looked up to meet Mister Tempest's gaze. He took the glass in his trembling hand and realised that he was shaking uncontrollably. He sipped the whiskey, trying his best not to slop it on the upholstery. Mister Tempest patted his shoulder paternally and went back to pacing.

The door opened and everyone, including Dahljeeling, looked expectantly at the physician as he finally emerged. The look on his face was not an encouraging one. He turned to address Mister Tempest.

"The bleeding has stopped, and I can find no broken bones. The skull is intact; however, I believe there might be some swelling of the brain."

"What does that mean?" demanded Mister Tempest.

"She has yet to regain consciousness. For now, there is nothing more to do but wait. Mister Tempest, depending upon the extent of the damage to your daughter's brain, you must prepare yourself that there is a possibly that she may never regain consciousness. I'm sorry."

Claus felt lightheaded and his vision blurred momentarily.

"That's not good enough!" boomed Mister Tempest. "There must be something that can be done!"

"Aside from waiting, nothing." The physician turned to leave.

Claus downed his remaining whiskey in one gulp and

ripped his watch from his waistcoat pocket, making Arabella jump with the suddenness of his actions. He gazed at her for a moment, gave her a hasty kiss and wound the watch back five hours.

18th Brevis, again

C laus vomited onto the carriage floor. He fought to catch his breath and looked around himself in confusion.

A carriage. He was in a carriage and it was moving. Moving to where? He was icy cold and shaking, his brow clammy with cold sweat. His stomach felt as though someone had replaced its contents with writhing snakes. He could taste whiskey. Why, and more to the point, *when* had he been drinking whiskey? Arabella and Dahljeeling sat beside him and they both looked stricken. In fact, Arabella looked as though she might faint. The carriage ground to a halt.

"The Edenia," announced the cabbie when his fare failed to dismount.

"The Edenia," Claus muttered. He noticed his puddle of vomit slowly spreading across the floor. He looked up at Arabella, ashamed, but she hardly seemed to notice, and they made a hasty exit before the cab driver could see the state of his carriage. Claus saw his friends waving at them and he stumbled towards them.

"Claus!" said Henrietta. "What on Cellanor is the matter?" She stared at Arabella for a moment. "You look perfectly dreadful! Both of you!"

"Perhaps we ate something that didn't agree with us," shrugged Arabella.

"Or maybe a touch of the ague," Claus mumbled.

"You look like a pair of ghosts! Get inside in the warm, for goodness sake," frowned Henry.

"You shouldn't have come out if you're unwell, we could have rearranged this for another time," Henrietta linked arms with her friends and squeezed them sympathetically. They moved inside the foyer and Claus stared around himself. He knew he'd never been to the theatre before, but the place looked so familiar.

"I think we should get some dinner right away," said Todorovich. "It might make you feel better."

Claus nodded, then remembered his manners.

"I'm so sorry, Mister Todorovich, how do you do?" he reached out and shook the scientist's hand.

"Better than you, I think! Let's get you both sat down in the warm."

Claus nodded and smiled distractedly.

Todorovich looked down and gasped at the presence of the monkey, who'd been huddled behind Claus.

"Dahljeeling? What's he doing here?"

Henrietta made hushing sounds.

"It's an odd story," said Claus and he rubbed his head. Todorovich looked intrigued as the group made their way to the restaurant. Todorovich led the way but Claus didn't need him to. He knew where he was going. He knew the restaurant would be pleasant and have paintings hung on the walls.

Henrietta tugged at Claus's arm, pulling him slightly away from the rest of the group.

"Did you go to visit Madam Nimueh?" she asked in a low voice.

Claus shook his head.

"Arabella was too tired to face it. We'll go tomorrow."

"I don't know how you can stand the suspense. Aren't you interested in finding out about this supposed estranged cousin of yours?"

"Exceedingly," Claus paused as another wave of nausea clutched at his insides. "But I dare say waiting another night won't change his diabolical plans."

Henrietta frowned and rubbed at her head.

"Claus, I do hope that I'm not coming down with the same illness as you and Arabella. I feel most peculiar all of a sudden."

The pair re-joined their party who were being shown to their table.

As soon as they were seated Todorovich began to thank them for their help. Claus knew that he was supposed to feel mollified about his injuries in the face of such earnest gratitude. He didn't. He felt like he was going to vomit again or pass out. He quaffed a large glass of wine in anticipation of the fabled medicinal qualities of alcohol.

"And now, you must tell me how you-"

"- came by William's monkey," Claus finished Todorovich's sentence.

Todorovich looked momentarily taken aback.

"Indeed," he smiled.

"It was the evening we disabled your machine."

Todorovich glanced at Arabella.

Claus waved an unconcerned hand at the scientist.

"It's alright, she knows everything. It seems that Dahljeeling followed me home from Cordage's," Claus's voice was emotionless, the words automatically coming out of his mouth without him considering them. "He was pursued by his doppelganger's who seemed intent on doing him harm, though we cannot work out why. He's living with me now. For the time being at least."

"Why would his duplicates want to harm him?" frowned Henry, directing his question at the scientist.

"I've no idea, although The Amplificator was never designed to augment a living subject. Even inanimate objects proved difficult to enhance to a satisfactory standard."

"They're certainly proving difficult to round up," said Henry.

247

Henrietta groaned and put her face in her hands. Her companions all turned to stare at her.

"Oh, don't tell me you're getting ill too?" moaned Henry. "Honestly, she's a nightmare when she's ill!" he complained to no one in particular. "She gets all grumpy and restless."

"Claus!" Henrietta looked up sharply. "You used *the watch,* didn't you?"

Claus began to shake his head and caught sight of Dahljeeling who was crouched upon the chair next to him. He was twitching in agitation and kept looking towards the doorway.

"I did," Claus breathed. "I did. But I forgot. But Dahljeeling remembers. He can remember a past which is yet to happen!"

"What's this?" frowned Todorovich.

"We have to leave," Claus sprang up from his chair as if it were arconized and grabbed Arabella's hand. Dahljeeling was making desperate keening noises and tugging at Claus's sleeve.

"Get out!" shouted Claus. "The monkeys are coming. Run. Don't look at me like that! Run!" He scooped Dahljeeling up into his arms and held him against his chest.

There came the sound of raised voices from the foyer before the restaurant door burst open and a horde of red coated monkeys poured in.

The twins needed no further persuasion and made a bolt for the door, Henry savagely knocking primates aside as he charged forth. Todorovich followed suit, with Claus bringing up the rear, pushing Arabella before him.

They ran as fast as they could in the confined space, the other diners following instinctually. They burst out onto road, ahead of the crowd. Giddy with relief, Claus let out a slightly maniacal laugh. Then he heard the sound of a horse screaming, followed by an abrasive, scraping noise of carriage wheels upon cobbles and a woman's shriek that preceded the shouts of the terrified diners, who were about to pour forth from the theatre.

Claus stopped laughing and swayed.

"She just ran out in front of me! There was nothing I could do!" pleaded the cab driver, who was scrambling down from his dickie box.

Henrietta lay motionless on the cobbles. The driver steadied his horse so that it wouldn't trample on top of her. Blood ran steadily from her head and into the gutter to mix with the frozen filth.

"I tried to stop the horse, but the carriage slid on the ice and hit her," explained the cabbie. No one was listening to him. The other theatre goers were tumbling out of the doors into the cold evening air, their shouts and screams drowning out Claus's agonised chant.

"No. No. No. No. No."

~

This time Claus didn't bother to count the panes of glass, nor the carpet tassels, nor the stripes on the upholstery. He didn't even glance at the Sergeant. Claus dearly wished that Dahljeeling could speak English. The monkey seemed to be able to remember what had happened *before* Claus had used his watch.

He decided that he would wait until after the physician had given his inevitable prognosis, before making an attempt to talk to Henry. Although, Claus doubted very much that his friend would be able to comprehend his words. Henry seemed to have gone into some form of shock.

Mister Tempest appeared with the whiskey which Claus politely declined. He couldn't face alcohol with his stomach empty and sore. His mouth felt like he'd been eating sawdust. Mister Tempest instructed one of his staff to make some tea and he swallowed the whiskey himself. He patted Claus on the shoulder. The physician emerged soon after.

When Mister Tempest had stopped shouting, Claus almost enjoyed the sensation of not knowing what was going to happen next. A servant brought up a tray of tea, not unexpected, but at least it was new. Claus, Arabella and Dahljeeling took a cup each and sipped quietly. Claus wondered how long he should give Henry before he interrupted his solemn vigil. As it happened, Henry emerged just as Claus began drinking his second cup of tea. There was something odd in his expression. If his countenance hadn't bore all the symptoms of a man in deepest turmoil, one might have called it hope.

"I need to talk to you," Henry's voice was barely above a whisper. "Not here," he gestured that his friends follow him downstairs and he led the way to the parlour.

"The watch!" he hissed, no sooner than he had closed the door behind his comrades.

Claus sighed.

"You could wind it back! Go back in time and change what happened and then-"

Claus threw his hands up to stop Henry from talking.

"Henry. I already tried that."

"What? What are you talking about?" he demanded, no longer speaking in a whisper.

"Do you remember what Henrietta said, just before the monkeys burst into the restaurant? She put her head in her hands and accused me of using the watch."

Henry opened his mouth, but no words came out. He stood in silent contemplation for a moment before a frown creased his brow.

"So…You *knew* they were going to attack? Why in the Vale of Lament didn't you do something?" he demanded.

250

"I couldn't remember turning time back!"

"Why? You could remember the other times! What was different?" Henry stamped over to the hearth in a way that was very reminiscent of his father. He picked up the iron poker and jabbed violently at the fire.

"I've never used the watch to go back more than a few minutes at most. This time I went back five hours. I felt ill and confused. I didn't know where I was, or what I was doing there."

Henry spun around to face him. His knuckles had turned white from grasping the poker so tightly.

"That's not good enough! You should have saved her!"

"Henry-"

Henry threw the poker down and stormed from the room.

"I tried..." murmured Claus.

19th Brevis

laus had expected to stay awake for the remaining hours of the night to formulate a plan. Thus, it was with some surprise that he awoke in the cellar of The Time Emporium, to the gentle clinking sound of cups on saucers. He raised his head from the workbench and noticed the blanket that had been wrapped around his shoulders, when it slipped off and onto the floor as he straightened.

Arabella was pacing up and down the available walking space and barely noticed that Dahljeeling had appeared with tea, two-day old scones and a pot of apricot jam. Claus took the teacup gratefully and drank the hot beverage in gulps and then got to work on a scone. It was stale but he didn't care, it just felt good to have something in his stomach. He looked up at Dahljeeling as the monkey butler poured him another cup of tea to wash down the desiccated cake.

"Thank you, Dahljeeling," Claus rubbed his eyes. He took the proffered cup and wrapped his hands around it in an attempt to warm his fingers. He stared around the workshop in a desultory manner until his eyes alighted upon the letters which Todorovich had written to William Cordage.

"That's it!" Claus jumped up and Dahljeeling sprang back a foot.

"What?" asked Arabella.

"I'll use the watch one more time and I'll write myself a letter to remind me what I've done!" Claus looked around to see Dahljeeling and Arabella frowning. "I know, I know! I shouldn't keep using it, but it is the only way to save Henrietta! I'll just try to change the details as little as possible. What could go wrong?"

Dahljeeling looked incredulous.

"Claus…" Arabella bit at her lip. "You said that Henrietta knew that you'd used the pocket watch. She was aware that you'd altered time. Does that mean that she's a Timesmith too? That she can remember the alternate version of the past?"

"No. She just gets this vague sense of Déjà vu, but she can't actually remember any of the particulars."

"Well, I could."

"What do you mean?"

"At first I felt very unwell, but when the monkeys arrived I could suddenly remember everything."

"How can that be? I don't understand," frowned Claus.

"Neither do I."

18th Brevis again. Again

Claus felt certain that there was something very wrong with himself. When he was a small boy, he'd been struck down with a violent bout of influenza, which had left him bedridden for more than a fortnight and painfully weak. His fever had raged, and he'd had no recollection of his actions for days at a time. When the fever had finally eased, he had been confused and discombobulated. That was how he felt now, although he wasn't coughing and sneezing, but he did ache all over.

He was supposed to be attending the theatre with Todorovich and the twins, but he was in two minds whether or not he should go. Arabella was also unwell, and he'd insisted that she go back to bed at once. The idea of getting in beside her was a pleasant one. He glanced at the clock on the mantelpiece. It was half past six. Claus sighed. It was too late to cancel now. He shrugged into his new greatcoat and turned to stare at himself in the looking glass. He had to admit that it looked rather good worn over his evening clothes and although it was fashionably cut, it was certainly too practical to look foppish. He shoved his hands in his pockets and moved around a little before the glass to get the overall effect. He felt something crunch between his fingers and pulled forth an envelope. He stared at the writing. It was addressed to him in his own handwriting. Perplexed, he tore it open and read.

Brevis 18th. Age of Cambion 13:7

Claus. The monkeys will attack The Edenia at around half past seven on the evening of Brevis 18th. Henrietta will be severely injured if you do not alter events. You are probably feeling rather unwell at the moment, I have deduced that this is a result of using the watch. It also seems to cause some short-term memory impairment and general confusion. Do not deviate too far from your original plans for this evening, as I'm concerned that there may already be mud on my shoes. Do not be in the restaurant at The Edenia at half past Seven. <u>*Save Henrietta.*</u>

Claus.

Ps. Arabella and Dahljeeling seem to be able to remember the changed past.

Claus read the letter three times in a row and then stuffed it back in his pocket. Now it was all coming back to him. He could remember writing himself this very letter. He raced into the bedroom.

"Arabella!"

Arabella looked as if she'd been dozing off, but her eyes sprang wide open at the sudden exclamation.

"Don't leave The Emporium! In fact, don't leave the bed! Stay here. Whatever you might remember!"

"What are you talking about?" she asked in alarm.

"Promise me!" he bellowed.

She nodded in a bewildered sort of way.

"Dahljeeling!" Claus cried as he thundered down the stairs and into the shop. "That goes for you too! Stay inside!" Then he ran out onto Sovereign Street.

Claus waved frantically for a cab. One pulled up a little further down the street and a gentleman made ready to climb in. Claus hurled himself towards the vehicle and yanked the door out of the gentleman's hand.

"I say!" exclaimed the disgruntled stranger.

"I'm sorry, Sir, this is an emergency!" Claus leapt into the cab and slammed the door shut. "Brandish Way, as quick as you can!" he yelled at the driver. The horses snorted as the cabbie applied the whip and took off over the cobbles. Several pedestrians had to scramble out of the road as the carriage thundered its way towards the Tempest house.

'*Please, let me be in time,*' Claus prayed under his breath to any divine power that cared to listen.

The cab slowed down as it drew closer to number thirty-one. Warm illumination shone through the curtained windows. Henry's room was at the front of the house and Claus could see that the lamps were lit, but that didn't necessarily mean that he was home. He jumped out of the cab before it came to a halt and thrust a handful of money at the driver. He hadn't bothered to count it, but the cabbie didn't yell after him as he ran off, so Claus assumed the payment was satisfactory.

Disregarding the bell pull, he hammered on the smart black door with both fists. One of the younger maids opened the door with a surprised look upon her face.

"Sir?"

"Where's Henry?" Claus blurted.

The girl stared at him with her mouth open.

"Where?!" Claus shouted.

"Upstairs, Sir."

Claus pushed past her and ran up the stairs two at a time. He burst into Henry's room without bothering to knock and thrust the letter beneath his friend's nose. Henry abandoned tying his cravat and looked up with startled eyes. Claus's sudden arrival and frenzied behaviour were so out of character that Henry didn't even bother to ask what had occurred. He simply took the piece of paper and held it at a distance which enabled him to read. His face paled as he read, and like Claus, his eyes passed over the words several times before his brain could fully appreciate the portentous content.

"What should we do?" he frowned. Claus said nothing but took a deep breath and dropped to his knees. "I say old chap, do you need to lie down?"

"No. No, I'm alright Henry. Just relieved that I caught you before you left for the theatre."

"But what's going to happen to Henrietta?"

"Nothing!" said Claus, louder than he meant to. "Nothing will happen to her. We'll make sure of it."

Henry nodded fervently.

"We should send word to Todorovich. Let him know that we cannot attend. I'll say that I'm ill. Or that you are. You look bloody awful."

Claus shook his head miserably.

"Henry, I think we have to go. In my letter, I warn myself that I shouldn't change events too much and I agree."

"You agree with yourself?" Henry looked confused.

"The Me of later on, the Me of *tomorrow* obviously knows what he's talking about because he's lived through *tonight*. I think we should listen to him-*me*- I mean," Claus shook his head as if to clear it.

"But you, I mean the you that's standing here now, can't remember going back in time? You can't remember what happened tonight?" Henry spoke slowly as if he were trying to get to grips with the problem of tenses.

"No. Remember what Madam Nimueh said? About that fellow using the watch too often and going mad?"

"Goodness, Claus. You don't suppose you're losing your marbles, do you?" Henry asked with sincere concern.

Claus almost laughed.

"I'm not sure."

"You said in your letter that Dahljeeling and Arabella remember going back in time. Do you mean they get a funny feeling? Like Henrietta does?"

257

"No. I can't speak for Dahljeeling, obviously. But he certainly seemed to know what was about to happen, even though it hadn't happened yet. As for Arabella, she said she couldn't remember to begin with. She just felt unwell, but later on it all came back to her, exactly the way it did for me."

"It's a safe assumption that Patrick- I mean, Niall- is a Timesmith, since the two of you are related. Why else would he want the watch so badly? But Arabella is only his *step*daughter... is Timesmithery contagious?"

"Timesmithery?" Claus allowed himself to laugh, though he had to be careful not to let it turn hysterical. "I think it's only passed on down the bloodline."

"Maybe it's a witch thing? Anyway, we can figure that out later. For now, we should go to the theatre, because we already did?" he raised an eyebrow as he spoke.

Claus nodded.

"Only, we should go a little later. In the letter he-*you,* say that the monkeys attack at half past seven, so we'll just make sure that we aren't in the restaurant at that time."

Claus let out his breath and stood up, relieved that Henry had grasped the situation.

~

"Really Claus, I don't know why you didn't just cancel. You look as though you ought to be in bed," admonished Henrietta.

"I'll be alright," Claus glanced at Henry as the carriage bumped its way over the cobbles towards Threefold Square. They had agreed that they would say nothing to Henrietta about the letter Claus had received from his future self. There didn't seem to be any point in upsetting her. Besides, who knew what repercussions that sort of knowledge could have?

"At least you've got Hattie now," Henrietta said, obviously fond of the woman. "She'll take good care of Arabella while you're away this evening. She makes the best soup when you feel under the weather, although cook used to get a bit crabby with her for muscling in on her territory. Her chicken broth has a way of warming you through and through. Gosh!" she suddenly exclaimed with a look of chagrin. "I hope Nikola hasn't been waiting outside the theatre for us all this time, he'll be frozen. I say! Driver!" she called out. "Would you mind putting a little speed on? We're dreadfully late!"

"Fashionably late," corrected Henry.

"We said we'd meet him at ten past seven! We're going to have to rush our dinner now if we want to see the show. What on Cellanor possessed you to ask Father about the way he keeps his invoice ledgers? You know once he starts talking about that he doesn't stop."

"Nothing wrong with a son taking an interest in the family's business," grinned Henry.

"I agree, but why tonight? And don't even get me started about the inventory accounts!"

"I thought it was rather interesting."

"You're an idiot," proclaimed his sister. She turned away in disgust to look out of the window. "You two! Look! What do you suppose is happening?"

"How should I know? I'm an idiot," replied Henry cheerfully.

Claus leaned over to the window and followed Henrietta's gaze. He could just make out the front of The Edenia, around which there seemed to be a mass exodus of people. He breathed a sigh of relief. The monkeys must have attacked by now and he and his friends were safely ensconced within the cab. Then he saw a tide of scarlet and brown pouring forth from the theatre. The monkeys seemed unstoppable as they charged down the street. An angry horde that raced closer with

259

every second until they were right in front of them. Claus could hear the cab driver shouting, the horses had gone mad with fear. The carriage didn't slow but the horses turned to avoid the tide of monkeys. The coach veered to the left, horse and gravity fighting over which way the cab would go. Neither was the victor as one of the front wheels struck an iron balustrade.

Claus suddenly lost the capacity to tell right from left or up from down. Then he lost consciousness.

20th Brevis

"**I** thought you were dead."

"I am. Leave me alone," Claus blinked to bring the room into focus. He'd expected to see his own bedroom ceiling, the dull, parchment colour paint and the dark wooden beams. Instead, this ceiling was high and white and there was an ornate plaster ceiling rose surrounding a large chandelier. A small brown furry face peered down at him.

"Ghar!" Claus sprang into a sitting position and felt the room spin. "You can talk!"

"Over here, dotard."

Claus looked to the corner of the room, where Henry was slumped in a chair, smoking one of his father's cigars. He got up and stretched and made his way over to the bed.

"We brought you back here and thought it best not to move you. Plus, it makes it easier on the physician, two patients under one roof. He's not getting any younger."

"Henrietta?"

"She doesn't wake up."

"How long have I been here?"

"Almost two days."

"Arabella?"

"She's asleep. She's been staying here too. Insisted upon watching over you."

Now that Claus had regained some of his wits, he took in his friend's condition. Henry had dark rings beneath his eyes, which normally twinkled with amusement, but now they were dull and sorrowful. He looked dishevelled and his breath smelt of strong liquor. His left arm was in a sling and his face and neck were covered in scratches and angry purple bruises.

"It didn't change anything," Claus said quietly. "Pass me my clothes Henry! I need my watch!" He began to kick his legs free from the bed clothes.

"You need to rest," said Henry firmly.

"I have to go back! I have to put things right."

Henry tried to push Claus back against the pillows with his good arm.

"And what's going to happen next time? You're going to get yourself killed!"

"But Henrietta-"

"May still come through this. She's an obstinate cow after all."

"You don't understand. I need to do this. I lost my mother. I lost Hans. I can't lose any more of my family."

"And what about me?" demanded Henry. "What am I supposed to do if I lose both of you? I need you here. I can't do this alone."

For one horrible moment Claus thought that Henry was about to burst into tears. He nodded in a placatory way and then groaned. He reached up to touch his aching head and discovered that it had been wrapped in bandages.

"Doctor Griffiths says you have concussion, but that there's no damage to your brain. I disagree," Henry forced a smile. "You woke up yesterday morning. You started ranting about monkeys and time travel. It was all a bit embarrassing really. Thankfully Doctor Griffiths put it down to the blow to your head, otherwise you might have been carted off to a padded cell."

"Perhaps I still shall," mused Claus.

"Are you hungry?"

Other than his aching head, Claus felt a curious sense of amputation from the rest of his anatomy. He tried to concentrate on his stomach.

"Yes," he decided.

"I'll get cook to whip something up. Just lay back down and rest, will you?" There was a definite note of pleading to Henry's words.

Claus nodded and Henry cast a worried look at his friend before leaving the room. Claus rolled onto his side and pulled the bed clothes up to his ear. The curtains were drawn and there was no light coming in from outside, so he deduced that it must be nighttime. Someone had built up the fire and the flames cast a warm orange glow upon the floral duck-egg blue wallpaper. There were flowers on the sheets too. Missus Tempest must really like flowers.

Claus couldn't remember when his body had ever felt so heavy, and he tried to work out when he had last slept (properly slept. Delirious insensibility didn't count) in a bed. He felt himself begin to drift, bits of his body were disappearing one by one, until he was just a floating mass of disjointed thoughts.

Threefold Square was upside-down. He knew that people were yelling, even though he couldn't make out the words. Feet were running around on the cobbles which were under his cheek. Sturdy police issue boots. He was laying with his torso hanging out of a cab window that was smashed. There was broken glass everywhere. He wanted to say something, but he couldn't speak. His vision blurred. Darkness engulfed him.

Claus was trying on his new clothes. He was getting in a cab. He was running behind his friends. Running out of the theatre. Henrietta had always been the fastest runner. Back when they were children, the three of them had snuck out of the house one night to explore one of the abandoned buildings down by The Wall. They were spotted trying to climb through a window by a policeman, who chased and caught the boys and gave them what for. Henrietta had been faster. She ran all the way home and never got in trouble.

She ran straight in front of the cab. The driver tried to steer his horses to the side, but the carriage skidded on the icy cobbles, swung about and sent her flying. Paintings on the walls of the restaurant. Claus tried on his new clothes. He got in a cab. Henry holding his sister in his arms. She was limp. She'd been trampled on. Her head was bleeding. They put her in a cab. Fifty-Seven bluebells painted on coloured glass. One hundred and fifteen gold-coloured tassels on either end of the carpet.

Claus gasped and opened his eyes. His brow was wet with sweat and his body shook.

"Henry!" he yelled.

He took ragged breaths and stared around with wild eyes. This wasn't the *second* time that Henrietta had been injured but the third. Claus could remember everything with perfect clarity. He was surrounded by patterns, choking on them and Missus Tempest's taste in soft furnishings was the least of it. The cab driver was always the same man. He'd picked Claus up the first time and delivered him to The Edenia. He was also the driver that had transported Henrietta back to Brandish Way, when she'd suffered her first head injury. Claus hadn't noticed at the time, but now the man's face stood out as clear as a candle flame in a dark room. The second time, Claus had been sick in the carriage, and it was the very same cab which, half an hour later, Henrietta was struck by. The third time the same cab was smashed with them all inside of it. It couldn't be a coincidence.

The bedroom door was flung open.

"Claus?" Henry panted as he rushed into the room.

"Henry. I need paper. And something to write with!"

Henry observed his friend's agitated demeanour with unease.

"Why?"

"I remember what happened! I need to write it all down!"

"Well…that's a good sign. Perhaps the concussion isn't as bad as we thought."

"No, not that!" Claus snapped. "I mean, yes, I can remember the accident, but I can remember everything else as well. Going back in time! It's always the same pattern. All the times that Henrietta has been injured!"

Henry rubbed the back of his aching neck.

"What are you talking about? What do you mean '*all the times*'? You only went back once, didn't you?"

"That's what I thought, but I was wrong!" Claus was almost shouting now. "Three times Henry!"

"You've turned back the watch *three* times now?" Henry was aghast and the glassy fervour in Claus's eyes did nothing to dispel his anxiety.

"She's had three head injuries and every time I go back to save her, *he's* always there!"

"*Who*?" Henry couldn't help but raise his own voice. Claus dropped his own to a vehement whisper.

"*The cab driver!*"

Henry backed away. He would never have imagined that he could be afraid of Claus. The man made clockwork mice, for goodness sake.

"'ll go and find you some paper," he mumbled and backed out of the room.

Henry shut himself in the study and began to look for unused journal. There were probably plenty to hand, but Henry was having trouble keeping focused. Also, he didn't really want to go back upstairs.

265

What if the old witch had been telling the truth? What if Claus had gone mad from using the watch too much?

Henry had never been interested in witchcraft and so he had dismissed the notion, but Henrietta believed in magic and fortunes and such. What if she was right? She usually was.

Henry let himself smile at the thought of his twin. He wished more than anything that she would wake up. She would know what to do for the best.

He fell into the chair, put his face in his hands and wept

21st Brevis

Henry was sat up in bed, holding a cup of tea in his clenched hands. It had gone quite cold. Without the aid of his sister, he would have to take matters into his own hands. Resigned to his only course of action, he placed the tea on the bedside table, next to the wooden clothes peg, and swung his legs out of the bed.

It was early. The rest of his family had yet to emerge from their sleeping quarters. Henry got dressed and tiptoed past his parents' bedroom. He could hear his father's snores from behind the closed door. It had been his mother's turn to spend the night in Henrietta's room, on a makeshift bed, which was basically just a sofa with extra cushions.

Only the staff could be heard going about their business. Henry left the house without anyone's knowledge. He moved with purpose down Brandish Way and waved his arm at the first cab to draw near.

"Where to gov'nor?" smiled the cabbie.

Henry shuddered as he looked up at the man on the dickie box. He would never be able to look at cab drivers in the same way again.

"Katamatown."

~

Henry approached the witch's shop with caution. He hadn't really worked out what he was going to say.

"Hello?" he called softly, as he opened the door. The little bell chimed above his head and startled him.

"I say? Are you there?" He slipped inside and his eyes were drawn to read the titles of the books which surrounded him. He wasn't sure what compelled him, but he felt an overwhelming desire to touch them. He reached out tentatively in spite of himself.

"Let me guess. He's in trouble because of the watch, yes?" came a voice from behind Henry. He whirled around to face the old woman.

"Yes," Henry removed his top hat. "How did you know?" He quickly riffled through his limited knowledge of the occult. "I suppose you saw it in the cards," he suggested uncertainly. The old woman let out a wheezing sound that resembled a laugh.

"Something like that."

"He needs help."

"That's obvious," growled Brenna.

"For that matter, so do I. My sister. She is…ill."

"Well, I'm sorry for it, but what to you want me to do? You want a spell for her? A potion? You don't even believe."

"No, nothing like that. I want…I would be very grateful if you could come and talk to Claus. I have him at my home."

"Talk to him?"

"You warned him that using the watch could make him…" Henry hesitated.

"Insane," supplied Brenna.

Henry opened his mouth and paused.

"He is…excitable. There was an accident. He sustained quite a blow to the head, which I think may have exacerbated his condition."

"And you think I can help him?"

Henry didn't know what to think. He shrugged impotently.

"I don't know. Please, will you try?"

"I'll come tonight."

"It's number Thirty-One Brandish Way. Will you be alright finding us? Since, well, you're...blind."

Brenna smiled sardonically.

~

Henry walked home, an unprecedented occurrence in itself. He felt that the air might do him good, or as much good as he could hope for, breathing in the smog and ash. He could barely see six feet in front of himself in the dense fog which had seemingly risen from nowhere. He mounted the steps to his front door with a feeling of dread. He was afraid of what he might find upon entering.

First, he checked on Henrietta. She looked peaceful, as though there was nothing wrong with her and that she was merely sleeping. He had hoped to find Claus in a similar condition, but when he peered into the guest room, it was empty.

"Claus?" Henry looked back into the hallway and caught sight of a maid. "Shirley?"

"Yes, Sir?"

"Where is Mister Vogel?"

"Oh, he left, Sir. Said he wanted to go and get something from his house. I told him the doctor would be angry."

Henry nodded and slipped into the guestroom, closing the door behind himself. The journal that Henry had given Claus the night before was laying on the bed. Henry didn't like the thought of invading his friend's privacy, but he consoled his conscience that these were mitigating circumstances. He opened the book to see Claus's spidery handwriting, scrawled heavily and without order, all over the pages. Most of the words were illegible, scribbled in a hasty frenzy with so much ink blotting that some of the words were entirely obliterated. If journals could be used to gain insight to the inner workings of one's mind, then

Claus was in trouble. Henry turned a few pages. There was much mention of patterns and references to the cab driver. There were three recurring sentences which stood out. *'Break the chain of coincidence'.* *'Eliminate the pattern'.* *'Eliminate the cab driver'.* These had been heavily underlined.

"Dantalis!" Henry breathed to himself. "He's going to kill a cabbie!"

"Where is he?"

Henry spun around to face the door. Arabella was stood with her hands on her hips and a stern look on her face.

Henry dashed forward and caught hold of her arm.

"We need to find him. Fast!"

~

Claus stood outside the Time Emporium and felt the cold weight of his grandfather's pistol within the pocket of his greatcoat. The last of the snow had melted away and the infinitesimal rise in temperature had encouraged, what the locals referred to as an 'Arcon's Fart'. A fog so dense that a person could lose their way home.

His breathing was ragged and caused condensation on the inside of the scarf which he had wrapped around the lower half of his face. He heard the cab approaching before he could see it. It loomed up alongside him out of the mists.

"Need a cab, Sir?"

Claus scrutinised the face of the driver. He was bundled up with hat and scarf, his coat collar turned up to protect the back of his neck.

"No," Claus shook his head and stepped back. The carriage moved on and was soon lost to view, swallowed up by the mists, the sound of the horse's hooves on the cobbles was the only indication that it existed at all. Claus knew that he was looking for the proverbial needle in a haystack, there must have been thousands of cabs in the city, but he felt sure that if he searched for long enough, he would meet his cab driver again eventually. He suddenly felt himself being accosted from behind and spun around to face his assailant, pulling the pistol out from his pocket as he turned.

"Dantalis's pants! Point that thing somewhere else!" hissed Henry.

"What are you doing here?" snapped Claus, irritably.

"I've come to help you."

Claus grinned and tucked his firearm away.

"I knew you'd see that I was right! You read my notes, didn't you?"

"Um. Yes," Henry looked up and down the street anxiously. Not that anyone would be able to observe them in the fog. "Shall we go inside?"

"I have to keep searching."

"I think we should get out of this damp. It's not good for the lungs. Arabella is with me."

Claus looked behind Henry and could make out Arabella's silhouette against the fog.

"She shouldn't be outside. Mister O'Connor- I mean, Mister McGrath could be anywhere."

"Precisely," Henry agreed, willing to use any advantage to deter Claus from shooting innocent cab drivers. "Anyway, this isn't going to work. We need to formulate a plan," he added, improvising wildly.

"Alright. Yes. A plan of attack!"

"Indeed," Henry steered his friend inside the shop before he could change his mind.

~

The Time Emporium wasn't much warmer than the street outside. It had

271

lain empty for the last two days while Claus had been unconscious at the Tempest's. Arabella and Dahljeeling had been residents at Brandish Way from the moment they'd heard about the disastrous cab journey, and Hattie had insisted that she come along too, acting as Arabella's lady's maid. The trio entered the office and Henry did his best to light a fire in the grate. He had never laid a fire in his life.

A mewling sound came from the doorway and Agatha ran in and began to wind her way around Claus's legs. He stooped to pick her up and then sat down in one of the armchairs.

"Aggie! You poor old thing! You've had no one to look after you!" Claus rubbed his face in the cat's fur, who purred in response to the attention. Henry felt a sense of relief to see Claus acting in his usual affectionate manner towards the animal.

"Henry, there's a tin of tuna in the cabinet upstairs, would you be so kind as to fetch it here and I will tend to that fire that you seem to be murdering."

Henry felt nervous upon hearing the word 'murdering' but since he was eager to restore some sense of normality to life, he hurriedly mounted the stairs. He located and opened the tin quickly, emptied the tuna into the first bowl that came to hand and raced back down the stairs. He was worried that in his absence, Claus would take it upon himself to disappear again. His anxiety came to nothing though, as when he returned Claus was crouched before the hearth, diligently encouraging the fire in the grate. Arabella looked anxiously at Henry, as if she was trying to speak to him without words. Henry placed the bowl of tuna on the floor and Agatha set about it with alacrity.

"You were right, you know," said Claus, his back turned to his companions. "It wouldn't have worked- me killing the cab driver. I don't know what I was thinking."

Henry sighed and exchanged a glance with Arabella. He sagged down onto the arm of the chair she was sat in.

"It gladdens my heart to hear you say that," she breathed.

"Indeed," nodded Henry earnestly. "And I can't imagine that Henrietta would thank you for it."

Claus stood up and turned around. Henry noticed a fevered, glassy look in his friend's eyes.

"What point would there be for me to kill him *now*? The damage is already done. I need to go back to the night Henrietta was injured. Shoot him *before* it occurs!"

"No! No more time travelling!" snapped Henry. "Don't you remember what the old witch told you?" He turned to look apologetically at Arabella. "I mean Missus McGrath, of course."

"What do you mean?"

"The watch is turning you into a lunatic!"

Claus frowned and shook his head angrily.

"But I must go back and change things! I have to save Henrietta!"

"Why must you?" Henry demanded. "For all you know, you might just be making things worse!"

"I'm a Timesmith Henry! If I can't make things better, then what's the point?"

Henry sighed in a defeated way. He stood up and moved casually towards the fireplace, then suddenly grabbed the blackened kettle from its home and swung it round. There was a dull thud as it came into contact with the side of Claus's head.

Arabella cried out in alarm as Claus fell, insensible, back into the chair.

"Sorry," said Henry. He meant it.

~

273

Henry paced up and down the parlour. Night had fallen and the mystic had yet to arrive. He was feeling quite nervous. His hitherto sedate and respectable household was turning into a menagerie of the unusual. He was playing host to a time travelling- potentially homicidal-watchmaker and the watchmaker's troubled beau, who happened to be a witch. There was a monkey in a suit, and a cat in the guestroom. And to top it all, he'd invited The Blind Seeress of Katamatown round. Someone was bound to notice.

There came a soft tapping at the door and Shirley the maid entered and bobbed.

"Sir? There's an old woman wanting to see you."

"Well show her in! Discreetly if you don't mind."

"Begging your pardon, Sir, but she came to the tradesman's door. We thought she was a beggar. Cook ordered her to go away but she won't. She's in the kitchen and she won't be moved."

"She held her own against cook?" Henry couldn't help but feel a little admiration. Even his own father tried his best to stay out of cook's way. "Very well."

Henry followed the maid down some narrow stairs and entered the warm, steamy confines of the kitchen. An unexpected sight met his eyes.

Brenna was sat down at the scrubbed kitchen table, a steaming cup of tea before her and a spread of cards laid out. Cook was sat next to her, leaning forward over the table with a look of anticipation on her flushed face.

"And this woman is going to bring me news of some benefit to me?" she was asking.

Brenna nodded and turned another card over.

"Any health issues?" she asked.

274

"My leg," frowned Cook. "Swells up something terrible sometimes. Why?" she demanded.

"Don't ignore it. I'd ask for some time off to rest it if I were you," Brenna glanced up at Henry and smirked. Cook followed her gaze and huffed.

"A chance would be a fine thing! Do you know how much these people eat?" she directed her words at Henry.

"I'll have a word with my father," he said in a placatory tone. "Madam Nimueh. Claus is upstairs." It was a polite way of telling her to hurry up. She stood and Cook looked disappointed.

"Come back any time, Madam. It's good to meet a genuine prognosticator for once."

Brenna's face twitched in her own version of a smile and she followed Henry out of the kitchen.

"*Must you?*" hissed Henry, when they were out of earshot.

They made their way quietly upstairs to the guestroom. Brenna sat down on the chair which Henry had placed by the bed.

"Has he not woken up from the accident yet?" she frowned.

"Oh yes but, he wasn't himself, so I..." Henry shuffled his feet guiltily, "Knocked him out again."

The mystic raised her eyebrows.

"What do you mean by 'wasn't himself'? Speak plainly."

"He got it into his head that the cab driver he encountered on the night of the accident was some sort of...catalyst for the events which took place," Henry whispered. He was afraid to wake Claus up, or rather, he was afraid of what Claus might do when he woke up. "In short, Claus was bent upon eliminating this catalyst."

Brenna snorted. She reached out a hand and placed it upon Claus's brow.

"He's burning up. Has he ever had a fever before?"

"When we were children," Henry nodded and crept closer.

"And how did it take him? What effect did it have?"

"Amnesia. Confusion, I think. Ramblings too," Henry shrugged. "It's difficult to remember, we were small."

Brenna bent down to search through her tattered carpet bag at her feet and pulled forth a tiny, amber coloured, glass bottle. She took the stopper out and waved it beneath Claus's nose.

"He has a brain fever," she commented impassively.

"He's not mad?" asked Henry hopefully.

"No more than you or I."

Henry silently debated this statement.

Claus's eyes flew open and he gagged at the pungent smell coming from the bottle held beneath his nose. He looked around and frowned.

"Missus McGrath? Why are you here?"

"Because you're a silly sod, that's why!"

Claus pulled himself into a sitting position against the pillows.

"I can't remember getting here."

"No, your friend here bopped you on the head."

Claus looked sharply at Henry.

"Was that really necessary old chap?"

"Yes," Henry nodded fervently. "You don't remember anything?"

Claus frowned and shook his head.

"You don't recall writing this?" Henry passed him the ledger. Claus stared at the pages with concern and shook his head again.

"But this is my handwriting!" he protested.

"I told you. Brain fever," Brenna shrugged.

"But this is wonderful!" cried Henry, almost dancing on the spot.

"I fail to see how me having a brain fever is wonderful," frowned Claus.

"It means that you aren't mad!"

"Here," Brenna produced another bottle. She tipped a little into an empty glass then mixed it with some water from the jug on the bedside table. "Drink this."

"What is it?"

"Fenugreek, feverfew, quinine and Indian snakeroot," she said. "There's no snakes in it," she added, as Claus peered dubiously at the proffered beverage. He took a sip and shuddered.

"It's awful."

"Just drink it," Brenna advised.

Claus had to concentrate on drinking the potion without vomiting. He knew that people advised swallowing foul tasting medicine in one go, but he felt sure he would be violently sick if he did that. He took small, shuddering sips as frequently as he could manage.

"Shall I get you some food, Claus?" asked Henry when Claus had finally emptied his glass. "Or tea? I noticed that Cook got some chocolate in for Matis Day, what about that?" he fussed. He felt very guilty for assaulting his friend with a kettle.

Claus shook his head, which was beginning to feel a lot clearer.

"You can tell me what has been going on," he gestured at the journal. "Seems to me that I wanted to commit murder."

"You did. It was most alarming! What do you remember?"

"We went to The Edenia for dinner and a show with Todorovich."

"No," Henry shook his head. "No, we never made it to the theatre. The monkeys ransacked the place and caused our carriage to crash as they ran away."

"I know all that. But you asked me what I can remember. I remember sitting down in the restaurant and the monkeys bursting through the door. We all ran, the other diners too. I made it outside, but Henrietta tripped and got trampled by the crowd. Todorovich hailed a cab and we brought Henrietta back here and sent for the physician. He said there wasn't much he could do, so I wound the watch back to try to save her."

"Were you very upset?" asked Brenna.

Claus stared at her for a moment.

"Of *course* I was very upset. One of my best friends had just been gravely injured."

"Hm. Your emotional state could have exacerbated the negative effects of using the watch."

"I turned the watch back five hours to the moment when I had been travelling to The Edenia. We had agreed to meet there at ten past seven. I was violently ill in the cab and very confused. I didn't remember that I had used the watch. I met with the others, but I felt as though I had been through it all before. What I mean to say is that I recognised the restaurant and I knew what my companions were going to say before they opened their mouths. Henrietta seems to feel the effects of the watch. Déjà vu she calls it. As we were sitting in the restaurant she suddenly accused me of using the watch and it was then that I remembered what had happened, but it was too late. The monkeys burst in and I yelled to my companions to run. We all made it outside, ahead of the crowd and I felt certain that I'd managed to change history, but then Henrietta ran into the road and got hit by a carriage which skidded on the ice."

Henry covered his open mouth with his hand, appalled.

"Poor Henrietta," he whispered.

"Then what?" urged Brenna.

"Then..." Claus frowned as he tried to put his memories in the correct order. "I used the watch once again, but not before I wrote myself a letter, warning me of the events that were to come. I had hoped that I would find the note in my pocket and have enough time to effect a change in events. I came here and spoke to Henry. We decided that we would arrive late, thus missing the attack. But it didn't go to plan and Henrietta is..." Claus merely gestured in the direction of her bedroom.

"So, you've tried to save this girl three times so far. No attempts have been successful, she has succumbed to three different head injuries and now you are ill." The mystic was silent and stared unseeingly at the embroidered flowers on the blanket.

"Claus. Do you remember when we spoke at your grandfather's wake?"

"Muddy shoes," Claus nodded.

"Destiny and the problems that might arise if some idiot tried to interfere."

Claus nodded again and then looked up sharply at the woman in horror as he realised what she was implying.

"It is not Henrietta's destiny to die!" he cried.

"It is everyone's destiny to die, silly boy."

"Not like this! Not now!"

"Why? Because you say so?"

"Yes!" exclaimed Claus. He didn't care if he sounded stupid or childish.

279

"Hear, hear," said Henry stepping forward. "Henrietta is my twin, the other half of me. I will do whatever I can to save her. I'm behind Claus all the way! Unless it involves killing innocent cab drivers," he added hastily.

Claus looked up into Henry's eyes and a silent pact passed between them.

"I can see that you are resolute," nodded Brenna. "There is nothing I can say that will dissuade you from this course of action."

"Nothing!" declared Claus.

"Then at least let me help you."

"We could use some help," Claus admitted. "How?"

"Mister Tempest, do you really wish to help Claus?"

"Of course," Henry sat down on the foot of the bed.

"Good. In that case, I think you should go back in time with him."

Her statement was met with bewildered looks.

"I am not a Timesmith, Madam," Henry replied, as if he were explaining to a dull-witted child that one plus one equalled two.

"No, but I am, and I'm also a witch," shrugged Brenna. "I can arrange for you to accompany him, so long as you are in physical contact when Claus winds the watch."

The boys stared at one another before turning their gaze on the old woman in mute confusion.

"You're a witch *and* a Timesmith?" frowned Henry. "That must come in handy."

"The Timesmith ability is passed on through the bloodline," said Claus "It's true then. The McGrath's are related to the Vogel's. That's why you've been helping me..."

"I am a Vogel," Brenna nodded. "Your great aunt, to be precise."

Claus stared at her.

"You're Hans's sister?" he asked incredulously.

"Half-sister. My father visited Irkland for a time, before running off, back to Skorda when my mother became pregnant. Vile dog of a man. I stayed with Hans and your mother when I first moved to Bitterend. You were very small."

Claus held out his empty glass for some more medicine. He felt he might need it.

"That's how you knew where to find me. That's why you turned up at Hans's wake."

The mystic nodded, solemnly.

"But Hans never mentioned you. Why didn't you ever come to visit?"

"We lost touch," frowned Brenna.

"The man you said about…the man who used the watch and went mad and, well …killed himself…"

"My father," nodded Brenna. "Your great grandfather."

"Arcon's arse," breathed Henry.

"And so, we are family then?" frowned Claus.

Brenna nodded.

"Who is Niall McGrath?"

Brenna twitched.

"How do you know that name?" she snapped.

"His stepdaughter is sat in the corner of this room," replied Claus.

Brenna turned in her seat as if to look for the girl. Claus gestured to Arabella to come closer. She hesitated for a moment before approaching.

"My name is Arabella McGrath," she paused for a moment. "Actually, it's Arabella Marley."

Brenna reached out and grasped her hand.

"Why Marley? Why not McGrath?" she demanded.

"I have disowned my stepfather."

The group was shocked to see Brenna smile.

"Then you truly know Niall."

"Missus McGrath, who is he to you?" asked Claus. "He told Arabella that he is my cousin. Can this be true?"

"Yes. Niall is my son," she said the words with a look that suggested she'd just taken a sip of the brain fever medicine.

"So, both of you can wield the watch."

"If I had a mind to," Brenna admitted grudgingly. "Which I don't."

"You said you could make Henry a Timesmith."

"I wouldn't go that far! He wouldn't be able to wield the watch by himself, but I can make it so that he can accompany you and assist you for a limited time."

"That would be helpful. Can't you come too?"

"Dantalis above! I'm too old for all that nonsense. And I haven't been getting much sleep with you putting time back willy-nilly."

"You can feel it? You can remember the past as it was, before I use the watch to wind back time?"

"Of course. I've had to have the same conversations with the same people over and over again!"

"You mean…time doesn't go back for you, when I use the watch? You just have to go through the same events again and again, knowing

282

that you have done them before?"

"Aye! I don't mind telling you that I was a tad annoyed."

Claus couldn't help but smile.

"I'm sorry."

"So you should be. I had to see to Mister Shipperton's in-growing toenail three times!"

Henry burst out laughing and Brenna scowled.

"We should come up with a plan," stated Claus.

"We're not doing anything tonight," stated Brenna. "You are unwell. You must rest and take some more medicine. One more night will make little difference in any case."

"And then?"

"Apart from this cab driver, are there any other patterns? Anything you can think of which links these events together?"

"Aside from Henry, Henrietta, Arabella and I?" Claus frowned and shrugged. "Todorovich?"

"Oh! Do we get to shoot Todorovich?" Henry brightened.

Claus laughed and gazed absentmindedly around the room. His eyes came to rest upon Dahljeeling who was sleeping peacefully on the sofa.

"Dahljeeling," he breathed. "The monkeys. That's how all of this started. We were investigating the escaped monkeys which had been terrorising the local tea shops. Henrietta met Todorovich and we destroyed his machine, and he took us out for dinner as a thank you!"

Brenna held up a hand in confusion. "The monkey plague is something to do with Todorovich? Nikola Todorovich the scientist?" She frowned.

"Indirectly," Henry said grudgingly. "Todorovich and Lord Cordage were friends. It seems that Cordage was interested in strange inventions. Todorovich made a flavour enhancement machine for him to experiment with his tea."

"Dahljeeling was Cordage's monkey butler," said Claus. "He is asleep on the chaise lounge behind you. He followed me home and lives with me now."

"You seem to have a habit of picking up waifs and strays, Claus," mused Brenna, inclining her head towards Arabella, who shifted uncomfortably.

"We think that Dahljeeling inadvertently duplicated himself in his master's device and now his genetically modified evil doppelgangers are terrorising Bitterend," explained Henry.

Brenna raised her eyebrows. She looked as if she might actually laugh.

"Lord Cordage was killed somehow-" he continued.

"Killed? It was murder, so I heard," said the mystic.

"Whatever happened to him, it wasn't suicide or natural causes. That was when this all got out of hand," nodded Claus.

"That's the key then. Cordage is the starting point of all this. You have to go back and stop him from tinkering with his monkey."

"To be fair, I don't think that he ever *intended* to 'tinker' with his monkey," frowned Claus.

"The machine!" Henry cried. "We should go back in time far enough to destroy The Amplificator, before it was ever used!"

Claus nodded and looked at his aunt.

"Seems reasonable," she sighed.

"You know though," said Henry hopefully, "If Todorovich was killed before he invented his infernal contraption, then none of this would have happened."

"We're not killing Todorovich," said Claus.

Henry sighed.

"So... You need to wind the watch back to before the monkey attacks began, which was when?" asked Brenna.

Henry whipped out his pocket notebook and riffled through the pages.

"Twenty Seventh of Moribund," he said promptly.

"In which case, you need to wind the watch back twenty-four days. Twenty-five if you leave it until tomorrow," Brenna didn't look at all happy. "Claus, I think you should take some of this medicine with you. Mister Tempest might need it, even if you do not."

"That's a bit uncalled for," commented Henry.

"Go back twenty-five days. Break the machine before Dahljeeling uses it. Stop Lord Cordage from dying," Claus counted the objectives off on his fingers as he spoke. "Missus McGrath? You will remember that this conversation took place when I go back in time, won't you?"

"I will remember everything, Claus," his aunt reassured him. "I will just have to put up with everyone else acting as if the last twenty-five days have not occurred," she sighed.

"Except for Dahljeeling and Arabella. You could always pop round to The Emporium for company," suggested Claus.

"What do you mean?" she asked.

"When I went back to save Henrietta, Dahljeeling seemed to remember the future. Arabella certainly can, can't you?"

Arabella nodded before remembering the old woman was blind.

"I can. I felt unwell at first, but then it all came back to me."

Brenna was quiet and looked thoughtful.

"Why?" asked Henry. "What is so strange about that?"

"A time travelling monkey?" Brenna cocked an eyebrow. "No, nothing strange about that. What puzzles me is why my step niece displays the abilities of a Timesmith when she's not a blood relation."

"I think what Henry meant was, do you think it significant?" smiled Claus.

"Most things are. But animals are very different to humans. They aren't as stupid for one thing. They don't have preconceptions of time and so they are less limited. Bodkin can sense it when you use the watch. He gets a bit grouchy. You said that Dahljeeling followed you home. Perhaps it was destiny that you two found each other."

"But if we go back and change everything, he'll belong to Lord Cordage again." The realisation made Claus miserable.

"Perhaps," Brenna patted his hand.

"So, Claus will take his medicine, we shall all get a good night's sleep and change history tomorrow," Henry summed up.

"Missus McGrath, would it be easier for you to stay here tonight?" asked Claus.

Henry blanched. There was no way the presence of the witch in the house would go unnoticed.

"I could have one of the maids make up another room for you," he agreed begrudgingly.

"No, I need to go back to my shop to collect some things."

Henry managed to withhold a sigh of relief. He stood up to show Brenna out.

"Forgive me, Madam, but this whole concept of me being able to travel through time, will it really work?"

"What do you think?" she asked.

"I think whatever I think is probably irrelevant."

"Glad we agree."

Brenna didn't turn up at Brandish Way until Ten o'clock the next morning, which was most acceptable to Claus, Arabella and Henry, who had all slept in late. She stood beneath Henry's window and cast pebbles at the glass until he came to investigate. He was relieved that she had not decided to gain access via the tradesman's entrance again. The staff would surely begin to talk. He made his way downstairs with all circumspection and let her in through the front door himself. Brenna opened her mouth to speak but Henry made quiet shushing noises and whispered that she should follow him up the stairs to the back parlour, which was seldom used. He winced as the stairs creaked beneath their weight, but they met no one as they ascended.

Henry opened the parlour door to find Claus and Arabella waiting in nervous silence. Brenna placed her ragged carpet bag upon a chair and extracted a small brown glass bottle, which she handed to Henry.

"I need you to put some of your blood in this," she instructed.

"Blood?" Henry was alarmed.

"Yes, blood. I've already put some of my own in."

Henry made a face and stared at the bottle in his hand with a look of deep mistrust.

"And what, may I ask, am I to do with this potion?" he said with evident dread.

"Drink it."

"I was afraid you were going to say that."

"Do you want to go back in time or not?"

Henry frowned and steeled himself.

"I need something to draw blood with," he sighed unhappily, but resolutely.

Brenna pulled forth a handsome looking dagger with a carved bone handle and offered it to him.

"We only need a drop or two," she uncorked the bottle and held it forth.

Henry took the dagger and pricked the end of his left forefinger. He turned a little pale as he watched his own blood drip into and mix with the unknown liquid in the bottle. Henry was not enthusiastic about the sight of blood, especially when it was his own. Brenna put the cork back in the top of the bottle and gave it a vigorous shake.

"What else is in it?" asked Henry, not sure that he really wanted to know. "Other than blood?"

"It's a mixture of..." Brenna hesitated. "Lots of things."

"Missus McGrath?" said Claus, "I was thinking, perhaps we should go back a little further in time than twenty-five days. It doesn't really give us much of an opportunity to intervene. Maybe we ought to go back to the day before?"

"The day that Hans died you mean?" she asked sharply.

Claus was silent.

"You realise that Hans died of old age, don't you? There is nothing to be done in such circumstances. Nothing you can do that will effect a change."

Claus said nothing.

"Anyway, didn't you make the watch after Hans was dead?" Henry frowned. "Would it not be dangerous to go back to a time when the watch didn't exist?"

Brenna raised her eyebrows in surprise.

"Hm. He makes a good point. Who would've thought?" she said.

Henry scowled and muttered to himself under his breath.

"The watch existed long before it was put back together," Brenna continued. "But your friend is right, Claus. We can't be sure what the repercussions would be if you went back to a time before you reconstructed it. It would be unwise, I think, to find out."

"Very well. I completed the watch some time in the early hours of the morning, after Hans died. I think we should go back as far as we deem safe."

"I agree," nodded Brenna.

"But what is our plan of action?" asked Henry.

"Arabella and I were up most of the night discussing this," said Claus. "I have broken into Lord Cordage's home before. I think we should stick to what we know. Scale the wall at the back of his estate, under the cover of darkness of course, make our way to the parlour, where we know for a fact that The Amplificator is, break in, disable the machine using the instructions we were given by Todorovich and then make a run for it."

"But, if we're going back to a time before we met Todorovich, surely we won't have his instructions, because he wouldn't have written them yet," frowned Henry.

"If I put the note in my pocket, before using the watch, it should travel back with me. Shouldn't it?" Claus looked at his aunt for confirmation.

"Aye. You could take any inanimate object along with you. As long as you have it on your person."

"That's settled then," nodded Henry.

"The sun won't rise until Eight o'clock and Lord Cordage, being a man of Bitterend society won't rise until mid-day. If we break in at say…Four o'clock?"

"I wish you would stop using the term 'break in'. You make me feel like a criminal. After all, we are doing this for Cordage's benefit as much as our own," complained Henry.

Claus smiled.

"Laudanum!" he suddenly proclaimed. "We shall need meat and laudanum. Lord Cordage has a particularly ferocious guard dog that will need subduing."

"I shall go to the kitchen to procure some meat. Will mutton do?" asked Henry.

"I really doubt it matters," Claus shook his head.

"And there is laudanum in the medicine cabinet."

"Good. Then all we need is a length of rope, a can of oil and some ill-fitting trousers."

Henry cocked an eyebrow.

"There are flower beds to crawl through."

"Aah," Henry nodded at this sage advice.

Claus turned back to his aunt.

"We were thinking, that is to say, Arabella and I wondered if she could come along with us? She'll be going back in time anyway."

"Hm. I've been thinking about that," frowned Brenna. "Where is she?"

"I'm here," Arabella stepped tentatively forward, and the witch reached out to clasp her arm.

"You're no Timesmith girl. That means you must be a witch."

"Um, yes, ma'am. My mother was too."

Brenna shook her head impatiently.

"There's power in you. Real power, I mean. Have you had any

291

schooling?"

"A little. Just what mama taught me. I know a lot about herbs and healing."

Brenna turned to her nephew.

"It's too dangerous to take her with you. She doesn't begin to understand her powers. Better that she come home with me, while the two of you go off gallivanting. She needs proper training, and I could use an able-bodied apprentice."

Claus nodded.

Arabella looked between the pair mutely while her fate was decided for her.

27th Moribund. Again

Henry lurched forward and vomited his breakfast (which, from a time travelling point of view, he had yet to eat) onto the floorboards. He staggered to the left and fell into his armoire as if he'd had too much brandy.

"That was singular," he commented to himself. He looked at his watch. Five minutes to four. The house was silent.

Twenty-four days ago, he had been fast asleep, without a care in the world. He ran downstairs and stopped dead at the sight of his sister, sat on a chaise with a cup of tea in one hand and a book in the other.

"What on Cellanor are you doing up and about at this hour?" she asked when she realised that he was stood in the doorway staring at her. "You look as if you've seen a ghost."

"I have to go," said Henry through numb lips. "I don't want to be late."

"Late for what?"

"Work."

"You don't normally worry about such things! And anyway, it's not yet dawn!"

"Why are *you* up then?" he said, deflecting her question with one of his own.

"I couldn't sleep. Something woke me and I felt…strange. I don't know, as if I had forgotten something vitally important," she frowned and shook her head as if to dispel the notion.

Henry dashed forwards and kissed the top of her head.

"Henry!" she grimaced, swatting him away.

~

Arabella opened her eyes with a gasp. Something about the room in which she was laying was wrong. It smelt wrong. It felt wrong. It even sounded wrong. It was too quiet, except for the caterwauling of seagulls beyond the window. Realisation washed over her. The feeling was akin to plunging one's head into cold water.

She was in Bightport Town again. The date was the twenty seventh of Moribund. She and Niall hadn't yet left for Bitterend. How could she have been so stupid? It hadn't even crossed her mind that a change in date would also mean a change of location. Her stomach dropped as she looked around the room for her stepfather, but she found that he wasn't with her. What had he been doing that morning? She wracked her brain.

Drinking. She remembered now. He'd come home drunk, happy with the stolen coin in his pocket. But Niall was a Timesmith. He would remember all that had passed. Like her, he would have been transported back to where he had been at that moment, only with full knowledge of events yet come to pass.

She stood up, unsteadily. There wasn't a moment to lose. He would come for her. What he didn't know was that she was also aware of the time shift.

She realised that she was wearing her old dress, and that it looked shabby in comparison with Henrietta's gowns. A tiny part of her wished that she could bring items back in time, as Claus could. Then she mentally admonished herself for being silly and worrying about something so frivolous at such a time. Niall could return at any moment. Could she force herself to pretend that she knew nothing of the events which would come to pass? Could she suffer herself to be in the same room as the monster Niall had become? She thought of her dear Claus and realised that she could not. There was only one course of action left available to her, and that was to flee. She hurried over to the corner of the room and pulled at the loose floorboard. She'd seen Niall hide his

294

ill-gotten gains there, when he'd assumed that she was too inebriated to notice what he was doing.

The cache was not insubstantial, and she stuffed as much as she could inside a small reticule. The rest she tucked down the front of her corset and down the sides of her boots. Then she fled as fast as her legs would carry her, her one thought was to get to the train station.

~

Claus sat up abruptly. The watch ticked serenely on the workbench before him. He felt slightly discombobulated and very sick, but that seemed to be the extent of his side effects. He could still remember everything that had passed. He took a sip of his great aunt's brain fever medicine, just to be on the safe side.

He looked around the workroom. It looked the same as it always did, except that the window had yet to be boarded up. If all went according to plan, there would be no need to board it up. The Emporium felt horribly empty. He'd quickly become accustomed to having Arabella at his side, Dahljeeling scampering around and Hattie busily trying to turn the building into a home. And now he had his aunt too. He had a family again. The thought spurred him into action. He picked the watch up and gazed at the hands as they moved around the face. Five minutes to four.

He and Henry had decided that they would meet halfway between their homes. It would be easier and faster than Henry having to wake his stable hand and coach driver and there was always a cab to be hailed in Bitterend, regardless of the hour. Claus pocketed the watch and cranked the Transporter up to the shop. He had donned his not-so-new greatcoat before turning the watch back, so that it came back in time with him. It had lots of deep pockets which would prove useful for the challenge ahead. He had grown rather attached to it and was quite upset to find that it hadn't fared well after the carriage accident. He doubted that climbing over walls and crawling through flower beds would do it much good either, but he could always get another one in the future.

He almost called out for Dahljeeling, before remembering that his hirsute companion belonged to Lord Cordage once more. He sighed and made his way out of the lonely Emporium onto the smoggy streets beyond.

It wasn't long before Claus saw a blacker outline of a man in the darkness ahead.

"Henry? Is that you?" he called out tentatively, at the same time as Henry asked if the figure approaching in the opposite direction was Claus. The pair greeted each other with evident relief and carried on walking down the road in the direction of Lord Cordage's abode.

"We need to find a cab," said Henry. "It'll take us forever on foot."

As if destiny had been waiting for these very words, a carriage became audible. Claus waved at it as it trundled up the street and the driver directed his horses to come to a stop.

"Late night gents?" The cab driver grinned down at them.

"Early morning, more like!" said Henry.

Claus felt the colour drain from his face as he glanced up at the man on the dickie box. It was the same driver from the night of the incident. The same driver that he, Claus, had intended to murder with the pistol that was still hidden in the pocket of his coat.

~

The cab ride to Lord Cordage's was a sombre affair. Whatever excitement the boys might have felt about their imminent act of derring-do was overshadowed by the very real prospect of arrest, or worse, failure and the impact it would have on Henrietta's future, or lack of it. Claus tried to concentrate on the scenery as they travelled, but it was so early that it was still as dark as night and he could make out very little of his surroundings.

The cab came to a halt and Henry and Claus exchanged a look as if

296

they had arrived at the gallows which awaited their pleasure.

"Have a good day, gents!" grinned the cabbie once the boys had climbed out. Claus flinched at the driver's loud farewell and looked around anxiously. The carriage moved away, and Henry rubbed his palms against the fabric of his trousers in an attempt to wipe away the nervous sweat which had accumulated.

"Do we go over this wall? It seems rather…you know, out in the open."

Claus didn't bother to answer but approached the aforementioned wall and unravelled the length of rope which he had concealed about his person. He swung the end towards the all too familiar tree branch which overhung the estate wall but misjudged the distance in his nervousness. The rope fell to the ground with a dull thud. He took a deep breath and tried again. This time the rope fell over the branch and Claus caught on to both ends. He tugged upon it to make sure that it would hold his weight, even though he already knew that it would, if his previous adventure was anything to go by, but he didn't want to leave anything to chance. He heaved himself up with his arms, his feet sliding ineffectually against the damp bricks and foliage of the wall, until he brought himself into a sitting position at the top. He gazed around the silent brumail gardens but could see no sign of life. He waved his hand at Henry to encourage his assent. Henry, being for the most part, a young man of leisure, had a little more trouble scaling the wall than Claus and when he finally attained his lofty position, he was breathless and red in the face.

"I swear that I'm going to take up fencing or something if we make it through this!" he puffed. Claus managed to conceal his scepticism and nodded supportively. He pulled the rope over the wall so that it dangled down into the garden. He lowered himself down carefully and crouched as he felt the frosty grass beneath his feet. Henry did likewise and they began to make their way across the lawn like a pair of brigands.

The rear of the house loomed into view and Claus thought that he could just make out the parlour doors, the glass was reflective even in the gloaming. He pulled out the laudanum laced meat and flung it onto the grass before gesturing to Henry that he should follow him through the flower beds. They attained the Bonancian doors which were once again, unlocked. They entered with as much stealth as they could muster. Henry lit a lamp and they proceeded towards Todorovich's Amplificator.

"Can you remember how to disable it?" whispered Henry.

"I think so. I brought Todorovich's instructions just in case."

"Alright," said Henry. He turned to set the lamp down upon the table and a precariously placed cup and saucer fell onto the floor and smashed. Claus sucked in his breath and Henry put his hands to his head, frozen in horror. They both held their breaths and strained their ears for a full minute. They heard no shouts, or voices raised in alarm and the door wasn't flung open, so the boys began breathing again.

"You get to work, and I'll keep a look out," sighed Henry.

"*What the blazers!*" came a booming voice, accompanied by the sound of a door being flung back with such violence that it hit the wall beside it. "Housebreaker's is it? Thieves! *Vagabonds!*" thundered Lord Cordage.

"No, no! It's not what it looks like!" protested Henry, holding his hands out in supplication. His eyes focused and became transfixed upon the blunderbuss which was being swung back and forth between himself and Claus like a pendulum of imminent death.

"Lord Cordage. Please, let us explain! We aren't criminals…" Claus trailed off as he wondered at the validity of his own words.

Lord Cordage advanced with his formidable weapon.

"*What are you doing to my Amplificator?*" he roared.

"I've got something here from Todorovich-" Claus improvised.

"Nikola?"

"Yes! Yes! Just let me show you!" Claus reached into his pocket to produce the slip of paper, his brain desperately scrabbling for some semblance of a rational explanation with which to appease the irate tea baron.

"Keep your hands where I can see them!" Cordage advanced threateningly.

Claus glanced to his side where the sudden movement of a dark shape had caught his eye. The monkey butler had sprung up upon the table. Their eyes met. Dahljeeling looked between Claus and Lord Cordage, screamed, picked up the nearest teapot and flung it with animal force. The teapot struck Cordage on the head and he dropped to the floorboards like a stone.

"Dahljeeling!" Claus reached out and patted the monkey on his little shoulder. "Thank you."

"Er...Claus?"

Claus turned to look at Henry who was leaning over the prone form of Lord Cordage. There seemed to be an awful lot of blood on the floorboards.

"He's dead. Just like before! This can't be good," Henry hissed.

Claus let forth a quiet, yet fervent, stream of profanities.

"Dahljeeling is wearing his red suit again," said Henry.

"This is the Dahljeeling from twenty-five days ago. He was still working for Cordage then. He doesn't travel back in time; he just remembers the future."

"So..." Henry began slowly. "There isn't a future version of him here as well is there? I mean, they're not going to bump into each other and cause a space-time continuum paradox, or something?"

299

Claus gave his friend a funny look.

"No Henry. There is only *one* Dahljeeling."

"If only *that* were true," Henry sighed.

"At this precise moment in time, *it is* true. He hasn't used The Amplificator yet."

"Should we just break the bloody thing and leg it then? After all, it's not our fault Cordage is dead. Dahljeeling killed him," Henry frowned suspiciously at the monkey.

Claus shook his head.

"It *is* our fault. If we leave things like this, we as good as killed Cordage ourselves. Dahljeeling was only trying to protect me. Besides, what if we're spotted leaving the house? We'll be hanged for murder, or worse, thrown over the wall."

"Spotted dick?" suggested Henry.

"Spotted dick," agreed Claus, and he pulled the watch from his pocket

~

Henry managed to withhold the contents of his stomach this time and merely stumbled a little.

"I'm not back at my house," he frowned.

Claus had wound the watch back to the point in time where he had met Henry out on the street.

"No, Henry. I only wound the watch back a little. We've already changed past events. We're back in the *second* past now."

"The second past," Henry said faintly and rubbed his forehead. "What now?"

Claus took a swig of brain fever medicine and offered some to his friend who declined, proclaiming that he was as sure of his own sanity

300

as he ever was, which wasn't saying much.

"We need a better plan," stated Claus. "I think we should go back to the workshop. I always find that I can focus more when I'm there."

Henry agreed and shuddered when he saw their infamous cab driver clatter past. He waved at the pair as if they were all old friends.

~

Arabella groaned and put her head in her hands. An elderly lady who shared the first-class compartment with her looked over in concern.

"Are you quite alight, dear?"

Arabella looked up and took in her surroundings. She was still sat in a moving train. Niall was nowhere to be seen. She'd used her new-found wealth to purchase a first-class ticket aboard an express train to Bitterend, in a carriage reserved for ladies.

"Yes," she answered. "Thank you."

Claus had obviously used the watch again, but only to go back as far as an hour or so. Things must not have gone according to plan. It was an ominous realisation.

~

The first thing that Claus did after entering the Time Emporium, was to make a pot of tea. The pair loaded up a small tray with teapot, cups, milk and custard cream biscuits and took it below ground to the workshop. They both agreed that breaking into Lord Cordage's abode was a bad idea. They couldn't risk yet another failure and so abandoned the idea entirely.

The pair sat around the workbench and sipped their refreshments in silence.

"I don't think house breaking is really our forte old chap," sighed

Claus.

Henry nodded and bit into a biscuit in a desultory manner, or as desultory as Henry could be when faced with anything edible.

"Do you think we should go and visit your aunt? Gosh that sounds odd!"

Claus frowned and nodded slowly.

"Indeed, it does. It might take me a while to get used to it. But I doubt she could help us any more than she already has."

"She's got a shop full of strange books and a bag full of strange potions. Who knows what she's capable of?"

"I thought that you didn't believe in that sort of thing?" Claus couldn't help but smile.

"Well, a chap is allowed to change his mind, isn't he? And after all I've seen lately…" he let his sentence trail off.

Claus nodded.

"I know she's a bit…stern-"

Henry snorted in laughter. "That's one way to put it! She's a cantankerous old git, just like Hans was!"

Claus smiled and continued. "-but I like her. And it's nice to know that I have family, even if they are cantankerous old gits."

"The Tempest's are your family too!" protested Henry.

"I know. What I mean to say is that it's good to know that I have blood relations."

"Well, you'll have lots of blood relations when you marry Arabella," grinned Henry.

Claus choked on a custard cream.

"I did have designs on making you wed Henrietta," admitted Henry.

"Ugh!" Claus looked aghast.

"What's wrong with my sister?" demanded Henry.

"There's nothing wrong with her!" said Claus hastily. "Apart from the fact that if I were to marry her I'd feel as though I were committing incest!"

"Fair enough," said Henry, somewhat mollified. "So long as she doesn't marry Todorovich," he dropped his voice conspiratorially "I think he fancies her you know."

Claus stared at his friend with wide eyes and his mouth slightly agape.

"I know. It's disgusting," frowned Henry.

"No! I've just realised! Todorovich! That's it!" Claus slammed his teacup down upon the workbench with unnecessary force and began searching in all of his pockets. He made a noise of victory as he pulled forth a crumpled piece of paper. "What say we add a spot of forgery to our portfolio of criminal activity?"

"What is that?" asked Henry as he reached out and took the paper. "Your letter? The warning that you wrote to yourself from the future. How is this going to help? I say, you must have been in some sort of frenzy when you wrote this, there's ink blotches all over the thing. And your punctuation is terrible!"

"Turn it over!" huffed Claus impatiently.

"You wrote it on the back of one of Todorovich's letters to Lord Cordage."

"You surmised correctly that I was, as you put it, in a frenzy when I wrote that letter. A frenzy and a dreadful need for haste. Todorovich's letter was the first piece of paper that caught my eye. With the instructions he gave us and this letter as a template..."

"You want me to copy his hand?"

Claus nodded.

303

"Can you?"

Henry shrugged.

"I've spent many a year forging my father's signature. I assume that you are proposing that we write a letter to Lord Cordage and sign it from Todorovich?"

"Indeed. Are you up to it?"

"I'll need to practice first, but I'll give it a try. What should we write? Another warning about using the machine?"

"No. That won't make a difference. I suspect that Dahljeeling merely set the thing off by accident. The maid told us he's fond of hiding in small places. When he was hiding from his doppelgangers in my attic, I discovered him sat inside an old tea chest."

"Yes, but that might be just another symptom of his obsessive tea disorder."

"He sleeps in a bedside cabinet, I think it's a safe assumption that he entered the Amplificator of his own free will," Claus smiled and departed to find some fresh paper from the office.

When he returned, he found Henry staring at Todorovich's letter with a look of consternation upon his face.

"Claus, you only have this letter because you had it upon your person when you used the watch, correct?"

Claus nodded.

"So, the rest of the letters we read...they are all back in Lord Cordage's parlour, because we haven't stolen them yet."

Again, Claus nodded.

"So, I was thinking… if we haven't *stolen* them yet, we cannot have *read* them yet. But we still know what is written in them," Henry rubbed his temples with his fingertips.

"Yes, because we read them in the future," said Claus.

Henry stared mutely at his companion.

"It's better if you just try not to think about it too much," he said. "Trust me."

Henry nodded emphatically. Claus passed him a fresh sheet of paper to practice his forgery. A few minutes of silence passed before Henry looked up, seemingly in great agitation about something but loath to mention it. He couldn't remain reticent for long.

"But this letter!" he cried, pointing at the one that lay before him on the workbench. "This travelled back in time, so that means that it is here with us, not with Cordage! He never received it!"

"No, no. We've never stopped Todorovich from writing it, nor posting it. Now there is two copies of the same letter existing in the same reality and time frame, one in the pristine condition in which Cordage received it and another with my note to myself scrawled on the back of it."

Henry opened and closed his mouth a couple of times but didn't make any comment.

"I told you, it's better if you-"

"Try not to think, yes," Henry nodded. "Gosh, no one has ever advised me to think *less*."

Claus took pity on his friend and poured him another cup of tea. They sat in silence for a while until Henry looked up from his task once more.

"I think I've got it. What do you think?" he turned the sheet of paper towards Claus who scrutinised the letters.

"Good enough I'd say. And we can't afford to waste any more time."

Henry gave him a funny look in response to such blatant irony.

"So, what should I write? You still haven't told me the plan."

~

Claus wasn't the least bit surprised when the cab that he hailed pulled over and he saw that it was driven by *The Cabbie*. In truth he probably would have been quite alarmed if he had looked up to see a different driver sat upon the box. When the boys disembarked at Lord Cordage's it was with great relief that the pair walked up the gravel path towards the front door, like any normal person would do and not as thieves trampling the begonias. They yanked on the bell pull and after a short pause, the familiar face of the butler appeared as he opened the door.

"Ah, you must be Mister Hogarth!" said Henry with as much authority as he could muster. The butler looked taken aback and opened his mouth to speak, but Henry cut him off before he had a chance to form a sentence.

"We are not salesmen, we have an *urgent* letter to deliver to Lord Cordage, on behalf of Nikola Todorovich. You must give this to him *at once!*" He thrust the counterfeit letter towards Mister Hogarth. The word 'urgent' was written, somewhat gratuitously, on the envelope.

"And whom, may I ask, are you?"

"We are friends to Mister Todorovich and have worked with him on occasion." It wasn't an out and out lie, but Henry was certainly stretching the truth. The butler grew a little more courteous upon hearing this proclamation and invited them inside. He told them to wait in the foyer while he delivered the message to Lord Cordage and disappeared.

Claus and Henry held their breaths while they waited. The forgery was a good attempt, but Henry would have preferred more time to practice before committing to writing an entire letter, even one so short. He wasn't entirely happy with the slant of his 'O's. Nevertheless, time was pressing. There was only four hours left before the first monkey attack was due and who knew what time Dahljeeling had had his misadventure with The Amplificator. His doppelgangers might have rampaged around Cordage's grounds for an hour or more before they made their way into town to ransack the local tea shops.

Claus tapped his foot in anxious impatience upon the tiles. He couldn't help it.

Lord Cordage came thudding towards them from the direction of the parlour. He looked a great deal larger when he wasn't lying dead upon the floor with a teapot shaped hole in his head, but curiously, he didn't look any less threatening than when they had seen him wielding a blunderbuss. Perhaps a look of anger was his default expression, or perhaps he had detected something was amiss with the fake letter and was coming to give them what for.

"So, you're the chaps, are you? You can fix it?" His Lordship demanded without bothering about the niceties or formality of greeting.

"That's us Gov'nor," smiled Henry, as he tipped his hat. Claus gave him a sideways look. He wasn't sure why Henry had suddenly adopted a Northwall accent, if indeed that was what it was supposed to be.

"Come along then. This way. Will this take long? I'm a very busy man, don't you know."

Claus realised that there was no hope of anything akin to gratitude from this man. He would never know that Claus and Henry were about to save his life and he supposed that was as it should be. Still, Claus ground his teeth a little. They entered the now familiar parlour and Claus pulled forth some tools that he had gathered from his workshop. They were not the same tools that Todorovich had supplied, as he had yet to even meet the man, but Claus judged that they could be put to a similar use. He didn't bother to look at the instructions, feeling that, by now, he really *did* know how to fix The Amplificator, or un-fix it, as the case may be. He set to work unscrewing various nuts and bolts. A small and somewhat pitiful noise from the corner of the room made him look up from his work.

"Dahljeeling," he breathed, as he met the monkey's sad gaze.

"What's that?" snapped Lord Cordage. "You can't want tea already! You've barely done anything!"

"Sorry? No," Claus shook his head and glanced at Henry. He hadn't realised that changing events would have such an impact upon poor Dahljeeling, who could remember all the time shifts and the time he had spent with Claus. Claus had a fierce desire to smuggle his fury friend out of the house.

He removed the arconian crystal and unscrewed the coil, then dropped both into his pocket with a huge sense of relief.

"There. All done. I suggest you wait for Mister Todorovich before you do anything with this," said Claus.

Lord Cordage didn't bother to thank them, and Mister Hogarth saw them to the front door. They walked down the pathway in silence. Claus felt as though his legs didn't want to work properly and no sooner were out of sight of the house, he sank to the ground in exhaustion. Henry began to laugh like an escaped lunatic.

"We did it! I can't believe that was so easy!" he crowed.

"Easy?" Claus looked up at his friend with an incredulous look. "Yes, it's been like a walk in the park." he scoffed.

"No, but, well it's done now!" Henry grinned. "It's done and there are no more maniac monkeys on the loose and nobody died, and Henrietta is going to be fine!"

Claus agreed that this was a very good thing.

"I suggest that we go and collect the girls and then head to Beverstone's for the heartiest breakfast conceivable!"

"The girls," mumbled Claus. "Henrietta won't know who Arabella is. How are we to explain her sudden appearance? Not to mention the fact I've suddenly acquired a great aunt."

"Erm…We'll think of something. Let's just get home."

Claus nodded and staggered as he got to his feet.

Henry supported most of his friend's weight as they made their way along the quiet, tree lined road. Cabs were not so easy to come by this far from town, but eventually they managed to wave one down.

"Sovereign Street," said Henry, as he bundled Claus into the carriage. He sighed with relief when he realised that he had never met the driver before. As the cab moved off, Henry heard a thud upon the roof. He peered out of the window but could see nothing amiss. He turned to Claus, but his companion looked so tired and drawn that he made no mention of it and let him nod quietly into the collar of his coat.

28th Moribund. Again

Brenna turned over the last two remaining cards. 'Justice' and 'Death'.

"These are the only two which never change," she grumbled and swore at her tarot deck.

Bodkin made a yowling noise. There was a bang on the shop door and Brenna stood up and shuffled out of the back room.

"I was beginning to think that you'd never turn up," she said as she pulled open the door.

"Aye. Well, you know what they say about bad pennies," Niall pushed his way inside.

"Why don't you come in?" muttered Brenna.

Niall looked around the shop interior.

"You've done alright for yourself old woman."

"I get by."

He glanced into the back room and saw the cards spread out upon the table.

"I don't know why you bother with those. I can tell you what your future holds."

"It isn't *my* future that concerns me," sighed Brenna. "Tea?"

Niall shrugged and sat down at the little table. Brenna poured them each a cup and joined him.

"I trust this isn't a social call?"

"I just want what I'm owed."

"Be careful what you wish for," she warned.

Niall laughed.

"So, did you buy this place with your inheritance money?"

"What inheritance money?" snapped Brenna. "I got this shop by hard work, my lad. You should try it sometime."

"Hard work?" Niall sneered. "Sure. The old codger didn't leave you anything in his will then?"

"Of course not! Not after you killed his daughter. Hans didn't want anything to do with me after that!"

"His own sister? I find that hard to believe. Are you sure he didn't leave you anything?"

"I saw him once before he died. He wanted me to have the watch, to destroy it, which I have done, so you can bugger off," she growled.

"The boy has it," said Niall, as if he hadn't even been listening. "What's more he keeps using it. Over and over. It's driving me mad. He needs to be stopped."

"On that at least we are in agreement," nodded Brenna.

"You'll get it for me, won't you ma?" he spoke reasonably, but there was an unmistakable undertone of threat in his voice.

"Why in the Vale of Lament would I do that?"

"Because I'm your son," he swilled his tea around his mouth as if he wanted to wash away the taste of those words. "All these years without a word. I thought you were dead. You should help me. You owe me that much. And because if you don't, I'll see to it that this place gets burnt to the ground, with you inside it."

Brenna snorted.

"You really think I'll respond to your threats? I have little fear of death and even less of you."

"The boy then. Perhaps you care what happens to him? Perhaps you'd care if his sorry carcass were to be washed up on the banks of The Dolorous?"

"And just how am I supposed to convince him to give me the damn watch? He doesn't even know who I am," she lied. "Our side of the family were cast out because of you, never to be mentioned again."

"The solicitor. He knows the truth. You must get him to uphold the will."

"I have no proof that I am family. I'm a *bastard* remember. Johannes Vogel's unwanted souvenir from Irkland. Hans only discovered my existence when he was sorting through his father's belongings after he died. If he hadn't found my mother's letters, pleading for money, he would have been none the wiser."

Niall waved his hand as if he were tired of the whole conversation.

"Get the watch or the boy gets a slit throat," Niall put his teacup down rather heavily upon its saucer and stood up. He swayed from side to side for a moment and clutched hold of the tablecloth before falling to the floor, dragging both cloth and crockery along with him.

Click Clack descended the stairs and looked at the man with the bright blue eyes. Brenna had been forced to explain her family history all over again since Claus had wound the watch back.

"I hope that was poison what you put in his tea?"

Brenna chewed at her bottom lip and shook her head.

"Valerian mostly. And laudanum. I thought it would take him quicker than that. I used to put it in his sugar water when he was a baby to stop him crying, the valerian I mean. Maybe he built up a tolerance to it."

"How long will he be out?"

"Long enough."

"Right then." Click clack rubbed his hands together. "Let's get to it."

"It'll all be for naught if Claus uses the watch. Niall is a Timesmith after all," Brenna signed in exasperation. "If Claus winds time back again after tonight, none of this will matter and worse still, Niall will be forewarned of what we have planned for him."

"But I thought you said that Claus had achieved what he wanted. That he'd managed to change the past?"

"He did," Brenna looked uncomfortable. "But that's not to say the temptation to use it again in the future won't arise."

~

Click Clack pulled Niall McGrath out of the shop by his ankles and was none too careful about the way his head knocked against the furniture. He heaved him up onto the back of the wagon, made sure he wasn't likely to roll off and covered him over with some sacking. He helped Brenna up into the seat and the pair headed towards the Lemon Street police station in Blacktemple. They passed many people on the way who paid them no attention. Even if the unconscious body in the back of the wagon had not been hidden, it was doubtful that anyone would have cared. They reached Lemon Street and Click Clack dragged the body to the entrance of the police station, where he propped it against the door. He took the gentleman's pocket watch and wallet, which he'd stolen earlier, from the inside of his coat and slipped them into Niall's pocket. Then he hurried away, took hold of the bridle and led the horse and wagon to a safe distance.

He stood beside Brenna and sipped from his hipflask and waited.

"Have they found him yet?" asked Brenna after a while.

"Not yet."

"Bloody useless buggers."

Click Clack passed her the flask.

"Hang on! Here we go."

313

A young police constable tried to exit the station only to find an insensible man slumped against the door. Click Clack watched as he knelt down to see if the man was alive and then signalled for his fellow officers to help him carry the figure inside.

"Do you think they'll notice the stolen goods?" asked Brenna.

"I recon they might. I stole them off Lord Cavendish myself. Felt strange picking a pocket after all these years. You don't have a dog and bark yourself after all, but picking pockets is a life skill. You never forget. Anyway, I'm pretty sure even the peelers will recognise that your son ain't Lord Cavendish."

"Will they hang him, do you think?"

"Hopefully. What do you care?"

Brenna shrugged and Click Clack put his arm around her shoulders.

"Nah. They won't hang him. Probably ship him off somewhere. Somewhere far away."

18th Brevis. Once More

The 18th of Brevis, Age of Cambion 13:7, was quite possibly the strangest day of Claus Vogel's life. He had already lived through it on several different occasions and wished heartily to be rid of it once and for all. Happily, this version of the day was turning out to be a great deal less traumatic than the others. He had awoken warm and cosy in his bed, and when he had ventured forth from his bedroom, he found Dahljeeling polishing the new silverware and Hattie busily cooking in the newly appointed kitchen.

The entire house was in various stages of renovation. The upper levels had been cleaned and aired, windows thrown wide, the sharp Brevis air dispelling the hitherto tomb-like petrification of the past, like spirits of the dead, released from bondage.

The peculiar circumstance of Claus re-living the past several weeks of his life was improved by the presence of Arabella and his Aunt Brenna. It was a comforting notion that they knew the truth of the matter. The fact that Henry was also going through the same experience was rather less comforting, as he had developed a habit of winking after saying or doing something that he had done previously, to the point that his sister was concerned that he had developed a nervous tick. He also kept stopping to stare at various occurrences that he remembered seeing before and commenting in a voice of wonderment, "This is *so* strange."

That evening, Claus, Arabella, Dahljeeling and the Tempest's should have been going to the theatre to meet Todorovich, but of course, none of them had ever made the scientist's acquaintance. Except for Henrietta. She had unexpectedly bumped into the man outside the science museum. Fortunately, Todorovich had made no mention of attending the theatre, although he had taken Henrietta out for dinner at Eldarn View. Henry was all in favour of using the watch to alter this turn of events, but Claus refused and counselled his friend that perhaps some things were just meant to be.

Claus had invited his Aunt round for dinner, an invitation which, of course, extended to Arabella, who was now living with Brenna and being schooled in witchcraft-whatever that involved. Claus was sat in the office of The Time Emporium, happily drinking tea with Dahljeeling, awaiting the arrival of his aunt and Arabella. Dahljeeling was wearing a very nice outfit of aubergine velvet, with a bronze and chocolate brown jacquard waistcoat and a top hat, set at a jaunty angle. Claus hoped that no one would recognise Dahljeeling as the monkey formally owned by Lord Cordage, who had gone missing under mysterious circumstances on the very same morning that two fraudsters had entered Lord Cordage's property and vandalised his flavour enhancement apparatus. It would certainly be a stretch of the imagination for anyone to believe that the monkey had absconded with the perpetrators, unbeknownst to them, and had travelled home with them atop their carriage.

Henrietta was more than a little confused as to where and furthermore, *why*, Claus had obtained a monkey butler. Henry and Claus had agreed that they would never divulge what had happened to Henrietta and so she was none the wiser about her accident. They also thought it prudent to conceal the entire sorry business of The Amplificator, the monkeys, and the peculiar watch. Instead, they carried on as though all was well and attempted to act normal, or in Henry's case, as normal as was possible. Henrietta complained of headaches, which was rather disturbing given the nature of her accident, and Claus felt terribly guilty each and every time that Henrietta put her hand to her head and complained of a sense of Déjà vu. In an attempt to ease his conscience, he allowed himself to be subjected to an all-day shopping spree, without a single word of complaint. His fears of introducing Arabella to Henrietta proved unnecessary, as she took an instant shine to the other girl and they quickly became firm friends.

Claus heard the bell above the shop door tinkle, and he smiled as he hurried to greet his guests.

He exchanged a slightly embarrassed greeting with Arabella, painfully aware that although his aunt was blind, she could still see.

"I've just brewed a fresh pot of tea," he announced.

Agatha appeared from nowhere and meowed in greeting. She seemed to have taken a great liking to Brenna, which was surprising as she was usually quite shy. Perhaps she could sense that the old woman was a devoted cat lover. Bodkin made his curious rumbling sound which meant that he was not displeased by the presence of the other feline.

"Shall we go to the parlour?" asked Claus. "Can you manage the stairs?" he added to his aunt.

"Don't fuss, Claus," Brenna stooped to sweep Agatha up into her arms. "I made it all the way here without some calamity befalling me, didn't I?"

"Oh. Yes, of course," Claus said, feeling a little foolish. "Dinner is almost ready. I re-employed Hattie last week. She's an excellent cook. I've a mind to hire a housemaid too, now that we've opened up the disused floors," he winced slightly as he spoke, waiting for an admonishment about wasting money.

"I always thought it a shame for a nice house like this to go to wrack and ruin," shrugged Brenna.

Claus raised his eyebrows. Clearly Brenna did not share her brother's attitude towards thriftiness.

"Anyway, we're having Bonancian onion soup, baked halibut, smoked pigeon pie and a buttercream torte with red berry compote for dessert."

Brenna nodded in approval and they all made their way upstairs. Since Claus had yet to resurrect the dining room, they had to eat in the parlour from trays upon their laps, but it was warm and informal, with a hearty fire burning in the grate. Dahljeeling joined them but insisted on getting

317

up after each course to tidy away the plates. Agatha and Bodkin ate beside them from their own dishes on the floor. It was a mark of how good the pigeon pie was that Agatha ignored the brass clockwork mice that kept whirring in and out of the room on their tiny wheels.

"There's something I've been meaning to do," said Claus after he patted his mouth with his napkin. He pulled out his watch and placed it on the coffee table in front of Brenna. She seemed to recoil slightly when she sensed its presence.

"I want you to have it," he said.

"I don't want it," she scowled as if the watch was her mortal enemy.

"But it is yours none the less. Grandfather stated in his will that the eldest member of the family should have it. He obviously meant you."

Brenna said nothing but stared at her great nephew in her disconcertingly penetrative and entirely un-blind manner. The silence stretched on until she sighed heavily and reached out. Her hand hovered over the watch for a moment, as though she was disinclined to touch it. Then she picked it up and wrapped it in a handkerchief before stuffing it unceremoniously into a pocket in the folds of her dress. The ticking noise it produced seemed uncommonly loud despite its wrappings. A crash from elsewhere in the Emporium startled them all.

"Dahljeeling getting the desert, no doubt," smiled Claus. He looked back at his Aunt. "What do you intend to do with it?"

"Eat it."

Claus huffed. "I meant what do you intend to do with the watch."

"Oh that. Chuck it in The Dolorous," she shrugged.

Claus couldn't conceal his wince.

"If that is your plan then I will accompany you. We can go tomorrow."

"I thought you were taking my apprentice out for dinner tomorrow."

318

"Er…um…" Claus blushed and looked at Arabella, who shrugged to convey that she had not divulged this information.

Brenna smirked.

"I think I shall go and see where our desert has got to." Claus stood up to go and retrieve the buttercream torte from the kitchen but came to a dead stop when he saw a dark figure stood on the landing.

"You?" he frowned.

"Good evening, Claus," said the man with the bright blue eyes, in an affable manner. He looked dishevelled and pale, a sheen of sweat lingered upon his brow and an unhealthy gleam, like marsh-light, burned in his eyes. "I've come here for my inheritance and my stepdaughter."

"Neither of which belongs to you," said Claus icily. He heard a shuffling of feet behind him and suppressed a groan as Brenna and Arabella appeared behind him.

"Oh look," smiled Niall. "We seem to have ourselves a little family reunion."

"What are you doing here?" growled Brenna.

"You mean, why haven't I been transported? Or perhaps you would have preferred me to go to the scaffold?"

Brenna winced.

"A witness finally came forward and testified that it was a Katamesian who stole from Lord Cavendish," Niall continued. "Since I am clearly not Katamesian, they had no choice but to let me go. Click Clack ought to hide his yellow face if he's going to do his own dirty work. Perhaps he's not as quick as he used to be."

Brenna ground her teeth together.

"And here is the slattern turncoat," Niall beamed, as if he'd only just noticed Arabella. She took a step behind Brenna, who grasped her hand protectively. "You abandoned the one person in this world that cared about you, to learn magic tricks from an old hag and to drop your drawers for this streak of piss who stole my inheritance. That's loyalty for you. I should've left you in Bightport. You could've earned your bread on your back, like the whore you are."

Claus couldn't control his temper and swung his fist at the unwanted guest. Unaccustomed to brawling, Claus was surprised that he managed to hit his target and it was with some satisfaction that he watched the man stagger back from the force, if only for a moment.

Niall retaliated almost instantly and lashed out with a more experienced fist, which caught Claus on the side of his head. He crumpled into the wall and lay dazed for a moment. The sudden explosion of pain very nearly caused him to regurgitate his pigeon pie. Niall reached down and hauled him to his feet by his throat.

"Leave him alone!" shrieked Arabella.

Claus could feel the iron like grip around his throat tighten. He felt his feet lose contact with the floor as he was lifted up and could do nothing to stop himself being shaken like a rag doll. Dahljeeling appeared in the doorway, roused by the shouting, buttercream torte in hand. Upon seeing his master's assault, he shrieked and threw the plate towards the assailant. The desert hit Niall square in the face and decorated the wallpaper with whipped cream, but it did little to improve the situation, other than to cause a temporary impediment to his vision.

"The watch! Give me the watch!" Niall bawled into Claus's face, bits of whipped cream and sponge spraying all over the place.

"Here!" screamed Brenna, and she tossed the watch towards her son.

Niall let go of Claus, who gasped and fell to the floor once more. The man with the bright blue eyes thrust out an arm to catch his precious prize. He cackled from behind his mask of buttercream torte, took a step back and trod on a clockwork mouse.

Without the aid of the watch, time seemed to slow down as Claus watched Niall's foot slide out from beneath him. He fell backwards, down the staircase behind him, with strangely muted thuds.

There was silence.

"What happened?" whispered Brenna. "Claus?" She sounded fearful.

"I'm alright, Aunt," croaked Claus. His hand went to his throat and gingerly touched the bruised flesh. "He fell down the stairs."

"I can't hear anything. Is he dead?" asked Arabella.

"I don't know."

No one seemed to be able to move in order to find out. Brenna reached out and took hold of Claus's hand and they all stood in silence for what seemed like a long time. In the showroom a great many clocks chimed midnight.

"Er...are you lot alright up there?" Rabbit called up the stairs to the figures who stood at the top.

"Aye. You one of Click Clack's boys then?" called back Brenna.

"Yes, Ma'am," Rabbit prodded at Niall with the toe of his boot. His head flopped unnaturally. "Reckon this bloke here is dead."

Claus looked sharply at his aunt to see if she were about to faint away with grief, but she nodded her head, as if the boy had merely confirmed what she already knew. There was a scuttling sound at their feet and Claus found himself surprisingly pleased when he looked down to see that no harm had come to the clockwork mouse. Claus, Arabella and Brenna descended the stairs slowly and had to climb over the broken body that was sprawled at the bottom. The office which had been cramped to begin with was now positively claustrophobic with four people and a corpse taking up floor space.

"Is that blood?" queried Claus, hoping that his voice didn't sound as shaky to the others as it did to himself.

Rabbit extended a forefinger, stuck it in the sticky red substance which covered the side of Niall's head, then put it in his mouth.

"Red berry compote," smiled the boy. "Shall I go and get Click Clack then?"

Brenna nodded. "How did you know to come here?"

"Click Clack has a contact down at Moarland Yard."

"Of course he does," Brenna almost smiled. "So he knew that Niall had been released without charge."

"Only found out this evening. He sent me on ahead of him, on account of me being fast an' all. I saw this fella breaking in here and I thought 'this looks like trouble' so I followed. Seems you lot can look after yourselves though. So, which one of you did for him?"

There was silence. Brenna crossed her arms over her chest and kept her mouth firmly shut. Claus realised with horror that his aunt would not have seen the clockwork mouse and so would naturally assume that Claus had pushed her son down the stairs.

"No one murdered him!" said Claus hastily. "He slipped on a clockwork mouse."

Rabbit looked as though he wanted to laugh. Claus realised how ridiculous his explanation sounded.

A short while later and under the blessed cover of darkness, the body of Niall McGrath was loaded onto the back of Click Clack's wagon for the second and, one could only hope, last time. Click Clack offered to dump the body in the river, but Brenna wouldn't hear of it. She felt she owed him a half decent burial at least, and so they trundled through the dark streets of Bitterend, towards Five Martyr's. Claus realised that any bystander would think them an unlikely band of travellers. An old blind woman wearing too much jewellery, a Northwall Katamesian in an Opal Road suit, a pick pocket and a watch maker, all riding along on an old wagon pulled by a dray horse. Not to mention the corpse. Click Clack had thought it prudent that the less people that undertook this particular endeavour, the better, but Claus had unremittingly refused to let his aunt go without him. Arabella had stayed at The Time Emporium, with Dahljeeling and Hattie. Claus was somewhat relieved. He really didn't relish the idea of Arabella being witness to what they were about to do.

"He really *did* slip on a clockwork mouse you know," Claus whispered. Brenna patted his hand.

"I know that you're no killer, my lad. Though I dare say he had it coming."

"You seem remarkably calm. I mean, he was your son."

Brenna grunted and was silent. Claus turned round on the bench to look at her. She seemed to be aware of his scrutiny.

"We went our separate ways a long time ago." Apparently, this was sufficient explanation.

"It wasn't an accident, was it," pressed Claus. "He killed my mother, didn't he? For the watch."

"Aye," said Brenna.

The horse was pulled up beside the iron gates of the Chapel of Galen, and Claus, Rabbit and Click Clack unloaded the body, which was rather heavy. Brenna pulled a couple of shovels from the wagon. Claus glanced around nervously, but the streets were empty. They staggered with their load into the cemetery and came to a stop beside the grave of Hans Vogel. Click Clack dropped the corpse unceremoniously and reached for a shovel. Rabbit took the other and the pair began shifting the soil from Hans's grave. Claus was amazed at the light work they seemed to make of it, and he couldn't prevent the disconcerting thought that the pair must have done this sort of thing before.

"Won't someone notice?" he hissed.

"Disturbed soil on a new grave?" smiled Click Clack. He shook his head. There was a dull thud as the head of his shovel met the wooden lid of the coffin. He looked up at Brenna.

"Ready when you are."

Brenna gave a brief nod, and the body was rolled down into the hole.

"I hope Hans doesn't mind," said Claus.

"I think he would find it quite gratifying," said Brenna.

"Do you want to say some words or something?" asked Click Clack.

"No," she said.

Click Clack gestured at Rabbit and the pair began to fill in the grave.

"Wait," said Brenna.

Everyone turned to look at her. She fumbled in the folds of her skirt and pulled forth the pocket watch.

"He wanted this so badly. Now he can have it," she tossed the watch into the grave. Claus wanted to protest, but the watch was no longer his to look after. In fact, it never had been. He couldn't deny that he felt a strange sense of relief to be rid of the burden.

He stood arm in arm with Brenna and watched as the soil was swiftly replaced.

"Phew," said Click Clack and he brushed the dirt from his hands. "I could do with a cuppa after all that. You two ready to leave?"

Claus nodded.

"No time like the present."

About the Author

~

Scottish born, but now living in the warmer climes of the South Coast of England, E J Shepherd frequently visits Cellanor to gather strange tales from the locals.

When spending time on Earth, E J enjoys committing regular social faux pas, long soaks in a hot bath, and cats. But not all at the same time.

Printed in Great Britain
by Amazon

54884829R00194